EVIL AT THE ESSEX HOUSE

PIPPA DARLING MYSTERY
BOOK 5

JENNA BENNETT

England, August, 1926

For months now, Pippa's and Christopher's neighbor Florence Schlomsky, the manhunter with the teeth, has been roaming London society looking for an opportunity to trade her father's American fortune for a British title. Both the Astley cousins, Christopher and Crispin, have landed in her marital sights, a fact which has not endeared her to Pippa.

But when Mr. and Mrs. Schlomsky arrive from America and Flossie is nowhere to be found, Pippa is first in line to offer assistance. She may not have liked Flossie, but she didn't want anything bad to happen to her. And when a ransom note arrives at the Essex House Mansions demanding fifty thousand American dollars in exchange for the heiress's safe return, Pippa determines to do everything she can to get Flossie back to her parents.

But when the trail leads from the glittering salons of Mayfair to the grimy streets of Southwark and beyond, Pippa discovers that there were aspects to Florence Schlomsky she didn't know were there, and perhaps it would have been better if she had never discovered certain details about a girl she thought she knew.

"Evil wears many faces, but its intentions are always the same."

NGAIO MARSH

CHAPTER ONE

WE WERE SITTING in the tearoom at the Savoy when a gentleman approached.

I use the word advisedly. He was clearly quality: his suit the equal of one of Crispin's—the Viscount St George, future Duke of Sutherland, has a penchant for expensive clothes, expensive motorcars, and expensive women—and his demeanor at least as entitled as St George's, as well. He looked at us down the length of his nose and intoned, without much apology in his voice at all, "*Entschuldigung,* but am I looking at *Fraulein* Philippa Marie Schatz?"

Heads turned, of course. Not only was the gentleman's voice penetrating, with a slight foreign accent that sent something warm swirling through my stomach for a second before icy discomfort replaced it, but the German honorific combined with the German surname (not to mention the German accent) still gets attention, eight years after the Great War.

"I'm Pippa Darling," I said, perhaps a bit coldly, and gave the gentleman my best fishy stare. It was less effective than usual, as I was seated at table and he was close to two meters tall.

Or perhaps not. Perhaps he was only an inch or two above six feet. But that still made him taller than any other gentleman of my acquaintance, except perhaps Uncle Harold, the current Duke of Sutherland. It put him at almost half a head taller than Crispin and Christopher.

The latter was sitting across the table from me, indulging in tea and hot buns, and looking from me to the German gentleman with a slightly puzzled, slightly suspicious—and it must be said, slightly awed—expression on his pretty face.

Crispin, just to have said it, was nowhere around. Christopher and I are best friends, the next thing to siblings. Christopher's other cousin and I are... not mortal enemies, certainly—not anymore, at least—but we're also not daily associates. Lord St George was, as far as I knew, in Wiltshire. It was a Tuesday, and Uncle Harold was no doubt keeping his son and heir chained up in his rooms at Sutherland Hall. St George does sometimes escape, and comes up to Town to carouse with his friends in the Society of Bright Young Persons, but that only happens on weekends, and then only occasionally. He'd only be in London midweek if something was going on, and if anything was, we'd probably have heard about it.

"*Freulein* Darling." The German gentleman clicked his heels together and bowed in a very precise, very dashing, and quite foreign way. He took extra effort with the R in the middle of my name, too. "May I introduce myself? I am *Graf* Wolfgang Ulrich Albrecht *von und zu* Natterdorff."

There was a moment's pause. More than a moment, if I'm honest, while I tried to come up with something to say.

In my defense, it wasn't just the fact that he was exceedingly foreign, nor was it the plethora of names and titles. Crispin has those, too, so I'm used to them. Christopher has his own string of names even without the honorific. But in addition to all that, there was the fact that *Graf* Wolfgang was quite possibly the best-looking man I had ever set eyes on. And I'm honestly not spoiled for choice as far as that goes. Christopher is quite attractive, and so is Crispin, for all his annoying ways. So, for that matter, is my elder cousin Francis.

And if I didn't happen to like the fair-haired and -complexioned, there's Lord Geoffrey Marsden, who is an awful cad, but with the glossy good looks and shiny black hair of a matinee idol.

There's also Thomas Gardiner, a Detective Sergeant with Scotland Yard and an old friend of my late cousin Robert's, although I have a feeling that Christopher might take it amiss if I extoll Tom's virtues too loudly. He's undeniably handsome, though, with brown, wavy hair and hazel eyes.

The *Graf* to and from Natterdorff was fair. His hair was parted down the middle and smoothed back from his face in golden waves, while his eyes were a dark blue. His face looked like something that might have been carved in marble, with a chiseled jaw, straight nose, and high cheekbones. The only thing marring its perfection was a scar, thin and white, long healed, that ran diagonally across his left cheek. It did nothing to destroy the overall effect, but instead added a touch of recklessness or danger to a face that might otherwise have been almost too classically handsome. I didn't need Christopher's foot nudging my ankle under the table to know that I was looking at something—or someone—extraordinary.

Of course I didn't let it show. If there's one thing I'm adept at, it's keeping a stiff upper lip in the face of unfairly charming men who do their best to throw me off balance. So I merely smiled politely and told him, "I'm pleased to meet you. May I present my cousin, Mr. Christopher Astley?"

The count—for that's what he was—clicked his heels together and bowed again. "*Mein Herr.*"

"*Graf* von Natterdorff." Christopher's eyes were enormous in his rapt face. "Won't you have a seat?"

He nudged one of the chairs with his foot so it moved slightly. The *Graf* eyed it for a second before putting a hand on its back. "*Freulein* Darling?"

"Of course," I said. "Please, be comfortable."

"*Danke.*" He pulled the chair out and seated himself. Up close, when I didn't have to stare up at the underside of his nostrils, he was even more spectacular-looking than I had originally thought. Perfect bone structure, perfect teeth, eyes of such a dark blue that they were almost navy. "I will not take up much of your time."

His speech was extremely precise, every word chosen with deliberation and placed carefully into the sentence. I knew what that felt like. It had taken me at least a year after landing in England at eleven to get over my habit of thinking in German and translating my thoughts into English before speaking them out loud. My mother was English, so I had learned the language at her knee, but we had lived in Germany all my life.

At this point, twelve years later, I hadn't thought in, or even spoken, German in at least a decade. The back of my mind was churning, trying to access old channels of words and sentence structure.

"Take up as much time as you want," Christopher said brightly.

The years since the Great War has, in many ways, been extremely kind to many of us. My skirts are short, and so is my hair. I smoke cigarettes and drink liquor in public. I'm unmarried at twenty-three, and not just that, but I share a flat in London with an unmarried man of marriageable age (consanguineous marriage is legal in England, so the fact that we're first cousins is not an impediment to our being romantically involved, theoretically anyway) without servants or a chaperone on the premises, and nobody (or nobody much) remarks on it.

Not that there's anything romantic going on, of course. Which is the point I was getting at. The post-War society that allows me the short hemlines and bobbed hair, also allows Christopher not to hide—or not to hide to an extreme degree—the fact that he prefers the company of other men. The buggery laws are still in effect, so he can't be too obvious about it—no hand-holding or kissing in public—but to many of us, it's not a matter worth much thought, and certainly no condemnation. Christopher is the way Christopher is, and I love Christopher like a brother, so why would I care on whom he bestows his personal affections?

He has bestowed them on Tom Gardiner, as far as I know. I'm fairly certain Christopher has at least a little crush on his late brother's best friend. I don't know whether Tom reciprocates, although I'm fairly certain he at least likes and cares about Christopher. He has yanked him out of a couple of uncomfortable situations that might have ended with Christopher's arrest and imprisonment for running afoul those buggery laws I mentioned, but I don't know if things have gone any farther than that, or whether they ever will. It could just be a crush on Christopher's part and goodwill towards a late friend's little brother on Tom's.

In any case, it didn't stop Christopher from being visibly taken with the *Graf*. He put his chin on his hand and eyed him admiringly from the other side of the table.

The *Graf* cleared his throat. "You do not remember me."

There was no question mark at the end of the sentence, but I suppose it might have been the German inflection.

"My apologies," I said. "I wasn't aware that we were previously acquainted."

Christopher glanced at me, question in his eyes. I glanced back. If I had ever seen the Count before, it was news to me.

"It was many years ago," the latter said. "Perhaps you were too young to remember."

He couldn't be more than a couple of years older than me—maybe three or four at most—so if I had been young, he hadn't been much older when—if—we'd met.

"You look very much like your mother," he added, "but you have your father's eyes."

Christopher shot me another look. I didn't return it this time, although I knew what he wanted. Yes, the *Graf* was correct. I looked like my mother had done at my age, but instead of her blue eyes, I had inherited my father's green ones.

And if he knew that—

"You knew my family?"

He sighed. "Alas. It was terrible, what happened."

Yes, it had been. When war broke out, my father had been conscripted for the German army. My mother had refused to leave him, but had sent me to her sister in England for safety. My father had died in the trenches, and my mother had succumbed to the Spanish Influenza the year after the Armistice. By then, I had settled into the Astley family as if I had always been a part of it. Losing both my parents before I was eighteen had been difficult, of course, but not as difficult as if I had been alone in a war-ravaged Germany when it happened. I was surrounded by people who loved me, I had surrogate parents in Aunt Roz and Uncle Herbert, and surrogate brothers in Francis and Christopher. Losing Robert during the war had been as hard as if he had been my own sibling. So compared to some, I was very lucky indeed.

"And you?" I asked politely. "Did you come through the war unscathed?"

He shot me a look, a quick flash of blue. "I was too young for conscription. My father was too old."

He'd have to be under twenty-seven, then, unless the Germans had had different rules for their conscription than the English. Here, my cousins Robert and Francis had gone to war, at eighteen and twenty respectively. No one younger than Robert had been conscripted, although I had heard that lads as young as fourteen had enlisted, more or less voluntarily, some of them under duress from the White Feather Brigade.

The *Graf* hadn't mentioned his mother, but I didn't think I ought to pry, so I said nothing about the omission. Instead, I asked, "When did we meet?"

He eyed me for a moment. "You were very small. Perhaps five or six. A little girl in a white pinafore with a white bow in your hair."

Quite a long time ago, then. I had some memories of being that age in Germany, but not many. He would have been seven or eight, I suppose. Perhaps a bit more likely to remember the incident than I was.

"And how did it come to be?"

"My parents and I visited you and your parents in Heidelberg," *Graf* Wolfgang said.

And that clinched it, because if he knew that I had spent my formative years in Heidelberg, he must have actually known my family back then. Or so it seemed, anyway.

"I'm afraid I can't recall meeting you," I said apologetically.

He nodded. "My apologies for intruding."

He pushed the chair back. I had my mouth open to tell him that he didn't have to leave just because I couldn't remember having seen him before—he was welcome to stay and tell me more about it; I wasn't trying to get rid of him—but then he added, "Perhaps it would be possible for me to call upon you sometime when you are not having tea with another gentleman?"

"Oh," I said, with a glance across the table at Christopher, "he's not—"

Christopher arched his brows, and I trailed off.

"Go on," he told me, smirking. "I'm not what, darling?"

"Don't do that," I told him. "You look and sound much too much like your cousin when you look at me like that and call me that."

He chuckled. "Sorry, Pippa. But what is it I'm not?"

"Nothing." Because of course he was a gentleman—fourth in line for the dukedom, after his cousin, father, and older brother—and he was also, indubitably, here.

All I had meant to say was that he didn't count, that I wasn't having tea with a gentleman in the sense that *Graf* Wolfgang had to vacate the premises to leave us alone... but that all became much too convoluted to try to explain, so I gave up. "Of course you may," I told the *Graf* instead. "We live at the Essex House Mansion flats on Essex Street. If I'm not there, you can leave a message with the commissionaire—his name is Evans—and he'll make sure I get it."

Graf Wolfgang nodded and clicked his heels together. "*Freulein.*" He turned to Christopher and did it again. "*Mein Herr.*"

"A pleasure," Christopher drawled, and managed, yet again, to remind me uncomfortably of his cousin Crispin, who drawls and smirks and arches his brows rather an excessive amount (if not in response to handsome young men).

If the *Graf* was bothered, he didn't show it, just turned on his heel and strode out of the Savoy tearoom seemingly without noticing, or at least without paying attention to, the stares and whispers that followed his passage. A table of young ladies eyed him the way young women everywhere eye handsome young men, exchanging glances and tittering behind their hands, while several gentleman, those a few years older than us, looked at him with rather less admiration and more resentment. They were, to a man, of an age where they had most likely spent some time in the trenches, and they weren't quite as ready to welcome the enemy with open arms into the Savoy tearoom quite yet, even if he was exceedingly young and handsome.

Christopher watched until the lobby had swallowed the *Graf*, and then he turned to me, eyes wide. "Well!"

"Well, what?" I inquired, picking up my teacup.

"Well, rather a lot, I'd say." He shot another glance at the door before fanning himself with his serviette. "Did you ever see anyone so handsome?"

"Geoffrey Marsden," I said, sourly, and returned the cup to the saucer without a noticeable click.

Christopher blinked. And thought for a moment before he conceded, "I suppose."

"But yes, I'll award you the point. He was definitely easy on the eyes."

Christopher nodded. "German, though." With all that that entailed, a decade after the Great War.

"Yes," I said. "German."

Christopher tilted his head to look at me. "Do you not remember him?"

"You heard me say that I didn't, didn't you?"

He nodded. "But I thought perhaps...?"

I shook my head. "If I've ever seen him before, he left no lasting impression."

"Hard to believe," Christopher said, with yet one more look at the door, "although, if you were five, he probably didn't look like that then."

"I'm certain he didn't," I said. "He would have been eight

or so, I assume. Too young to serve, so he must be younger than Tom. He's older than us by a couple of years, wouldn't you say? So twenty-five or -six. When I was five, he would have been seven or eight."

Christopher nodded. "I imagine he was a handsome little boy."

"He might have been, although it doesn't necessarily follow, you know. You and Crispin were both buck-toothed and scrawny at eleven, and look at you now."

He smirked. "So you'll admit that Crispin is handsome."

"I'll admit that *you* are," I said. "That was a singular 'you,' not a plural one."

He looked at me, eyebrows arched, and I sighed. "Of course he's handsome, Christopher. He wouldn't have half the young women in the Bright Young Set chasing him otherwise. There's the title and money, yes, but they've all got titles and money of their own, don't they, so there must be something more to it. And it can't be his personality, since he's an abhorrent prat. So what's left?"

Christopher grinned. "I knew it!"

I rolled my eyes. "You're making something out of this that absolutely isn't there. He looks enough like you to be your brother. Your *twin* brother. You don't need to be told that he's handsome. Or that you are."

"But I never thought *you* would admit it, Pippa."

"I've told you that you're handsome before," I said.

He nodded. "Of course you have. But you've never admitted that Crispin is."

"But as I said, you're practically identical. So how could he not be?" I shook my head. "You're getting off the subject, Christopher. We were discussing the *Graf von und zu* Natterdorff, not your cousin Crispin. And while he may have been a handsome child—or not—I still don't remember him."

Christopher gave up the pursuit of annoying me to ask, seriously, "You don't suppose he was lying, do you?"

"Why on earth would he lie? He recognized me. Knew my name, even." My former name. My father's last name of Schatz had been anglicized to Darling when I landed on English soil, ostentatiously German surnames being a bad idea in 1914, and not really a much better one now. But the *Graf* had known it.

I continued, "He knew that I look like my mother but with my father's eyes. Knew where in Germany we lived when I was five. Besides, what would be the point? I'm nobody important. What would be the purpose of lying to get an introduction to me? And between you and me, Christopher—"

I shot a look at the door to the lobby myself, "—looking like that, he doesn't need an introduction. He can just turn up and say hello, and we'd all be delighted to make his acquaintance."

Christopher nodded. Fervently.

"Better not let Tom see you look at another bloke like that," I told him, and he flushed.

"Tom and I are friends, Pippa."

"Of course you are," I said fondly. "At any rate, I'm sure I did meet him when I was a child. It's so long ago that it's no wonder I don't remember. And it might not have been a very momentous meeting."

"Unlike when you met us."

He smirked. I smirked back. "Quite unlike."

The meeting between myself and the family that was to become my own had taken place on the passenger docks in Southampton in the very early days of August 1914. Things took some time to get going after the assassination of Franz Ferdinand at the end of June of that year. Kaiser Wilhelm II went on vacation to Norway for the best part of a month, and it wasn't until he came back—and was unpleasantly surprised at the war machine that had been gearing up in his absence—that things really got going.

Wilhelm, in justice to him, did try to avoid the whole mess, but when war was declared between Austria-Hungary and Serbia in late July, there was very little choice, especially when Russia came down on Serbia's side. Germany declared war on Russia on August 1st and sent troops into Luxembourg on August 2nd. They declared war against France on August 3rd, and England declared war on Germany the following day, after Germany invaded Belgium overnight.

After that, as the saying goes, it was just one damn thing after another. Austria-Hungary declared war on Russia on August 5th; Serbia on Germany on August 6th; Montenegro on Austria-Hungary on August 7th and on Germany on August 12th. France and Great Britain declared war on Austria-Hungary on August 10th and August 12th, respectively. Japan declared on Germany on August 23rd, Austria-Hungary on Japan on August 25th, and on Belgium on August 28th.

By then, I was installed in a room at Beckwith Place in Wiltshire, after the infamous meeting on the Southampton docks earlier in the month. My mother had taken me as far as Bremerhaven, and had put me on a steamship bound for England, while she returned to Heidelberg to await news about my father.

Uncle Herbert and Aunt Roz had a bigger motorcar back then, a seven-passenger Pierce Arrow Touring Car with room for the entire family. When I came down the gangplank, still wearing the same clothes I had left Heidelberg in three days earlier, everyone was on the dock, holding flowers and flags and a banner that read *WELCOME HOME, PIPPA!* written in several colors and different hands. Christopher was waving the Union Jack, and Robbie—home from Eton between Summer Term and Michaelmas, along with Francis—had a horn he was blowing into, the next best thing to my own marching band.

I burst into tears, of course. I was eleven years old, and had just spent two and a half days alone on a steamship, after having left my father and mother and the only home I had ever known. I was frightened and overwhelmed and exhausted and sad, and it was the first time anyone had called me Pippa, and this woman I didn't know, who looked a bit like the mother I had left behind but not enough to make me actually comfortable, just stared at me as if she had seen a ghost—I didn't learn until much later that I looked very much like my mother had done when she was my age—and there were people everywhere, and noise, and everyone spoke in a language I wasn't used to hearing, and eventually it was Christopher, little, scrawny Christopher, who took the first step forward and bowed and offered me his handkerchief as he told me, formally, "Good afternoon, Philippa. I'm your cousin Christopher."

Francis woke up after that, and so did Robbie, and so, eventually, did Aunt Roz. Francis called me Pipsqueak—a nickname that has lingered to this day, I'm sorry to say—and he and Robbie hauled my trunk to the Pierce Arrow and fastened it to the luggage rack in the back, and then they all bundled me into the rear of the vehicle with the three boys and we started on the long drive home to Wiltshire, while Robbie occasionally blew his horn at other motorcars on the road.

I shook the memories off and smiled at Christopher. "Definitely nothing like that. Nothing like when I met St George for the first time, either."

That had been a few weeks later. We had been invited to Sutherland Hall, I assume so Duke Henry could get a look at the upstart German girl his youngest son had been saddled with, thanks to his daughter-in-law's unruly sister—not that I realized any of that at the time. I had managed to settle into the family a bit by then. I still missed my parents, but my aunt and uncle had done a good job of making me feel welcome, and I had formed a fast friendship with Christopher. He was just a few months younger than I was, and he delighted in showing me his world. His older brothers both adored him, and they transferred that feeling to me with no questions asked, but they were both old enough to do things, and to be interested in doing things, that Christopher couldn't do, so Aunt Roz and Uncle Herbert were happy to provide him with a playmate of his own age, one who would be around more permanently than Crispin was.

Upon arrival at Sutherland Hall, the latter eyed me narrowly, and then suggested to Christopher that we should play hide-and-seek. Christopher said yes, and that experience set the tone for most of my interactions with St George from then on. He coolly informed Christopher that he, Christopher, was *it*, and then, when Christopher covered his eyes and began to count to a hundred, Crispin grabbed my hand and pulled me behind him into the hedge maze.

I suppose I trusted him because he looked so much like Christopher, and because everyone else in the family had proved themselves to be lovely. I soon learned different. The yew hedges of the maze went by in a blur, and I had no hope of remembering the left and right turns he pulled me around with lightning speed, until we were in the middle of the maze, where he pointed to a wrought iron bench, said, "Wait there," and ran off again.

And didn't come back.

By the time Christopher found me, I was sobbing. I can still see Crispin's smirk, and the malicious satisfaction in those cool, gray eyes.

"Bastard," I said half-heartedly.

Christopher chuckled. "Hasn't he ever apologized for that?"

"You know, I don't believe he has. He may have uttered the words, 'my apologies, Darling,' at some point, but that's hardly the same, is it?" Not when there was nothing sincere whatsoever about the drawled delivery.

Christopher shook his head.

"Not too long ago," I added, "he informed me that it's been a long time since he did anything truly awful to me, so I assume I'm supposed to let bygones be bygones, but I'm not sure I ever received an apology, no."

"You'll have to rectify that," Christopher said with a smirk of his own, and I rolled my eyes.

"Enough, Christopher. I'm sick and tired of everyone insinuating that there's something going on between me and St George. I wouldn't have him gift-wrapped with a bow around his neck, and you know it."

"It's less about that—" Christopher began, and I shook my head.

"Spare me. Lady Laetitia is welcome to him."

"No, she isn't," Christopher said.

No, she wasn't. There was no part of me that wanted Laetitia Marsden as part of the family, and it wasn't because I wanted Crispin for my own, to be clear. She had been told that he was in love with someone else, and she was determined to wed him in spite of it. One of these days I was concerned that she'd succeed in wearing him down. His father was rooting for it, and so, of course, was her mother. The rest of us thought it a fate worse than death, but if he wouldn't stand up for himself, there was nothing any of us could do to prevent it.

I shook off my misgivings, since there was nothing whatsoever I could do about them. "Are you ready to go home?"

"I suppose we'd better," Christopher said with a glance at

the window. "Tea-time is over. And so is the excitement, it seems."

If the excitement had been the *Graf* from and of Natter-dorff, then yes. The excitement was definitely over.

"We'll have to see whether he contacts me with an invitation," I said, as Christopher pulled my chair out and helped me up.

He shot me a glance from under his eyelashes. "Will you go, if he does?"

I shot one back. "Is there any reason I shouldn't go, if he does?"

"Not unless you don't want to," Christopher said and offered me his arm. I took it and headed for the lobby and the street outside.

CHAPTER TWO

AS I HAD TOLD the *Graf von und zu* Natterdorff, Christopher and I shared a service flat in the Essex House Mansions. When we entered the lobby, Evans the commissionaire was waiting.

"Miss Darling." He inclined his head. "Mr. Astley."

"Evans." He looked expectant, and I tilted my head. "Is something going on? Did someone stop by? No..." My eyes narrowed, "—don't tell me. Is Lord St George upstairs, waiting? Did he talk you into letting him into our flat while we were out?"

"No, Miss Darling," Evans said, while Christopher chuckled. "This arrived for you, Mr. Astley."

He handed Christopher a note. The latter took one look at the handwriting and turned pink.

I hid a smile and turned my attention back to the doorman. "So no one is upstairs, Evans?"

"No, Miss Darling."

Next to me, Christopher opened the note. It hadn't been

tucked inside an envelope, merely folded and sealed, and as he unfolded the paper, I slanted my eyes that way.

It wasn't a long note, just a line and a half of script I couldn't make out, but with a rather informal signature that I could: *Tom.*

"If you have to leave..." I told Christopher, who gave me a distracted look before dropping his eyes to the note and skimming it again.

Behind us, the door to the street opened, letting in the sounds of early evening in London before the door shut again. "Pardon me, Miss. Here you are, guv'nor."

A slim figure in a natty gray suit, a lad no more than fifteen, slipped past me to hand Evans another missive. "Telegram for Miss Florence Skl..." He peered down at it. "Shhh..."

"Schlomsky," I said. "Miss Florence Schlomsky."

He glanced at me. "Right you are, Miss Schlomsky."

"No, *I'm* not Miss Schlomsky. The telegram is for Miss Schlomsky."

He rolled his eyes. "Yes, Miss. See you later, guv."

He slid past in the opposite direction and was gone. The door shut behind him while Evans stared at the telegram. Christopher was still peering down at his own note, too, seemingly deep in thought.

I turned back to Evans. "Would you like for me to take that upstairs to Miss Schlomsky? I'm going that way anyway."

Evans hesitated before handing it over. "If you wouldn't mind, Miss Darling. That way Miss Schlomsky won't have to wait for it. I'm not supposed to leave the lobby in the middle of a shift."

No, of course he wasn't. I took the thin envelope between two fingers and flicked my cousin a glance. "Coming, Christopher?"

"As a matter of fact, Pippa—" He shot me a look back,

distracted. "I think I'd better respond to this as soon as possible."

I tilted my head. "And you don't want to come upstairs where we have pens and paper and penny stamps?"

He shook his head. "I'm just going to run down to the public call box for a minute."

I tilted my head the other way. "Everything's all right, isn't it?"

He smiled. "Of course, Pippa. Just a quick ring for Crispin."

"St George? What does Tom want with him?"

And why hadn't he just contacted Crispin himself, instead of involving Christopher? Tom knew where to find St George.

After a second I added, suspiciously, "He's not coming up to Town, is he? Remember what happened the last time one of us went somewhere with him."

(In a word, murder. Or in a few more: driving around London with a dead body in the back of the motorcar, and almost getting caught in a police raid, before leaving said body under a tree in Hyde Park. It's a long story.)

His lips twitched. "That was your fault, Pippa. You were the one who convinced him to put on a gown and crash a drag ball. None of that was his fault. Or mine, either."

I rolled my eyes. "He's the one who wanted to go out and celebrate his birthday. And we wouldn't have been there in the first place if not for you."

Although seeing the most eligible bachelor in England, heir to the Sutherland dukedom, in a beaded evening gown and makeup had almost been worth what came later.

Almost.

"At any rate," Christopher said, "I'm going to run down the street to the call box. I'll be up in five or ten minutes."

I nodded. "Give him my—"

He smirked, and I made a face. "Regards, Christopher. Give him my regards. I have no love to spare where St George is concerned, and you know it. Stop trying to pretend something is going on when you know there isn't."

"Yes, Pippa." But he was still smirking when he turned for the door.

"You'd better not, Christopher," I told his back threateningly. "If I find out that you've been telling St George that I'm sending him love, I'll make sure you regret it."

"Yes, Pippa." He ducked through the door and out. I huffed and turned back to Evans.

"I'll take the telegram up to Miss Schlomsky, Evans. Any message?"

Evans shook his head. "No, Miss Darling. You were here when it was delivered. You know as much as I do."

Of course. "I'll see you later, then, Evans."

I headed for the lift.

MISS FLORENCE SCHLOMSKY has been a neighbor of Christopher's and mine in the Essex House Mansions since we moved in early in the year. At that point, I believe she had been in London just a few months herself. We never have gotten on well, as she's everything I particularly abhor in a woman. Or practically everything, anyway. Since meeting Flossie, I have met a few other specimens that have actually been worse, but she's still not one of my favorite persons.

She's American, for one thing. And while being an American doesn't necessarily indicate that someone is vulgar, Flossie is definitely vulgar. She's brash, and loud, and approximately as delicate as sandpaper. She also has the personality of a steam roller, and she doesn't slow down for anyone or anything. She latched onto Christopher as soon as she realized that he was the grandson of a duke, and I had to spend time making certain that she wasn't terrorizing him. And then, a few months later, she made Crispin's acquaintance, and while she—thankfully—turned her attentions to him instead of Christopher, that didn't endear her to me any further.

She is also a gold-digger.

Or perhaps that's not fair. Flossie has plenty of gold of her own. Her father is a big deal in America, somewhere she calls Toledo. Florence is the Toledo dime store heiress. So while she's definitely mercenary, she's not actually looking to marry for money. She is looking to trade her father's money for a British title instead, or so it seems. She might have settled for Christopher, had he been interested. He *is* the grandson of the Duke of Sutherland—or was at the time—and he's both young and handsome, something which isn't necessarily true of all the unmarried gentlemen in England.

But then, of course, she met Crispin, and decided she'd rather have him instead.

And Crispin, being Crispin, was disinclined to discourage her. So the last time he'd been to the flat—on the aforementioned occasion when we'd gotten involved in the murder—I had had to take him away from her. In this very lift, in fact. She had had him backed into the corner by the button panel, and was busy assaulting his mouth (and possibly other parts of his person) when the lift arrived on our floor. I had had to physically remove him from her, and I doubt he had ever been able to remove her lipstick from his collar.

All of which is to say that Florence Schlomsky and I will never be bosom buddies. She is, however, a neighbor, and a very friendly sort, and I don't think she actually minds that I do my best to remove both Christopher and Crispin from her clutches when she gets her hands on either one of them. When she pulled the door to her flat open, she gave me a big smile. "Hullo, Pippa!"

"Hello, Florence," I said.

Christopher's nickname for Flossie is 'the American manhunter with the teeth,' and it's not inaccurate. We've all got teeth, of course, but Florence has more than the usual number, all very white and straight. And she's not a bad-looking girl, for all that she is, again, a bit vulgar. She has bouncy, brown curls, and pink apple cheeks, and she loves anything that flutters, or sparkles, or shines. Tonight's evening dress was a delicate shell pink, with a scalloped hem and sparkling beads in a fish-scale pattern all over the skirt. It must have cost a fortune, and I'll admit to giving it an admiring glance or two before I told myself firmly that it was all the wrong color for me—shell pink makes me look washed out—and stuck my hand out.

"Telegram for you. I was in the lobby, so I told Evans I would take it up."

I had glanced at the front of it in the lift. It was there in my hand, and there's nothing else to look at in the lift, so I didn't feel bad about it. I'm sure Evans had glanced at it, too, before he handed it over to me.

Not that there was anything to see. Just a perfectly plain envelope of the same sort that Christopher and I had received a month ago, announcing his brother Francis's engagement to my friend Constance Peckham.

In this case, it was Florence's name and direction behind the crinkly plastic on the front, and the usual post office logo in the corner. There was no reason at all that she would turn pale, although she did.

So had Christopher and I, when our telegram arrived. We'd all gotten so used to bad news during the war, and I guess we hadn't quite recovered yet.

"Go on," I told her bracingly. "I'm sure it's not as bad as you fear. And even if it is, it's better to get it over with quickly."

She gave me a look before she ripped open the envelope and pulled out the single sheet of paper. I tried to read upside down, but I'd gotten no further than *SURPRISE!* before she made an inarticulate sound. Her hand convulsed on the paper and when I looked up, shocked, her healthy, pink cheeks had turned a pasty white.

I put a hand under her arm for support and felt her tremble.

"Florence?" I tried gently. "Is everything all right?"

It clearly wasn't, and I craned my neck in an effort to get another look at the telegram, but she had crumpled it in her fist and it was unreadable. For a moment she looked at me as if she had never seen me before, before she seemed to pull in a very deliberate breath and straighten up. "Yes, of course, Pippa. Thank you."

The accompanying smile was so forced it looked more like a grimace.

"Is there anything I can do?" I dropped my hand since support seemed unwanted. She had taken a step back from me. "Would you like to talk about—?"

"No." She shook her head. "No, thank you. This is something I—" Her voice broke and she cleared her throat, "—this is something I have to deal with on my own. Thank you, Pippa."

She stepped back, and a second later, the door shut in my face. I stared at it for a moment, annoyed, before I harrumphed and headed down the hallway towards the door to my own flat.

THE FLAT THAT Christopher and I share is a two-bed, single-bath with a foyer, a sitting room, a dining room, and a kitchenette. The sitting room is directly behind the foyer when you walk in, with the dining room and kitchen to the right and a hallway with two bedrooms and the washroom to the left. Mine is the first bedroom. I went into it and removed my cloche hat and matching jacket, and unbuckled my shoes in favor of quilted slippers. After a quick fluff of my hair in the vanity mirror—brown and bobbed, not as curly as Flossie's, but not sleek, either—I headed back into the main part of the flat, only to intercept Christopher coming in. His telephone call to Wiltshire really hadn't taken more than the few minutes he had promised.

I looked from the note still crumpled in his hand—shades of Florence Schlomsky—to his face. "Is everything all right?"

He nodded. "Yes, Pippa. Everything is perfectly fine."

"What did Tom want? The note was from him, right?"

"To cancel an appointment," Christopher said and crossed the foyer towards the hallway to his room.

I trailed after him. "Tom and Crispin had an appointment? Anything I should know about?"

He smirked at me over his shoulder. "No, Pippa. Tom and I had an appointment, and Tom had to cancel."

"What does that have to do with St George?"

"Nothing whatsoever," Christopher said. "They were two totally separate issues."

I narrowed my eyes. "So why did you ring him up? Or was ringing up Crispin just an excuse, and what you really wanted, was to contact Tom? If so, you could have just been honest about it, Christopher. Nobody cares." I certainly didn't.

Christopher chuckled. At least I chose to interpret it as a chuckle and not a snigger at my expense. "No, Pippa. Tom's flat isn't on the telephone. You know that. I rang up Sutherland Hall and spoke to Crispin."

I trailed after him down the hallway. "Is St George in

trouble with Scotland Yard?" Had Tom's note contained some sort of warning?

Christopher shook his head. "Not at all." He gave me another look just as he reached the door to his room. "Now go away, Pippa. I'm going to take my clothes off."

The door shut in my face and I growled and went for the knob. "You know, Christopher..."

He sighed. "Just wait until I come back out, Pippa."

"I've seen you in your unmentionables before," I told him.

"That doesn't mean you'll get to see me in them now. Go pour us a couple of drinks. I'll be there in a minute."

"And you'll tell me what happened?"

"Nothing happened!" He took a breath and added, "Yes, Pippa. I'll tell you what happened. Even if it was nothing. A Gin Rickey, please."

"Fine." I shut his door with a little more force than necessary and took myself to the sitting room, where I got busy at the bar cart. By the time Christopher came back into the sitting room in his stocking feet and *sans* jacket, I had a cocktail waiting for him on the table, and was sipping one of my own. "Tell me everything."

"You're like a dog with a bone, Pippa." He sank down on the Chesterfield and folded one elegant leg over the other as he lifted the glass to his mouth. After taking a sip, he added, "And not one of those cute lapdogs, either. A bulldog or something like that. All possessive and growly."

"I'm not possessive," I said. In a tone that might have led someone to call it a growl.

Christopher sniggered. It was definitely a snigger this time. "Of course, Pippa."

"I'm not! I'm just curious. First Tom sends you a note—and don't bother denying it, I saw the signature—and then you rush out to ring up Crispin. You can't blame me for being worried."

"I don't blame you," Christopher said, "but there's nothing to worry about. I swear. They're not related. Tom's note wasn't about business. He canceled an appointment we had made for tomorrow. He had to go away. And it was my idea to call Crispin. I thought he would like to know about the *Graf* von Natterdorff."

"The...?" My eyes bugged out. "Why on earth would you tell him about that, Christopher? You know he can't be trusted with that sort of information."

St George would cling to it like a bad odor, and rib me about it every chance he got.

"I thought he'd like to know," Christopher said.

Fine. I rolled my eyes. What was done was done, and it probably wouldn't matter, anyway. I might never hear from Wolfgang Albrecht *von und zu* Natterdorff ever again. "How is he, then?"

Christopher shrugged. "He's bored. Stuck in Wiltshire with nothing to do and no one to talk to. I offered to visit, but he declined. Said his father would never allow it."

"Why on earth not?" It's not like Christopher's a bad influence. He was hardly likely to turn Crispin queer simply by spending time with him—St George had absolutely no proclivities in that direction, so it would take a lot more than simply Christopher's presence to accomplish it—and while he does have a tendency to want to seduce anything that moves (anything female, that is) he wouldn't try to seduce me if I came along (which I certainly would). And since neither Christopher nor I have any particular inclinations towards dope or excessive drinking, or gambling or any of the other vices Crispin had a tendency to fall victim to, it seems as if Christopher and I are among the safest visitors Uncle Harold could introduce to the Hall to keep his son company.

"It all seems to be part and parcel of my uncle's plan to get Crispin to do the right thing vis-à-vis Lady Laetitia," Christopher said.

I arched my brows. "The right thing, is it?"

He made a face. "You know what I mean. The right thing according to Uncle Harold. He thinks it's time Crispin settles down. Laetitia Marsden meets the requirements. And he did—"

He drew quotation marks in the air with two fingers on each hand, "—ruin her earlier this year."

I scoffed. "I hardly think that she'd agree with you that she's ruined, Christopher. She was the one who seduced him, wasn't she, and not the other way around."

"So it seems," Christopher said.

"It's the nineteen-twenties, for goodness's sake. We're all very modern now."

He didn't respond to that, and I added, "And it's not as if he got her with child, is it?"

"No," Christopher agreed, "it doesn't appear as if he did."

No, it didn't. "If they were together in January, she'd be as big as a Zeppelin by now."

And she wasn't. Or at least she hadn't been as of a few weeks ago. Lady Laetitia had been as willowy and beautiful as always during my cousin Francis's engagement party in July.

"That's if he hasn't been with her since," Christopher said.

I stared at him for a second before I opened my mouth. "When would he have had the chance? They weren't together during that weekend at the Dower House. We were there, and he spent every night in a room with you and Francis. And he said no to her during the weekend at Beckwith Place. She announced it right out loud, remember?"

"But Uncle Harold invited the Marsdens to stop at Sutherland Hall on their way back to Dorset," Christopher said. "People do have relations when you and I are not around too, you know."

"Of course they do, Christopher. But they're not going to misbehave at the Hall with his father and her parents there, surely?"

"I didn't get the impression that her parents or Uncle Harold would mind if they did," Christopher said dryly. "At any rate, the solitude at the Hall is chafing at him. You know how he gets."

I did. The Viscount St George enjoys excitement. When he's kept from it, he wilts, the poor, delicate flower. "But nothing's wrong?"

He shook his head. "Nothing aside from his being bored and alone. I'm more interested in Flossie Schlomsky right now. What on earth was in that telegram, Pippa?"

"I have no idea," I said. "I tried to get a look at it, but between reading upside down and the flimsiness of the paper —" not to mention Flossie's hand shaking, "—all I caught was the first word. *Surprise.* She turned as white as a sheet, though, so I don't imagine it could have been good news."

"It didn't look like it," Christopher agreed, and took another sip of his Gin Rickey. "She swept through the lobby just as I was on my way back inside. I held the door for her, and she barely took the time to say thank you—no smile, no, '*Hello, Mr. Astley—*'"

He delivered the last three words in Florence's saucy alto, "—before she was out the door and on her way up the pavement."

"She must have run out almost as soon as she shut the door in my face," I said.

He arched his brows. "Did she really?"

I nodded. "I didn't say anything about it, because I could see that she was shaken, but it was quite rude. Even for her."

There was a moment's pause while we both sipped our drinks. Then—

"I hope she's all right," Christopher said.

It was my turn to snigger. "Why, Christopher. I didn't know you cared."

He sent me a dark look. "I don't, Pippa. But I don't wish ill on anyone."

"I do," I said. "Quite a few people, as a matter of fact."

"Name one."

"Uncle Harold," I said. Christopher arched his brows, and I continued, "I don't like the way he treats Crispin. He's a bully, and he needs to keep his hands to himself. I was sincerely concerned that he had given Crispin a concussion last month at Beckwith Place."

Christopher grimaced, but didn't protest.

"And Laetitia Marsden, as well. Flossie is an irritant, and I would hate to have to look at her across the Christmas goose for the next forty years, but there is no chance that he'll want to marry her, and I don't think I'll have to worry about him being forced into it against his will, either. Lady Laetitia, on the other hand..."

Christopher nodded. "She definitely has designs on Crispin, as well as Uncle Harold's blessing to get him to propose by any means necessary. And she would kill you as soon as look at you if you got in her way, so you'd better be careful if that's your plan."

I rolled my eyes. "If he's willing to let himself be pushed into proposing to a woman he doesn't love simply because he lacks the backbone to say no, that's his problem. I'm just listing off people I would enjoy seeing with a painful and embarrassing rash."

"And you would like to see Laetitia with one of those?"

"I would be delighted," I said. "Flossie, on the other hand... Well, I don't suppose a rash would hurt her, either. But I wouldn't rejoice in it, I don't think. And as for anything worse... Well, I hope you're right, and nothing terrible is wrong."

Christopher nodded and raised his glass. "To Flossie."

I raised mine, too. "If you insist."

CHAPTER THREE

"YOU REALLY HAVE no idea what the telegram was about?"

I shook my head and put the glass on the table. "None. As I told you, all I saw was the first word. And that didn't appear like bad news, but she certainly behaved as if it was."

"Well, it's too late now to follow her," Christopher said. "She's long gone."

I nodded. "None of our concern, either, really. Unless she asks for help, anyway."

"Of course. But it's interesting. It's been an interesting day all around."

I supposed it had. "It isn't every day you meet a handsome young gentleman—and a *Graf*, no less—who remembers you from when you were small."

"No, it isn't." He tilted his head. "Didn't the Weimar Republic do away with the German noble titles a few years ago?"

"In 1919. Or they did away with their nobility, anyway. If you were the *Graf von und zu* Natterdorff before that, I believe you're still the *Graf von und zu* Natterdorff now. It's just that being the *Graf von und zu* Natterdorff doesn't make you any better than anyone else."

"Socialism," Christopher scoffed, and shifted so he could fold the other leg over his other knee. "So riddle me this, Pippa: If there's no nobility, but the *Graf von und zu* Natterdorff takes a wife, will she still be the *Gräfin von und zu* Natterdorff? Or would she be just plain *Frau* Albrecht?"

"I have no idea," I said, "and I don't know that it's an incentive either way. But good for you, knowing that the *Graf*'s wife is the *Gräfin*."

He sniffed. "Of course, Philippa. I am the grandson of a duke, after all."

"Of course you are." I smiled at him fondly. "Did they teach you that at Eton?"

"I have no idea where I learned that," Christopher said, dropping the affectation. "I imagine my mother probably told me at some point. Or my father. Or perhaps my grandfather. *Noblesse oblige* and all that."

Yes, of course. "Well, everything you learned about Germany at your mother's knee is defunct now. It's not the same place it was when we were small."

Christopher shook his head. "How are you really, Pippa? Coming face to face with your past like that?"

I sighed. I hadn't wanted to think too deeply about it—hadn't had the opportunity, either, honestly—but I supposed it was inevitable that I'd have to. "It was a shock. I didn't expect to see anyone I knew back then ever again. Not with both my parents dead and me in an entirely different country with a new name, not to mention the war and international relations and everything else."

"Do you remember him now?"

I shook my head. "But that's all right. He clearly knew me."

"What does he want, though?" Christopher wondered.

I peered at him. "What do you mean? He recognized me, and wanted to introduce himself."

He nodded. "Of course. But beyond that. What was he doing at the Savoy? He wasn't taking tea with anyone. I didn't notice him in the tearoom when we came in, and believe me, Pippa, looking like that, I would have."

I would have, too, most likely. The *Graf* was definitely eye-catching.

"Perhaps he saw us cross the lobby," I suggested, "and thought I looked familiar. Perhaps he's staying at the Savoy."

"He has to stay somewhere," Christopher agreed, "so perhaps he is. I wonder what he's doing in England?"

"He has some sort of business here, I expect. We're doing business with Germany again, aren't we?"

"Germany's in the League of Nations now," Christopher nodded, "and there was the Locarno treaties last year. I think things are back to normal as far as that goes."

Normal as in before the Great War, I supposed, when Germany was just one of many European countries and not a threat to world peace.

I had my doubts about it, honestly. About things going back to normal, I mean. That madman *Herr* Hitler was out of prison again now, after serving his sentence (or part of it) for planning the Beer Hall *Putsch*, and it had taken the German government just two years to lift the ban on his National Socialist party. He wasn't the type to give up that easily. The manifesto he had penned while incarcerated had been chilling, to say the least, and I was certain we hadn't heard the last from him.

Christopher nodded when I said as much. "Stay with us, Pippa, where it's safe. Marry Crispin, or marry someone else, but stick with England."

I fully intended to. However— "I need you to stop saying

that, Christopher. Uncle Harold would sooner disinherit Crispin than allow him to marry someone like me, not to mention that I don't like him that way. You—all of you—have to stop it. Even your mother asked me, last month, whether I was sure I couldn't just marry Crispin and rid us of Lady Laetitia."

Christopher's lips twitched, and I added, severely, "He and I don't get along, and he's in love with someone else. Besides, I don't think the rest of you would approve of it either, no matter what you all say."

"If it was what you wanted," Christopher said, "we'd all be delighted for you. We all want you to be happy. If marrying Crispin would make you happy—"

"It wouldn't."

"—we'd all be happy for you."

"Well, it's moot," I said. "I'll marry you before I marry him."

"Famous last words," Christopher responded. "As for His Highness, five quid says we'll hear from him tomorrow."

His Highness? "Do you mean Crispin?"

"I mean the *Graf*. Although I wouldn't be surprised if Crispin showed up tomorrow, too, just to remind you what he looks like."

"He won't have to show up for me to remember what he looks like," I said. "He looks like you. And that's too soon to hear from the *Graf*." If we heard from him at all, that was.

"Five quid on tomorrow," Christopher repeated.

I shook my head. "Don't be vulgar, Christopher."

"What's vulgar about betting on when my flat-mate will hear from a bloke who took her fancy?" He grinned.

I rolled my eyes. "First, he didn't take my fancy. He was pretty, yes, but otherwise, not my type. And secondly, that wasn't the part I thought was vulgar."

"Quid is Latin, darling."

"And here I thought it came from the papermill at Quid-hampton," I said dryly. "Don't call me darling, Christopher. You sound too much like your cousin when you do."

"His has a capital D. Or so you always tell me." He leaned forward to put his empty glass on the table. "I'm serious, Pippa. Five pounds sterling says he'll be in touch tomorrow."

I shook my head. "Thursday, at the earliest."

"Shake on it?" He stuck his hand out across the table.

I took it. "You're on."

AS IT HAPPENED, we were both wrong about the time it would take Wolfgang, *Graf* Natterdorff, to get in touch with me. He must have gone directly home—or up to his room at the Savoy, or wherever else he was staying—and penned the note, because it arrived an hour later by messenger. Evans rang up from the lobby to let me know it was there while Christopher and I were in the middle of indulging in beans on toast, and I ran downstairs to pick it up, with Christopher's laughter in my ears.

"What does he want?" he asked when I walked back into the sitting room, note in hand. And then his eyebrows rose when he noticed that the envelope was still sealed. "Don't tell me you waited until now to open it?"

"I wanted to hold your hand," I said. "What if it's bad news?"

He rolled his eyes. "How can it be bad news? It's a young, good-looking gentleman asking for some of your time. I wouldn't turn him down, let me tell you, but you can always say no if you don't want to meet him."

"You're certain that's all it is?" I turned the envelope over in my hand.

Christopher nodded. "What else could it be? Just open it and get it over with, Pippa."

Fine, then. I took a breath and tore the envelope open and pulled out the notecard with the Savoy's insignia in the corner. The *Graf*'s handwriting was sloped and elegant, flowing across the paper in tidy lines.

"What on earth?" Christopher said, staring at it, his eyes wide.

I glanced at him. "What?... Oh. It's *Kurrentschrift*. A bit different from English cursive, isn't it?"

He glanced back. "You can read it?"

"Of course I can. Can't you?"

"That's a lowercase F," Christopher said, pointing to it, "but that's also a lowercase F, and it looks different. And that, and that, and that—" he indicated, "are all capital letter Ls, and they're all different."

"That's because that F," I pointed to it, "is a lowercase H, and the three Ls are an L, a B, and a C, respectively. This F is actually a capital I."

"That's mad," Christopher said. "But you understand what it says?"

"Yes, of course I do." It was a bit more difficult to make out than it would have been a dozen years ago, admittedly. I hadn't dealt with German *Kurrentschrift* since I left Germany. "He's inviting me to have supper with him tomorrow. Seven o'clock in the Savoy's dining room."

"Oh, lovely," Christopher said. "He didn't waste any time, did he? You owe me five pounds."

I sighed. "Of course."

He made to push up. "Guess I'd better go ring up the Hall again."

I put my hand on his arm. "Don't be stupid, Christopher. I could understand it if you wanted to ring up Beckwith Place to let Aunt Roz and Uncle Herbert know that a German count is sniffing around me. That's something your parents might actually want to know. But Crispin won't care."

"Shows what you know," Christopher said. "Although you're right. I should ring up Beckwith Place and let Mum and Dad know."

"Not until afterwards, Christopher. Please. It's dinner with a gentleman I barely know in a public setting. Nothing to worry your parents about."

"He's German," Christopher said.

I refrained from reminding him that so was I.

"That will only upset Francis," I said instead. "There is no need to let them know. Not now. Please, Christopher."

My cousin stuck his lower lip out and folded his arms across his chest, mutinously. "Fine. But if he asks you out again, I'm phoning home. And you will absolutely tell me everything that happens tomorrow. Every word, every gesture, every look."

I promised I would, since I didn't expect there to be anything very exciting to report. As I had pointed out, it was supper in the Savoy's dining room, in full view of everyone there, with someone I had no recollection of meeting before. It was hardly an intimate occasion.

"And I'll help you decide what to wear," Christopher added. "And do your face."

"I can do my own face, Christopher."

"Not as well as I can," Christopher said, which was true. "I won't have anything to do tomorrow anyway. Not unless Tom makes it back from Sussex or Surrey or wherever it was he went. The least you can do is distract me."

I rolled my eyes. "Very well, then. You can do my makeup. And pick out my frock. And make sure I look presentable for the *Graf*."

"Thank you, Pippa." He rubbed his hands together glee-fully. "This will be fun."

IT WASN'T, of course. It was an hour of agony, sitting in front of my mirror while Christopher painted my face and fluffed and curled my hair and made sure every aspect of my appearance was as perfect as it could be. He picked out my frock—green silk with diamante accents, the same frock his deviousness, the Viscount St George, had once informed me made me look like a Bramley. A frock I could not now wear without hearing his voice in my head.

Christopher shook his head, as he leaned into me with an eyebrow pencil in his hand and the tip of his tongue sticking out as he concentrated. "You look nothing like a Bramley, Pippa. Besides, what Crispin said, at least according to Constance, was that you looked edible. Crisp and tart and good enough to eat, wasn't it? Which is—"

"Rude," I said. "Completely improper. Indecent, even." Lewd, to make a rhyme of it.

The corner of his mouth turned up in a smirk worthy of his cousin even as his eyes stayed on my eyebrows. "Oh, certainly. But it's a compliment, isn't it? 'You look like a Bramley' is no compliment. But saying that you look good enough to eat means that he's not opposed to a taste—"

"Ewww!" I made such a face that Christopher had to stop drawing and lift the pencil away from my skin. I flapped my hands at him. "That's vile, Christopher. Disgusting. Horrid! As if I'd want St George's mouth anywhere near my person. God only knows where it's been!"

He sniggered. "God and Crispin, I assume."

If the latter remembered everything he'd done with that mouth, and I doubted it. "I can't believe you'd say something like that to me," I said. "That's repulsive, Christopher. How can you suggest such a thing?"

"I wasn't the one who suggested it. He did."

He leaned in with the pencil again and motioned to me to shut my eyes.

"He absolutely did not." But I closed my eyes obediently. "That may have been what he said, but it wasn't what he meant."

"It was one hundred percent what he meant," Christopher said, the strokes of the pencil light against my skin.

I wanted to shake my head, but refrained, since I didn't want to end up with a streak of black across my forehead. "He can't be that stupid."

He let out a puff of laughter. It was warm against my face and smelled of cloves. "Oh, of course not. He knew you'd respond the way you did. But it was absolutely what he meant."

"So why say it?"

"Because he knew it would get under your skin," Christopher said. When I slitted my eyes he was peering intently at my eyebrows. I closed my eyes again, but not before I had seen the corner of his mouth tilt up. "Just look at you. It's three months later, and you're still thinking about it. He got what he wanted."

"To ruin my enjoyment of my new dress?"

"For you to think about him every time you put it on," Christopher said. "Or at least every time someone pays you a compliment when you're wearing it."

I shook my head, and he hissed in annoyance. "Do that again, and you'll end up with stripes."

"Sorry. But you know St George doesn't care about my opinion of him."

"Sometimes, Pippa," Christopher told me with a sigh, "for being such a smart woman, you can be very thick."

"Excuse me?"

"Dense, darling."

"I told you—"

"You're being stupid," Christopher said bluntly. "And what's more, I suspect you're being stupid on purpose."

I opened my mouth, and then closed it again when he went on. "Of course Crispin cares about your opinion. We all care about your opinion. Although that's not at all what this is about."

"What is it about, then?"

"The fact that my cousin would dearly love for you to spend twenty-four hours every single day thinking about him. He would like nothing better."

He took a step back and eyed me critically.

"I knew it," I said. "He's trying to ruin my life."

Christopher sighed. "Yes, Pippa. That's what he's trying to do. Ruin your life."

He gestured. "Up you go. You're as lovely as I can make you."

I got to my feet and peered at myself in the mirror. "Well done, Christopher. You made me quite lovely indeed."

"I had a good canvas to work on," Christopher said as he started to put away the various pots and brushes he had used. "So you won't go anywhere with him after supper. You'll let one of the doormen at the Savoy put you into a Hackney, and you'll come home alone."

I nodded. "As discussed."

Call me paranoidal—call both of us paranoidal—but neither of us knew the *Graf* well, and we had no idea what his motives were for wanting to spend time with me. Hopefully they were innocent, and I would simply have a nice meal with someone who remembered me from my previous life and perhaps wanted to get to know me better, but Christopher had been adamant that I be careful.

In fact, he had threatened to lurk in the lobby of the Savoy all evening, to make sure nothing untoward happened to me. I had told him that that was unnecessary—nothing was likely to happen during supper at the Savoy, of all places—but he was still worried.

"And you'll be careful about what you eat and drink," he told me, not for the first time. "Don't leave your glass unattended so he can put anything in it."

I shook my head. "I think we've both learned that lesson."

Back in May, Christopher had unintentionally imbibed a glass full of Veronal that someone had hoped would kill me, and he hadn't woken up for days. It was lucky he had several stone on me, since I probably wouldn't have woken up at all, had I been the one to drink it.

"Say it," he told me sternly.

I sighed. "I promise. I'll keep an eye on my glass at all times, and I won't let anyone but the waiter put anything into it. The food from the kitchen should be safe, don't you think?"

"It should be," Christopher said grudgingly. "Look out for needles—don't let him jab you with anything—"

"Of course not."

"And don't let him share your cab. If he offers to, say no. I don't care if he's offended."

I didn't care, either. If it's between offending someone, especially someone I didn't yet care about, and being safe, I'll choose safe every time.

Not that we had any reason to think *Graf* Wolfgang wasn't exactly what he purported to be. I would probably be perfectly safe, because the idea of putting something in my food or drink or jabbing me with a syringe wasn't likely to have crossed his mind at all.

"And come straight home," Christopher admonished. "Don't dilly-dally. If the *Graf* offers to canoodle—"

"I'll turn him down, never fear."

"I was going to suggest that you canoodle in a corner of the lobby, where there are other people," Christopher said with a grin, and I made a face.

"He won't want to canoodle, Christopher. He was as stiff as a board yesterday, and I don't intend to give him any encouragement. Not on a first date."

He nodded. "Then tell him goodnight and let the doorman send you home in a Hackney by yourself. Any problems, make a scene."

"Of course. Do you still insist on seeing me there?"

"What kind of best friend would I be if I didn't?" Christopher wanted to know, and I rolled my eyes.

"You're just hoping for another glimpse of the *Graf.*"

He grinned. "How can you blame me? He's about the most decorative specimen I've seen in my entire life. Not that there aren't plenty of attractive blokes in London. But it isn't every day I get the chance to ogle someone like that."

I shook my head. "Please don't ogle him. In fact, I would prefer it if he didn't notice you at all. I don't want him to feel as if he has to include you in the dinner invitation. No offense."

"None taken," Christopher said blithely. "If he were my dinner date, I wouldn't want to share him, either."

"That's not why, and you know it. But if he has something he wants to say to me privately, he won't say it if you're there."

"That's true," Christopher agreed, and offered me his arm for the walk to the lift. "Do you suppose there is anything like that? Does he have something to say he doesn't want me to hear?"

"I have no idea," I said, tucking my hand through his elbow, "but he did invite me to supper. He might have something to say."

Christopher nodded and pushed the button to call the lift. "I'll take you to the Savoy and hand you over. And then you'll tell me everything when you come home."

"Of course I will," I assured him, and let him hand me into the lift.

CHAPTER FOUR

HIS HIGHNESS, the *Graf von und zu* Natterdorff, was waiting in the lobby of the Savoy when we walked in off the Strand. His face lightened when he saw me, and then closed up again when he spied Christopher coming in behind me.

"This is far enough," I told the latter and pulled him to a stop just inside the doors.

He flicked a glance in the direction of the *Graf* and nodded. "Be careful, Pippa. I'll be waiting up for you."

Of course he would be. I lifted up on my toes—not a far distance, as I'm not particularly short and Christopher isn't particularly tall—and pecked his cheek. "I'll see you at home."

"See that you do." He squeezed my hand and nodded to the *Graf* across the lobby, and then turned and walked back out the doors. I waited until he was outside in the street before I started my own trek across the checkerboard lobby floor towards Wolfgang.

He put out a hand as I approached. When I placed my own in it, he clicked his heels together and bowed over it. "*Freulein* Darling."

"*Graf* Wolfgang." I had no idea whether that was the correct address or not. I hadn't grown up rubbing elbows with the German nobility—the *Graf*'s assertion that we had met before notwithstanding—and I had arrived in England at the beginning of a war against Germany, at a time when no one cared about addressing any German, even the nobility, properly. So whereas Aunt Roz had instructed me in how to speak to His Grace, Duke Henry, and to Uncle Harold, the then Viscount St George and his wife, Lady Charlotte, I had no grounding in how German noble titles worked. "You may call me Philippa," I added graciously, "as it seems we're old friends."

At this, Wolfgang's lips curved up in the kind of smile that made an older lady crossing the lobby stumble over her own feet. "You must call me Wolfgang, then. No need to stand on ceremony."

"I would be delighted," I simpered.

He offered me his arm. "Shall we?"

I put my hand on it. "Let's."

A few minutes later we were seated at a table in the River Restaurant, watching the Thames flow lazily by outside the tall windows, surrounded by white-topped tables under an ornately carved ceiling.

"I am transported that you would allow me the pleasure of your company," Wolfgang told me, a bit too formally, after the waiter had watched us decide between the shrimp and the caviar for an appetizer, and between *Tortue Claire* and *Borscht* for soup. (The entire menu was in French, of course, as was *de rigueur* at the Savoy. Except for the *Borscht*, which is Russian and not German, in case you wondered.)

"It's my pleasure," I told him, sincerely. "It's not every day you meet someone who remembers you from when you were small." And half a continent away. On the opposite side of a war.

A shadow crossed his face, as if I had said those words out loud (I hadn't). "But you don't remember me?"

"I don't," I said honestly. "If what you told me was true, I was probably too young."

His face grew another shade darker. "Of course I told you the truth. I am not a liar."

"I didn't mean to suggest that you were," I said. "Of course you told me the truth. You have no reason to lie."

He looked just marginally mollified by that. "Is that why your friend, your cousin, escorted you here? Because you do not trust me?"

"I don't know you," I said. Politely but honestly, since I'm not the type to beat around the bush or, for that matter, the type to flatter a gentleman needlessly. "I have no reason to think you're untrustworthy, but I have no reason to trust you, either. Not yet."

He didn't seem to like that much, although he nodded, as if conceding my point.

"Christopher went home," I added. "He's not going to lurk in the lobby until our dinner is over so he can escort me back. He isn't like that." And I had firmly put my foot down so he wouldn't.

"Tell me about yourself," I added, since I know that all gentlemen like to discuss themselves. "What are you doing in London?"

He was on some sort of diplomatic mission, it seemed, or if not anything that specific, at least a trip during which he was supposed to meet people and talk to them and rebuild relations between Germany and England after the war. It might have been a personal mission, not a patriotic one. A way to get the

Natterdorff family back in good standing again after the aggressions. He wasn't terribly detailed, to be honest, and I didn't ask for specifics, partly because I thought laying out the answers might be awkward for him, and partly because I truly didn't care all that much. It was enough to sit and watch his lips move and have the timbre of his voice, and that almost-forgotten accent, the accent of my father, flow over me like a warm breeze.

"And what about you?" he asked eventually. "How has your life been since you arrived here from Germany?"

By then we were into the main meal—duck for Wolfgang, quail for me—and we spent the rest of that course talking about the Astleys and the Sutherlands. I brushed lightly over Crispin, but I did pay attention in case this whole thing was in some way about using me to get close to Duke Harold and his heir, for some nefarious purpose of Wolfgang's own. I had no idea what that purpose might be, but the possibility was there at the back of my mind, so I paid attention to it.

It was during this recitation that the *Graf*'s eyes focused on something over my shoulder and I saw his eyes narrow.

"Something wrong?" I broke off in the middle of the story about how I had gone to the Godolphin School in Salisbury while Christopher (and Crispin) were away at Eton, and how my old school chum Constance Peckham was now engaged to marry my cousin Francis.

Wolfgang's deep blue eyes flicked to mine for a second. "I thought I saw your cousin out there in the lobby."

I shook my head, without bothering to turn around. "Christopher bennet home."

"Does he always do what he says he'll do?"

Of course he didn't. Not always. However—

"There was no reason for him to lie about this. If he had wanted to hang around to make sure I was safe, he would have told me so and we would have worked something out. He wouldn't lie about it."

Wolfgang withdrew his eyes from behind me and focused on my face, but not without maintaining a tiny wrinkle between his brows. "You are close."

"Cousins," I said. "Best friends. The next thing to brother and sister."

He looked relieved. At least I thought so.

"I'm sure it was just someone who looked like him," I added. "London is full of fair-haired young men in evening kit."

Especially this time of day and in this sort of setting.

Wolfgang shot a last look over my shoulder in the direction of the lobby, but he must have decided that I was most likely right, because he didn't say anything else about it.

"So you went to secondary school in Salisbury—" he prompted, and we were off again, talking about Godolphin and Constance and the weekend party at the Dower House in Dorset where Constance and Francis had gotten to know one another.

At the end of the meal—Peach Melba; one can't really sup at the Savoy without finishing with it—Wolfgang walked me through the lobby and out on the Strand. "May I see you home?" he asked politely, while clasping my hand in his.

"If it's all the same to you," I answered, keeping Christopher's admonition in mind, "I think I'll just take a Hackney cab. I don't want to put you to any trouble."

"It's no trouble—"

But that was as far as he got before a motorcar swept up behind me, close enough that I could almost feel its front fender brush the backs of my legs.

Or if not that, I could at least feel the passage of air as the fender passed within three inches or so of my calves.

I squealed and jumped, and Wolfgang pulled me towards

him with a guttural growl, no doubt a German curse I hadn't had the pleasure of hearing before I left Heidelberg.

His hands were hard on my arms, and I could feel his breath flutter the hair at the top of my head. His heart beat strongly inside the chest I was leaning on.

It took me a moment to gather myself enough to pull away. And when I swung on my heel, it came as no surprise to see the blue Hispano-Suiza idling behind me in the Savoy's drop-off and pick-up lane, and to see Crispin Astley smirking at me from behind the wheel. "Hello, Darling."

Wolfgang's eyes narrowed into slits, and so did mine. "What's the big idea, St George? You normally manage to refrain from out and out attempting to murder me."

The smirk turned into something more like a sneer. "Let's not exaggerate, Darling. If I wanted to murder you, I wouldn't have missed."

"Says you," I retorted. "Perhaps I simply got out of the way faster than you had anticipated, and you weren't quick enough to hit me."

He inclined his head politely, or it might have looked like politesse to someone who didn't know him the way I did. "Yes, Darling, that must be it. Because if I wanted to kill you, I'd certainly do it in front of the Savoy, in full view of at least a hundred people who know exactly who I am."

He had a point. Wolfgang was staring, of course, but so was everyone else. And if there weren't a hundred of them, there were a lot. Crispin and his motorcar are well known all over London. I'm sure the doormen at the Savoy knew him—and it— by sight.

"What are you doing here anyway?" I wanted to know. "Did you slip your leash and run away from home?"

It wasn't even a weekend, although perhaps that had made it easier to escape.

"Father had business out of the house this evening," Crispin answered, civilly enough, "so I thought I'd take the opportunity to run up to Town for some entertainment."

"It's rather a long drive just for an evening's debauchery, isn't it? Won't you have to be back in your own bed by the time your father gets up tomorrow morning?"

"I'll manage," Crispin said. "It won't be the first time I've stayed up all day and night and the following day, too."

"I'm sure it won't be. Don't let me keep you."

I flapped my hand at him. He smirked. "You're not keeping me, Darling. As always, I'm exulting in your company. Aren't you going to introduce me to your friend?"

"I'm sure you already know all about him," I said sourly. Christopher would have told him everything he needed to know on the phone last night, no doubt. Or on the phone this morning, perhaps, if he had rung up again, which I rather thought he must have done, for Crispin to be here now. Or perhaps they had discussed it in person when Crispin arrived in London, if they had seen each other at the flat before Crispin made his way here.

I glanced around, discreetly. There was no sign of Christopher anywhere. That probably meant that if Wolfgang really had seen one of them earlier—and he probably had—it had probably been Crispin. He wouldn't be the first person to get the two of them mixed up on short acquaintance.

Crispin's smirk widened. "Indubitably, Darling. But if you'd prefer that I do the honors myself…"

"No," I said. Definitely not. Best not to let Crispin do anything whatsoever himself. He can't be trusted. There was no knowing what he'd say if I gave him free rein.

I turned back to the *Graf*. "Wolfgang, this is Crispin Astley, the Right Honorable Viscount St George. Christopher's cousin. Crispin, the *Graf von und zu* Natterdorff."

Wolfgang smacked his heels together with a noticeable click and inclined from the waist. "*Mein Herr.*"

This time it was Crispin's eyes which narrowed. "*Graf* von Natterdorff."

A quick primer for those of you who don't know the intricacies: a *Graf*, as Christopher had pointed out yesterday, is the equivalent of a count. There are no counts in the British noble ranks. There are, however, countesses. Lady Laetitia Marsden's parents, Lord Maurice and Lady Euphemia, are the Earl and Countess of Marsden. Thus, Wolfgang was the equivalent of an earl. And an earl ranks above a viscount in the hierarchy.

Now, once Uncle Harold kicked the bucket and Crispin became Duke of Sutherland, then he'd rank above the earls and marquesses. Dukes are at the top of the social ladder, only just below royalty. But for now, Crispin was a step below Wolfgang on the nobility scale, and I could see it grate. Especially since Wolfgang had addressed him as if he were an inferior, something the Viscount St George is definitely not used to. His jaw clenched and fury flashed in his eyes.

I'm sure it didn't help, either, that Wolfgang was taller, and older, and—it had to be said—better-looking. Or more classically handsome, at any rate.

Not that Crispin is ugly. Not at all, in fact. He quite lovely to look at. So is Christopher. They both have heart-shaped faces with big eyes and long lashes and cupid's bow lips and high cheekbones and slightly pointy chins: a bit elfin, if you want to be fanciful. But at twenty-three—and a fairly new-minted twenty-three in Crispin's case; his birthday had been just two months ago—they both look boyishly charming, soft and a bit pretty, while Wolfgang was a man.

An exceptionally handsome man. Of higher rank than a viscount. And with that dashing scar on his cheek.

It took a few seconds, but then Crispin pried his jaws apart to do the right thing. "Delighted to make your acquaintance."

He has lovely manners when he bothers to make use of them. Of course, he couldn't make it sound like he meant it, but the sentiment was nicely appropriate.

There was a curve to Wolfgang's lips that suggested that he was well aware of the effort it had taken Crispin to get the words out. Thankfully, he didn't see the need to rub it in, which wouldn't have gone over well. Instead, he simply nodded, as if the response had been his right and there was no need, nay, indeed any reason for him to reciprocate the compliment. I saw Crispin's eyes turn flinty, but he refrained from letting his mouth run away with him. I could tell he wanted to —had it been anyone else, he wouldn't have bothered to restrain himself—but instead, he turned back to me. "May I offer you a lift, Darling?"

"You may offer," I said dubiously, and he smirked.

"Let me rephrase. Hop in and I'll take you home."

"*Freulein* Darling can make her own way home," Wolfgang said stiffly, and Crispin shot him a look.

"Of course she can, old chap. Does it every day, doesn't she?"

He turned his attention back to me. "But I'm here, and the motorcar is at your disposal, Darling, and so am I, of course; entirely at your disposal—"

He blinked innocently as he turned back to Wolfgang, "—and it occurs to me that you probably don't have a motorcar at the ready, *Graf* von Natterdorff..."

My eyes narrowed. "You're horrid, St George."

He sniggered. "Of course, Darling. But after I made the drive all the way from Wiltshire to ensure you get back to Kit safely, would you really deprive me of the pleasure of your company?"

"Horrid," I repeated. "You lie like a rug, St George. Like a flatfish. Like a cheap watch. You certainly did not drive here all the way from Wiltshire just to—"

He raised his voice. "Darling."

In fairness to him, he had to, because once I get going, it can be difficult to derail me.

"Yes?" I said.

"Get in the motorcar."

I sighed. "Stop ordering me about, St George. You know it doesn't work."

He sighed back. "Yes, Darling. But you know what they say. Hope springs eternal."

"Of course." I turned back to Wolfgang, who was looking from one to the other of us with his brows lowered. "I'm sorry. But he's right, I should let him drive me home. He's here, and it makes sense to go with him rather than paying for a Hackney."

"I would be happy to pay for the Hackney," Wolfgang said.

"It's not the money." I could pay for my own Hackney. It's not like I'm destitute. Aunt Roz and Uncle Herbert keep Christopher and me in more-than-adequate pocket money. "But he's here, and he's offering, and I know that he knows where he's going, and that I'll be safe with him..."

A corner of Crispin's mouth curved up. Wolfgang withdrew his attention from him to look at me. A second passed, then two. Then he nodded. "Of course."

"I had a lovely time tonight. Thank you for inviting me."

I extended my hand, a bit hesitantly. Crispin's appearance may have destroyed all the goodwill that had developed over dinner, and if so, it would be hard to blame Wolfgang. St George is difficult to stomach under the best of circumstances, and these weren't those. I could hardly hold it against Wolfgang if he never wanted to see me again, if only so it would ensure that he'd never have to deal with Crispin again.

The latter, of course, watched our exchange like a hawk. Wolfgang seemed to hesitate for a moment, too, before he took my hand in his and gazed deeply into my eyes. "Perhaps I may impose on you for supper again sometime?"

"I would be delighted," I said, with a lot more feeling than Crispin had been able to manage. I could hear him snort behind me. Thankfully, it was soft enough that Wolfgang didn't seem to notice, or if he did, it was soft enough that he could pretend to ignore it.

"I shall send another note," he informed me.

"Please do." I simpered.

He clicked his heels together and bowed over my hand. This time he raised it all the way to his lips, and let his mouth linger on my knuckles for a long moment before he brushed his thumb over the spot where they had been. It was a classic Crispin-move—I had seen him employ it before, and had seen young women titter and blush when he did it, too.

I tittered, and I probably blushed. Wolfgang smirked. "Let me assist you into the motorcar."

He opened the door and seated me, carefully. And then he finally, reluctantly, withdrew his hand from mine before he shut the door behind me. "I look forward to seeing you again, Philippa."

"Likewise," I breathed, "Wolfgang."

He clicked his heels together and bowed sharply one last time, one hand spread over his heart. And then Crispin, giving in to his bad mood, took his foot off the clutch and stomped on the gas pedal, and the Hispano-Suiza took off from the entrance to the Savoy with a roar that scattered car park assistants and pedestrians and enveloped Wolfgang in a cloud of exhaust as we shot onto The Strand and away.

I giggled, of course. It was impossible not to.

Admittedly, it took me a minute to get to that point—my

heart had jumped into my throat as soon as he started driving, and it took a few seconds to force it back down where it belonged—but once we were a couple of blocks away from the Savoy and he had slowed to a more decorous pace, much more suitable for the busy London streets, I told him, amused, "I had no idea your jealousy extended so far, St George."

He slanted me a look of dislike from under lowered brows. "Don't be ridiculous, Darling. I'm not jealous."

"No? What would you call it, then?"

He sniffed. "Concern. Obviously."

"Concern? You looked ready to call him out."

He shot me another look, this one with less dislike and more incredulity. "Call him out? To a duel, do you mean? Have you lost your mind, Darling? You think I would duel another man for you? Especially one who looks like that?"

"Looks like...? Oh, you noticed the bragging scar, did you?"

"Who wouldn't?" Crispin said. "The Germans were mad for them before the war, apparently. Thought it made them look brave."

He sneered.

I wanted to sneer back—it's automatic—but I found I couldn't. "I imagine they've learned better now." After a war that had resulted in far more grievous injuries than neat slices across the cheeks.

"My father had one," I added.

Crispin flicked me a look. "A dueling scar?"

I nodded. "I'd forgotten all about it until now. But he did. It was smaller than Wolfgang's, and a bit lower. About..." I reached over and dragged a fingertip along his jaw, "—here."

If that sounds flirtatious, or like I took an opportunity to touch him because I wanted to, I can assure you that such was the furthest thing from my mind. I simply didn't want him to take his eyes off the road for something as frivolous as watching me point to the place on my own face.

And yes, perhaps there was a small part of me that wanted to see his reaction. Last month, at Beckwith Place, I had put my hand on his cheek for a moment, as part of a (if I do say so myself) rather well calculated bit of tit-for-tat, and he had practically stopped breathing. So I'll admit I wanted to see if I could do it again.

I couldn't, although for a second he didn't say a word. Then he cleared his throat. "No offense, Darling, but I'm not risking my pretty face for you."

"How deplorably ungentlemanly of you," I told him, and folded my hands in my lap.

"Well, he's a *Graf*, isn't he, and I'm a lowly Viscount." The corner of his mouth turned up in a smirk. "I suppose it's all right if I'm not as much of a gentleman as he is."

"He put you in your place rather neatly," I said, "didn't he?"

"He was certainly rude enough about it," Crispin agreed. "And you did nothing to defend my honor. This is the last time I'll come to your rescue, Darling."

"I shall certainly hope so," I told him. "What you 'rescued' me from was in all probability something I would have enjoyed."

He sneered. "Wanted the handsome count to kiss you, did you?"

I rolled my eyes right back. "As if you have any room to talk, St George. You'll kiss any girl who'll let you."

He didn't respond to that, and I added, "I wasn't going to go upstairs with him. Christopher made it clear that I was to go nowhere that wasn't public. Not up to his room, not into a cab, nowhere."

Crispin muttered something. I think it might have been, "Good for Kit."

"Ridiculous," I said. "I can't believe Christopher talked you into—"

"He didn't. I was coming up to London anyway."

"That's not what you said earlier."

He shrugged. "Perhaps I told a small fib."

"Of course you did." I made a face. "Let me guess. The lovely Lady Laetitia Marsden is in Town from Dorset?"

His mouth curved. "She might be."

"Well, thanks for nothing, then, St George. You cad." I stuck my bottom lip out.

He sniggered. "Dear me, Darling. Did you want me to drive here from Wiltshire for you?"

"I didn't want you to drive here from Wiltshire for Laetitia Marsden," I said. "You know my feelings on the subject, St George. You'll regret it if you marry her. You might have fun with her—"

As she had told him once, on one of the occasions I had overheard her try to talk him into accepting her; the words still made my face pucker when I repeated them, if I'm honest, "—but you don't love her, and all the fun in the world isn't going to make you happy in the long run. If fun is what you want—"

Because it wasn't as if I didn't know what she meant by that reference, was it? "—you can have it without being married. You've had plenty of fun so far, and entirely without a wife. There's no reason why you can't simply continue to do what you're already doing."

"There's my father," Crispin said.

"Blast your father. If he'd rather have you married and miserable, he doesn't deserve your consideration. Damn him."

He didn't answer, and we drove the rest of the way to the

Essex House Mansions—just a few blocks by then—in silence. Crispin pulled the motorcar up in front of the front door. "Here we are."

"Indeed."

I waited for him to turn off the engine and come around the car to open the door for me, but when he didn't, I added, "I suppose she's waiting for you? You don't want to come up and see Christopher?"

"I've already seen Kit," Crispin said, "and had my weekly dose of Miss Schlomsky, too."

So he *had* stopped by and talked to Christopher before he went to the Savoy.

"I don't see any lipstick stains on your collar," I remarked, with a searching glance.

"She seemed distracted," Crispin answered. His eyes twinkled, as if he found my examination amusing. "She took the time to back me into a corner of the lift to have her way with me, certainly, but her heart didn't seem to be in it."

"That must have been disappointing for you."

"Indeed." He smirked. "My goal in coming here is always to provoke some young lady to passion."

"If that remark is intended for me—" I subsided when his smirk broadened.

"Oh, indubitably, Darling. You turn so gloriously incandescent when you want to murder me. Such a thrill."

"Hmph," I said. "I don't suppose she said anything to you, did she?"

"What do you mean, 'anything'? She said," and here his voice climbed into the range of Flossie's strident alto, "'Oh, Lord St George, aren't you just the cutest thing—'"

And then it dropped back down to his regular smooth tenor before he added, "But other than that, no, Darling. She didn't."

I flicked a glance over his black jacket, white waistcoat, and perfectly knotted bowtie. Cute? "That's rather uninspired."

"It's Florence Schlomsky," Crispin said. "Of course it was uninspired."

Of course. "I'm sure Laetitia will do a better job of complimenting you when you see her."

He flicked me a look. "You could do a better job of it too, you know."

"I could," I said, and opened my door, since it seemed obvious by this point that he wasn't going to come around and do it, "but I won't. Are you quite certain you don't want to come up?"

"As I said," Crispin said, "I've already seen Kit. And he must be simply slavering to hear every detail about your time with the *Graf*. You go on up."

While he went off to meet the lovely Lady Laetitia, I presumed.

I nodded. "Thanks for the lift, St George. And while it was unnecessary, I appreciate the rescue, as well."

"Any time, Darling. Have a good evening."

"You too," I told him, and shut the door to the Hispano-Suiza. "Safe home, St George."

"Thank you, Darling. I'll give Tidwell your love, shall I?"

Tidwell the butler was the very best part of Sutherland Hall, if you asked me. I nodded. "Please do. No need to remember me to your father, however."

"No, Darling." His lips curved. "He's not likely to forget."

He probably wasn't. "Drive carefully," I told him. "And if something happens and you can't get out of London and you don't want to go to Sutherland House," and he couldn't spend the night with Lady Laetitia, although it was difficult to imagine an eventuality where that wouldn't be an option, "come back here and we'll put you up for the night."

"Thank you, Darling. I'll see you next time, shall I?"

He didn't wait for my response, just put the H6 in gear and rolled off down the road. I waited for him—for the car—to vanish from sight, and then I went into the lobby and greeted Evans.

CHAPTER FIVE

CHRISTOPHER WAS SITTING on the Chesterfield with a cocktail when I walked into the flat.

He was also sitting with Tom Gardiner, who was ensconced in an armchair with a drink of his own. It looked like straight bourbon or brandy, unlike Christopher's sparkling concoction. When I showed up in the doorway to the foyer, they both looked up at me. Christopher had a slight flush across his cheekbones that might be guilt because of Crispin, or embarrassment because I had interrupted something, while Tom gave me a bland smile that didn't quite reach his eyes.

"Philippa," he said. "You look lovely."

I looked down at myself. "You don't think I look like a Bramley?"

Christopher sighed. "Let it go, Pippa." To Tom he added, "Crispin once told her the dress made her look tart and crisp and edible. She took it as a slight and has been telling me he compared her to an apple ever since."

Tom's lips curved. "No, Philippa. You look nothing like a

Bramley, and I doubt Lord St George was telling you that you did."

"Speaking of Crispin—" I said, and turned to Christopher.

The flush went immediately more guilty, although he tried to hide it behind an insouciant front. "He found you, then?"

"I wasn't exactly hard to find," I said. "All he had to do was loiter outside the Savoy and wait for me to come out. And then he had the nerve to almost take me out at the knees when he swept up behind me. I think the H6 missed me by two or three inches, no more."

"That was careless of him," Tom commented. "I would have expected better."

I huffed. "I wouldn't. It's exactly the kind of thing he would do. I'm just surprised I'm not limping."

I turned back to Christopher. "Why on earth would you drag him all the way up here from Wiltshire, Christopher? If you wanted someone to spy on me, couldn't you have done it yourself?"

"You told me not to," Christopher said.

"That was because I didn't want anyone to! It certainly wasn't a suggestion that you should induce St George to make the drive to London so that he could do it instead!"

"I didn't," Christopher protested. "I simply phoned him and let him know about the invitation to supper. I didn't know that he was going to drive to London until I came back home after dropping you off and he was waiting outside."

"You didn't have to tell him where I was! Why didn't you tell him not to bother?"

"Have you ever told Crispin not to bother when there's something he wants to do, Pippa?" He gave me a look. "He's spoilt, which you very well know. And he doesn't like to be told what to do or not to do. In fact, if you tell him what to do, he frequently does the opposite, just to spite you. If he wanted a look at the *Graf,* I certainly wasn't going to be able to stop him."

I rolled my eyes. "Well, he got one. After he nearly broke both of my legs, he tried to insult Wolfgang and was insulted in turn. And then he drove me home and went off to see Laetitia Marsden."

"Laetitia Marsden?" Christopher shook his head. "She's not—"

I cut him off. "Never mind Laetitia Marsden, Christopher. Although— no, never mind. He knows how I feel about that whole situation, and so do you. He can do whatever he wants."

As Christopher had so eloquently pointed out, Crispin was spoilt and prone to not taking advice. Perhaps I would just stop telling him to stay away from Lady Laetitia and hope that a spot of reverse psychology would do the trick.

"Dinner was lovely, thank you for asking," I said instead.

Tom's lips twitched. "You've met someone, I hear."

"If you want to put it like that." I crossed the floor and sat down next to Christopher on the Chesterfield, crossing my legs. "His name is Wolfgang Albrecht, and he's the *Graf von und zu* Natterdorff."

Tom nodded. "So Kit told me. He knew you when you were a girl, Kit said?"

"That's what he told us. I still can't remember him, but he knew my parents' names and where we lived and that I look like my mother but with my father's eyes. It would seem that he's at least seen us all—or them, at least—at some point."

"Is there a reason you're suspicious?" Tom wanted to know.

"I don't know that I am," I told him. "Not specifically. But I can't remember him, and he's German. And while that's probably hypocritical of me—" since I was half-German too, "it's too soon after the war to feel completely comfortable with that, I think."

"But he hasn't said or done anything that sounds out of character?"

"I have no idea what would be in or out of character for a German *Graf*. My parents weren't wealthy, you know. Apparently it was a scandal when my mother left England and married a commoner in Germany. I have no idea why we would have hob-nobbed with a *Graf* in the first place. But no, I wouldn't say so. Nothing he said today contradicted anything he said yesterday."

"No reason to think he isn't who and what he says he is?"

"None I can think of," I said. "Why would he bother to approach me saying he's the *Graf* von Natterdorff if he isn't? I'm nobody!"

"You're one step removed from the Sutherlands," Tom said, with a glance at Christopher, who sipped his cocktail calmly. "You're living with the Duke of Sutherland's nephew, you were more or less adopted by the Duke's younger brother, and you're involved with the Duke's son and heir."

"I'm not *involved* with St George."

Christopher chuckled.

"Not romantically, perhaps," Tom allowed. "But you're friends, or something like it."

I opened my mouth to protest—I'm certainly not friends with St George, and besides, what did he mean, *perhaps?*—and he waved me down. "You're an access point to the Sutherlands, Pippa. You're also an access point to Francis."

I closed my mouth again. "Why Francis?"

"Francis was in the trenches during the War," Tom said. "Aside from you, he's the only one in the family with a bona fide connection to Germany."

That was true. And it was only too easy to come up with reasons why someone might want a go at Francis, from the far-fetched to the blatantly obvious. Something had happened during the war, he had seen something or heard something, or he had killed someone or maimed someone or simply taken part in the fighting.

"Do you have any reason to think that he doesn't simply want to get to know me better?" I asked.

Tom shook his head. "None at all," he said cheerfully. "It's just part of the job, you know. We're deeply suspicious bastards in the CID."

Of course. "Well, if you want to look into him, be my guest. But do it quietly, please. If he truly is who he says he is, I don't want to upset him. Even though I don't remember him, it's nice to have a connection to my former life."

Tom nodded.

"I see you made it back from Sussex," I added. "Or was it Surrey?"

"It was Bristol," Tom said, "actually."

"Bristol?" That's nowhere near Sussex or Surrey, nor does it sound like it. "County or city?"

"Both," Tom said. "Second time in a month, too."

"What were you doing in Bristol a month ago?"

"Dropping off Baby Bess with the Doles," Tom said.

Baby Bess—or Elizabeth Anne—was a roughly six-month-old baby girl we had thought might belong to Crispin, or if not, perhaps to Francis. She hadn't turned out to belong to either of them, and when her mother died, Tom had driven the baby to her grandparents in Bristol. I hadn't inquired into the specifics at the time. I'd honestly just been relieved to know that none of my nearest and dearest was responsible for the baby, or for her mother's demise.

"Is something wrong?" I asked now.

Aunt Roz had impressed upon Tom that if Baby Bess

wasn't going to be happy with the Doles, or if the Doles weren't nice people who would take good care of the tyke, Tom was to bring her back to Beckwith Place post haste, and Aunt Roz would flout convention and take her in herself, be damned to anyone's prurient thoughts on the subject.

"Not with the baby," Tom said. "Or I assume not. That wasn't part of this."

"What was?"

He exchanged a glance with Christopher, who lifted a shoulder. Tom turned back to me. "I got a summons from the Bristol police. One of their dead was in possession of one of my calling cards and they wanted to know why."

"One of their—?"

"Dead," Tom nodded. "A woman was killed in an alley in Bristol three nights ago, and my card was in her reticule. The Bristol police wanted to know why."

"Why would someone kill someone in an alley and leave her reticule? Was she—?" I stopped and swallowed.

"No," Tom said, his own voice tight. "She was not harmed in any way."

"Other than being dead?"

He nodded. "And you're right, it's strange that someone would have accosted her in an alley and then left her purse with her money behind. Usually when people are accosted in alleys, it's for their money."

Precisely. "So who was she? Why did she have your card?"

And then something occurred, and I added, my face pale, "Oh, God. It wasn't Abigail Dole's mother, was it? Her father has certainly been through enough."

"Undoubtedly," Tom nodded, while Christopher winced, "but no, it wasn't her. It was Margaret Hughes."

"Margaret who?"

"Aunt Charlotte's lady's maid," Christopher said. "Remember? She went with Tom and the baby last month."

Of course. After Aunt Charlotte's death, Uncle Harold had sacked her maid, or perhaps it was that Hughes had decided to leave on her own when there was no work for her to do. Neither Uncle Harold nor Crispin were in need of a lady's maid.

However it had come about, she had ended up at Beckwith Place the same weekend as Abigail Dole and her baby. There, she had proceeded to blackmail my Uncle Herbert for a thousand pounds, before going off with Tom and little Bess and a hefty cheque. I found it difficult to muster up much sorrow that she had come to a bad end.

"What about the money?" I asked.

"The money?"

"The thousand pounds from Uncle Herbert. We talked about this."

"*We* didn't talk about this," Christopher said, looking from me to Tom and back.

It was my turn to wince. "You had just found out that you had a half-brother and then he was dead. It didn't seem necessary to tell you that Hughes had blackmailed your father with that information."

Not to mention with the information that not only had Uncle Herbert sired a son with one of the maids before he had married Aunt Roz, but apparently he'd done it again at some later point, after Francis and my late cousin Robbie had been born, and while Christopher was either a gleam in his mother's eye, or perhaps not yet conceived.

He scowled. "What's the big idea, not telling me something like that?"

"You seemed upset enough when we found you outside the study window," I said, "and then there was the whole business with the gunshot. I suppose it slipped my mind for a while, and then I didn't see the point in bringing it up. It doesn't actually matter to anything. Except perhaps to her death."

I turned back to Tom. "Had she cashed the cheque?"

"That all happened last month," Tom said. "Of course she had. And opened herself a nice, fat account with a local bank for the money. It was still there. Or most of it was."

"So if it wasn't for the money, and it wasn't for..." I hesitated, "amorous purposes, why kill her?"

"Who knows?" Tom said. "It's the Bristol PD's problem, not mine. They didn't want my help with the case, just with information. When they found my card, the local constables rang up the Yard and I went down to Bristol to give them what information I could. Which was precious little, other than how she came by my card."

"Did you happen to mention...?" I trailed off delicately.

"They assumed the money had been severance," Tom said evenly, "or perhaps a settlement in Lady Charlotte's will, and as her possession of it didn't seem germane to her death, no, I didn't see the need to bring it up."

There was a moment's pause before he added, "I stopped at Beckwith Place on my way back to Town. Your mother put me up for the night."

It took a second, but then Christopher flushed up. "Checking my father's alibi? Really, Tom?"

"Not just his," Tom said coolly. "But you don't have to worry, Kit. They were all home together on the night in question. Your father, your mother, Francis, and Constance."

Christopher eyed him like this wasn't really the point, and of course it wasn't. Or it was only part of it: the other part was that Tom had dared to suspect them in the first place.

"Well, of course they were," I said. "Uncle Herbert would never kill anyone, and besides, he probably didn't even know where Hughes had ended up. He and Francis had already left for Southampton when you and Hughes took the baby to Bristol."

Tom nodded.

"That still doesn't mean I appreciate it," Christopher declared with a scowl.

Tom sighed. "I'm a detective, Kit. It's what I do. Margaret Hughes blackmailed your father out of a thousand pounds. It would be a motive for murder for anyone. If she did it once, she could do it again. Anyone would want to avoid that, and some people would kill to do so."

Christopher couldn't dispute that, of course, since it was obviously true, but he still stuck his bottom lip out in a pout.

"At this point," I said, "what Hughes was holding over Uncle Herbert is pretty well out in the open anyway. We all know about the affair with Maisie Moran and what came of it, and as for the other thing, Uncle Herbert assured me that Aunt Roz already knew and that there were extenuating circumstances..."

Christopher and Tom exchanged a look.

"Yes," Tom agreed after a moment. "I suppose that's true. Your uncle isn't the one who has the most to lose there, in any case. Nor is your aunt."

Perhaps not. I wasn't up on the details of that particular issue, since Uncle Herbert hadn't seen fit to confide the details to me. I looked from one to the other of them—Tom certainly knew, and I suspected that Christopher knew more than I did, too—but now didn't seem like the best time to bring it up for clarification, so I didn't.

"I don't think I care who killed Hughes as long as it wasn't someone we care about," I said instead. And then I realized how cold that sounded, so I added, "I mean, I don't wish murder on anyone, of course, but—"

"I get it," Tom nodded. "The Bristol police are working the case. I told them what I could—it wasn't much—and left them to it. It'll probably turn out to be quite simple. People kill for a lot less than we think sometimes. She might have had ten pounds in her reticule, and for some people, that's enough to justify murder."

We sat in silence a moment.

"Was everything all right at Beckwith Place?" I asked.

"Everything was perfect," Tom answered. "I stayed for dinner and spent the night. Francis looks healthier than I've seen him since the war, and Constance was glowing."

"Well, I'm sorry to have interrupted your discussion." I pushed to my feet. "Carry on with what you were doing before I came in. I'm going to go to my room and change."

"I was just updating Kit on what had happened in Bristol," Tom said. "Feel free to come back and sit with us. I'd like to hear more about your evening."

Christopher nodded. "Yes, please, Pippa. Every word."

"Of course." I headed into the hallway towards my room and left them alone.

WOLFGANG DID NOT SEND a note that night. He didn't send one the following morning, either. I tried not to think unkind thoughts about Crispin, whose fault it surely had to be —I had been a delight, hadn't I? We'd had a perfectly lovely time all through dinner, and it wasn't until St George showed up outside the Savoy and started to throw his weight around that things had taken a turn for the sour, wasn't that so?—but as the hours passed with nothing, I started to second-guess my own appeal, too. Perhaps I hadn't been fawning enough? Perhaps Wolfgang was used to women who succumbed to his charms in short order, and the fact that I had gone off with another man at the end of the meal instead of upstairs with him, had grated?

Christopher told me I was being ridiculous, that Wolfgang would be contacting me again, I just had to be patient. It wasn't as if he'd want to look too eager, was it, when I had left him to stand there outside the Savoy whilst I left with another man, which made perfect sense. I kicked myself again, mentally, and did the same to Crispin. What was his problem, anyway? It wasn't any of his affair if I had dinner with a handsome gentleman who evinced interest in me. He had his hands full with Laetitia Marsden, not to mention all the other women who buzzed around him like bees around a flower, and he had no business whatsoever to meddle in my affairs.

The next time I saw him, I was definitely going to tell him so.

I did a bit of marketing in the middle of the day—visits to Fortnum & Mason and to Twinings, among other things—and then I asked Evans again on my way inside, "Any messages, Evans?"

"I'm afraid not, Miss Darling."

He made to shut the front door behind me, but hesitated when a Hackney cab swung off the street and made to pull up to the front door.

I hovered too, of course. I'm curious by nature, and besides, what if it was Wolfgang?

It wasn't. Enough time passed for whoever was inside to pay for the fare, and then the back door opened. A stout gentleman in a pearl gray suit with an enormous gray mustache popped out of the back. He carried a silver-topped cane in one hand, and turned to offer the other to his companion, a lady a few years older than Aunt Roz, short and sturdy with black hair that sported white threads through the front.

The Hackney's door shut behind the lady, and the black

motorcar rolled away. The lady and gentleman turned to Evans. "Howdy," the gentleman said, in a broad American accent.

I think I knew right then who he was; I didn't need the next sentence.

"My name is Hiram Schlomsky, and this is my wife Sarah. We're looking for our daughter Florence."

CHAPTER SIX

THE SCHLOMSKYS WERE NOT what I had expected. I
thought they would be like everyone's—or at least like my—
image of the stereotypical American couple. Loud, and brash,
and dressed just a degree or two over the top from what was
tasteful. A bit like Flossie herself, to be honest, with her indul-
gence in fluttering pink panels and beads and tassels. But they
weren't. Not even close. Mrs. Schlomsky wore a perfectly plain
and boring summer ensemble in navy and white, off the rack
instead of haute couture, and without a flutter or a tassel in
sight. The skirt was several inches too long to fit with current
fashion, and so was the lady's hair. No bob for Mrs. Schlomsky.

She and her husband were clearly used to people bowing
and scraping to them, however. When Evans didn't jump
quickly enough, the millionaire Mr. Schlomsky poked at him
with his walking stick.

"My daughter. Where is she?"

"I don't believe Miss Schlomsky is in the building," Evans
said as he skipped away from the point of the cane.

"Not home?" The parents exchanged a glance.

"I knew we should have sent another telegram," Mrs. Schlomsky muttered. "The first one probably didn't make it here. If she'd known we were coming, she'd have been here."

"If she knew we were coming," Mr. Schlomsky added, "she would have been at the hotel last night. Or at least first thing this morning."

I cleared my throat, and they both looked at me as if the vase of flowers on the sideboard had given voice. "Hello," I said, feeling a bit awkward about it. "My name is Pippa Darling. Flossie and I are... um... friends."

Or at least Flossie had always been friendly to me, and more than friendly to Christopher and Crispin. Christopher had always been terrified of her, and although Crispin was far more capable of taking care of himself, I still didn't appreciate her constantly throwing herself at him.

Naturally I didn't say any of those things to the Schlomskys, who were eyeing me up and down. "Friends?" Mrs. Schlomsky echoed, a bit blankly. "Flossie?"

I narrowed my eyes. "Is there a reason I shouldn't be friendly with your daughter?"

She didn't answer immediately, and I added, "She's my neighbor. We're around the same age. She's quite open and welcoming, you know." A bit too welcoming with certain people, perhaps, but we wouldn't go into that. "And my flatmate is the youngest nephew of the Duke of Sutherland," I added, "so it's not as if we're unsuitable company—"

"No, no," Mrs. Schlomsky waved me into silence. "You misunderstood me. I'm delighted that Florence has made friends. She was always so quiet and studious at home."

Quiet and studious?

"The change of scenery must have been good for her," I said, because quiet and studious were two of the last words I would have used to describe Flossie.

Then again, most parents probably have no idea of what their children get up to when left to their own devices. I didn't think Uncle Herbert and Aunt Roz knew that Christopher dressed in drag and went to monthly balls under the guise of Kitty Dupree, and Uncle Harold hadn't had any idea of the excesses Crispin indulged in until Simon Grimsby, the late Duke's valet, exposed them back in April. And Wiltshire is only a few hours from London, so Uncle Harold, Uncle Herbert, and Aunt Roz had less excuse than the Schlomskys for not knowing what their offspring was up to.

For a second it occurred to me to wonder whether my own parents, had they been alive, would have recognized the person I had become. Would I even be the person I was now had the war not derailed everything in Europe?

Probably not, I had to admit. If I had spent a peaceful life with my parents in Germany, I would be a different person than I was. I had become Pippa Darling instead of Philippa Schatz from leaving home at an early age, and from being integrated into the Astley family from then on, and from Christopher, around whom most of my existence had revolved for the past twelve years.

No, coming to England had changed my life, and had changed me into someone different than I would otherwise have been, and it wasn't unlikely that the same thing had happened to Flossie, on her own for the first time in a strange country.

"When do you expect our daughter back?" Mrs. Schlomsky inquired of Evans, who looked mildly surprised.

"I wouldn't know, Mrs. Schlomsky. Miss Schlomsky didn't tell me where she was going or when she was returning."

I hadn't seen Flossie this morning. I hadn't seen her yesterday either, although Crispin had said he'd done. Now that I thought about it, I hadn't seen her since I'd delivered that telegram two evenings ago.

"Did you say you'd sent a telegram?" I asked the Schlomskys.

They both stared at me, startled, but after a moment, Hiram Schlomsky nodded. "We did, young lady. We crossed from New York to Southampton on the RMS Berengaria, and spent a night at the Star Hotel before we came up here to London yesterday. We telegrammed Florence from Southampton the first night. We assumed she would come and find us at the Savoy when we got here, and when she didn't, we decided to give it a night. And now here we are."

He spread his hands. Or at least he spread one, the other still held the walking stick. The head was shaped as some sort of animal, I saw. Something monstrous and curly with horns, perhaps a yak or a bison.

"I think I saw your telegram arrive," I told him. "Or at least I saw *a* telegram arrive. I was the one who brought it upstairs to her. Did it begin with the word *surprise?*"

They both nodded. "We didn't tell her we were coming," Hiram Schlomsky rumbled. "We haven't seen her since she left Toledo last fall. We wanted to surprise her."

"Well, unless someone else sent a telegram that began with *surprise* on the same day, it got here. I stood right in front of her when she opened it."

"Then she should have come and found us," Mrs. Schlomsky said, her tone somewhere between peevish and worried.

I nodded sympathetically. "I'm not sure why she didn't, but she was alive and well as of yesterday evening. I haven't seen her myself since the telegram arrived, but Christopher saw her later that evening, and Crispin saw her yesterday. Lord St George."

I exchanged a glance with Evans, who nodded. "Your daughter was on her way out at the same time as Miss Darling's cousin last evening. That was the last time I saw her, as well. The door is locked at eleven, when I go off duty. She must have come in after that."

Or not come in at all, although of course I wasn't insensitive enough to actually say that.

"Perhaps you'd be so kind as to open the door to her flat for us, Evans?" I asked. "I'm sure Miss Schlomsky would want her parents to be as comfortable as possible while they wait for her."

Evans hesitated, and I added, "They're probably the ones paying for it, you know."

Flossie hadn't a job, so her parents' fortune surely provided her rent and spending money, in the same way that Uncle Herbert was the one paying for Christopher's and my flat and our allowances. Evans would have let Uncle Herbert up with no questions asked if my uncle were to show up here and wanted to go upstairs. Evans had even sent Uncle Harold up without announcing him just a month or two ago, and Crispin's father had nothing whatsoever to do with the financials for the flat. In justice to Evans Uncle Harold is, of course, a duke, and his son and heir had been crashed out in my bed at that point, so there were mitigating circumstances.

And no, it wasn't the way it sounds. I slept on the Chester-field in the sitting room that night, in case you somehow got the idea that we'd been sharing. Naturally, that was what Uncle Harold had been worried about. As if sharing a bed with me could have ruined his son and heir any further than Crispin had already ruined himself.

"Of course," Evans said. "One moment."

He disappeared behind the counter to dig out the keys to Florence's flat. I turned to the Schlomskys and smiled politely.

"I trust your trip to London was uneventful? And you're staying at the Savoy, you said?"

They nodded.

"I had dinner there just last night," I said brightly. "And tea the day before. Lovely place, isn't it?"

"It's adequate," Sarah Schlomsky informed me, as if it was likely that Toledo had anything better to offer.

"No trouble on the ocean voyage, I hope?"

"A bit of bad weather south of Greenland," Hiram Schlomsky said with an expansive wave of his cane. "Nothing to worry about."

Indeed.

By then, Evans had returned, jingling Florence's keys enticingly, and we headed into the lift. "Florence and I live on the same floor," I explained as the lift took us up two stories. "She's to the left down the hallway and I am—we are; I share a flat with my cousin—to the right, but Florence and I see one another rather frequently going up and down. And she'll knock on our door occasionally and come in for a drink."

"A drink?" Mrs. Schlomsky said blankly. She glanced at her husband.

I nodded. "Cocktails are rather the thing among the younger set here in London. It might be different where you are from. Florence tried to explain to me where it's located. The mid-west, she said?"

I had absolutely no idea where the mid-west might be—somewhere in America, obviously, although Flossie's directions had made no sense whatsoever. One of them had included the words, 'drive west for eighteen hours,' which would have put us in the middle of the Atlantic if we had tried to do it from here—but it sounded rather corn-fed. Millions of dollars aside, the Schlomskys might not be familiar with London society, or any other society, either. There might be no society to speak of in Toledo.

"Our daughter doesn't drink," Sarah Schlomsky said, as the lift doors opened and Evans got busy pulling the grille back from the opening.

I opened my mouth, and closed it again. Of course Flossie drank. I had watched her do it, in my very own flat. I had also seen her come home rather giggly on more than one occasion.

I didn't insist on my version of reality, though. If the Schlomskys wanted to believe that their daughter was a studious and quiet teetotaler, to try to convince them otherwise would only annoy. They'd see the truth for themselves once Flossie turned up.

So I trailed behind instead, as Evans led the way down the hall towards Flossie's door. And then I waited as he knocked on the door, and fitted the key in the lock, and twisted it, and pushed the door open. "Miss Schlomsky?"

Sarah Schlomsky pushed past him with Hiram right behind. "Florence, darling? It's Mother!"

She headed into the flat while Evans wiggled the key back out of the lock and stood for a second, undecided, with it in his hand.

"I'll give it to them," I said, holding out my hand. "I know you're not supposed to leave the lobby empty."

Evans hesitated. "It's the only spare key, Miss Darling. If it gets lost..."

"Just leave it on the table, then." I nodded to the small console sitting by the foyer wall under a modern painting of colorful blobs. "We won't lose it. We'll need it to lock the front door again, for one thing. So no chance it will be locked in here."

Evans nodded.

"I'll tell them to drop it off with you on their way out," I said, and lowered my voice. "Listen, Evans..."

"Yes, Miss Darling?"

"The last time you saw Miss Schlomsky—"

He eyed me.

"When she went out last night, with my... with Lord St George, was there anything about her that you noticed? Anything—" I hesitated, "unusual?"

"No, Miss Darling," Evans said.

"Nothing? Crispin said she seemed distracted...?"

"No, Miss Darling." The doorman shook his head. "She appeared just as normal. Came out of the lift chattering to Lord St George as usual."

"And clinging to him," I said sourly, "I suppose?"

"Yes, Miss Darling."

Yes, of course. "I don't suppose you have any idea where she was going?"

Evans shook his head. "No, Miss Darling. Lord St George helped her into the motorcar and I watched them drive off, but I don't know where they were headed."

"They left together?" Crispin hadn't mentioned that part.

Evans nodded. "Yes, Miss Darling. To the left down the street."

In the direction of the Savoy Hotel. And also in the direction of quite a few other things. There's quite a lot of real estate in the area between the Essex House Mansions and the Savoy Hotel. There are also Hackney cab stands, and entrances to the Underground, and at least one train station. Flossie could have been headed anywhere in London or beyond, really. The fact that she'd left with St George didn't mean anything. She hadn't been with him when he brought me home a couple of hours later, so at some point they had parted ways.

"Thank you, Evans," I said. "That's helpful. I'll make sure

you get the key back." I shooed him gently out the door before I went off in search of the Schlomskys.

FLOSSIE'S FLAT was in most respects a mirror image of Christopher's and mine. Parquet floor in the foyer, sitting room beyond. In this flat, the bedrooms were to the right and the kitchen and dining room to the left, while in Christopher's and my flat, it's the opposite.

And Flossie's tastes ran to the more modern and—dare I say it—garish. Christopher's and my flat is mostly furnished with castoffs from Sutherland House. When Uncle Herbert had agreed to let us move out of Beckwith Place and in together in the Essex House Mansions, he had raided the attics of Sutherland House for anything he thought we might need. A few small things had been brought up from Wiltshire, but most of the bigger pieces had merely made it across town from the surplus in Mayfair. As a result, our flat was furnished in semi-threadbare heirlooms and almost nothing later than 1870.

Flossie, on the other hand, must have bought everything new. It was all streamlined, very art deco and modern, and all mixed with Florence's favorite pink. The array of pillows on the Chesterfield ran the gamut from palest shell pink to hot fuchsia, and from velvet to silk and everything in-between. There were enough tassels and flourishes to outfit the entire mansion block, not just Flossie's flat.

I averted my eyes politely from the stack of gossip magazines on the low coffee table. I recognized the covers, and knew that several had images of St George inside; I had seen them myself, and the fact that Flossie had a collection of them on her table struck me as foreboding.

Or at least it would have struck me as foreboding had I had the slightest fear that she would succeed in her attempts to vamp Christopher's cousin. I didn't. If St George ended up married to someone who wasn't his secret lady-love, it was more likely to be Lady Laetitia Marsden instead of Florence Schlomsky.

The Schlomsky parents were back in the bedroom wing. I could hear their voices in the background as I made my way across the parquet floors, past the too-modern, too-flashy furniture, and to the hallway.

Flossie must have claimed the slightly bigger back bedroom —Christopher's in our flat—for her own. Christopher had tried to talk me into taking it—it had a window looking out on the courtyard, while the front bedroom, closer to the hallway, had no natural light—but I had insisted. I was only living there through the generosity of Uncle Herbert, and I wasn't going to deprive Uncle Herbert's son of the nicer bedroom. Besides, I sleep better when it's dark, anyway. Might as well avoid the ambient light from outside and make it easier. It's never really properly dark in London at night, with all the street lights.

What was my bedroom in the other flat had been turned into Flossie's closet, I discovered as I got closer. I glanced through the open door on my way past, and then stopped as my brows climbed up my forehead.

Where I had fit an entire bedroom set into the room—bed, tallboy, dressing table and chair—Flossie's front bedroom held nothing but apparel. Clothes and shoes and handbags and hats, hanging on racks, piled on shelves, lining the walls. Christopher would have been in heaven—or at least he would have been if he and Flossie were anywhere close to the same size. To me, it looked excessive to the point of obsession. Not to mention how very pink it all was.

And it wasn't even well-maintained. Silk scarves were piled in baskets, shoes without shoe-trees were tossed on the floors with no attempt to line them up neatly. Unmentionables in pretty pastels—mostly shades of white, cream, and pink—over-flowed their drawers. And in the middle of the room, Sarah Schlomsky stood with her mouth open, taking in the mess with wide, shocked eyes.

I smiled sympathetically. "Was she more tidy at home?"

Christopher had certainly been more tidy at Beckwith Place than he was now. I was mostly the same, I thought, but then I hadn't spent so much of my time suppressing who I really was, either.

Not that Christopher is careless. All of Kitty's parapher-nalia is housed in my wardrobe and on my dressing table. Living alone, in a flat in London, made it much easier for Christopher to do what he wanted and to be who he was, but we did still get occasional visits from family, and there was no point in flaunting his monthly cross-dressing.

Mrs. Schlomsky was clearly shocked down to the toes of her very sensible shoes to see her daughter's excesses. She looked around as if she had never seen anything like it.

"This is—" She ran down and looked around one more time before turning to me. "Is this really my daughter's apartment?"

Flat, I translated in my head. And nodded. "Yes, Mrs. Schlomsky. This is Florence's flat. There's another bedroom in the back. I'm sure she's sleeping in that one."

There was no room to sleep here.

A tiny wrinkle appeared between her brows. "Where does Ruth sleep?"

"Who is Ruth?" I didn't think Flossie had a flat-mate. I had certainly never seen one, and surely I would have, when we had lived in the same building for half a year now.

"The maid," Sarah Schlomsky said, as if it were obvious, when in fact it was anything but.

"I don't think Florence has a maid," I said, since I knew

very well that she didn't. "She's never mentioned a maid, and I've never seen one, either."

Mrs. Schlomsky sniffed. "Of course she has a maid, you silly girl. We wouldn't have sent our daughter halfway around the world without a maid."

"Of course." I nodded politely. "It's just that I've never met the maid. And I don't know where she'd be sleeping. There are only two bedrooms in this flat, and if this one is in use as a closet..."

There was the pantry, I supposed, if Florence was heartless enough to relegate her maid there just so she herself could make use of both bedrooms. But that didn't explain why I had never seen or heard of Ruth.

Mrs. Schlomsky glanced around again, but there was no way to deny what I had just said.

"Hiram!" She brushed past me without so much as a by-your-leave. "Hiram!"

Her voice disappeared down the hallway to my right. I stayed where I was long enough to take another look around the room—around Flossie's closet—before I followed, past the lavatory and to the bedroom at the end of the hall.

I reached the doorway in time to see Mrs. Schlomsky confront her husband, both hands on his arms. "Ruth, Hiram! Where is Ruth?"

Mr. Schlomsky looked around, as if expecting the missing Ruth to materialize out of thin air. She didn't, and it's hard to say whether she could have, had she wanted to. The room was chock full of furniture, to such a degree that there was hardly any floor space left. I stayed in the doorway, since doing anything else would have put me as close to Hiram Schlomsky as his wife was currently, and that would have been practically indecent.

Flossie had a reproduction four-poster bed with gauzy

hangings—I knew it was a reproduction because I have slept in the real thing at Sutherland Hall—along with a matching tallboy and a makeup table with a chair, and a small loveseat and a footstool and of course a night table or two—one on each side of the bed. The loveseat and footstool were both uphol-stered in rose velvet, while the draperies and bed-hangings were shell pink. A fussy lawn nightgown, dripping with ribbons and lace, lay across the counterpane.

At this point, the sheer level of pinkness was overwhelm-ing. I knew that Florence favored the color—had seen her in dress after pink dress—but I hadn't realized that everything else inside her flat would be in shades of pink, also. It was cloying and too sweet and a bit like being inside someone's mouth after they'd sucked on a peppermint.

I tried to push it aside to focus on the Schlomskys and their dilemma. No Florence, and now no Ruth.

"I don't know, dear," Hiram told his wife. "She's not here."

"But she has to be here, Hiram!" Flossie's mother clutched at her husband's forearms, her voice turning shrill. "They both have to be here!"

"I'm sure it's nothing," I said from the doorway, and they both turned to me. Sarah frowned, and Hiram pursed his lips. I added, "Honestly, it happens to a lot of young people when they get out from under their parents' thumbs."

They both narrowed their eyes, and all right, it might not have been the most diplomatic way of putting it. I soldiered on. "Your daughter probably decided to enjoy her freedom while she was away from home. So she let go of the maid and started to take care of herself. It's not a bad thing. Independence and an ability to take care of oneself are healthy."

Sarah Schlomsky drew breath, her chest inflating like a pouter pigeon, and I braced myself. But instead of letting the breath out on invective in my direction, Mrs. Schlomsky merely informed me, in a tight but civil voice, that, "Our daughter is not the independent sort."

"She came all the way to England by herself," I pointed out. "Someone wouldn't do that who wasn't at least a little bit interested in independence."

"Florence came to England for her health," Mrs. Schlomsky said stiffly.

"Her health?" There's nothing healthy about the British climate. It's chilly and gray and wet most of the time.

Hiram Schlomsky put a hand on his wife's arm to stop her from responding. "Didn't you say you know our daughter, Miss...Sweetling, was it?"

"Darling," I said, while I thanked my lucky stars that St George hadn't been around to hear that. He would never let it go.

Hiram nodded. "Miss Darling. Of course."

"And I do know your daughter. She has lived down the hall from me for as long as I've been in the Essex House Mansions. And she's a friendly sort, so I've seen rather a lot of her."

They exchanged a look. Mrs. Schlomsky murmured something, and her husband shook his head. "You're sure we're talking about the same girl?"

Who else would we be talking about? "She's around my age," I said. "A little shorter than me, a bit more curvy."

I have what is generally known as a boyish figure, with not much in the way of hips or a bust. Perfect for the current fashions. Florence, meanwhile, took after her mother; both of them shaped in the traditional mold.

"She has brown bobbed hair and a round face with pink cheeks," I continued. Mrs. Schlomsky opened her mouth and then closed it again. Perhaps Flossie had acquired the bob since she left America. Nothing unusual about that, either, especially if her mother didn't approve of short hair. "She has an American accent. And lots of... um..." I flushed, "she has a big, bright smile and very nice teeth."

They both nodded. "That does sound like our Florence," Hiram Schlomsky said.

Well, of course it did.

"I don't know where she might be," I added. "We don't spend much time together outside of the Essex House. But I'm sure she'll be home safe and sound by this evening. She does keep a busy schedule. She probably just spent the night with a friend."

"Do you know any of her friends?" Sarah Schlomsky wanted to know, and I had to tell them both that I didn't.

"I'm afraid we don't travel in the same circles. Christopher and I stay away from his parents' generation—" We hadn't come to London to deal with the peerage, had we, nor to make advantageous marriages, "—but we're also not terribly keen on the Society of Bright Young Persons."

I saw enough of St George as it was. And I had seen entirely too much of Lady Laetitia Marsden and her ilk.

"Is she—" Sarah Schlomsky's brows drew together. "Does Florence spend time with the Society of Bright Young Persons?"

"Not as far as I know," I assured her. The stories about the Society's exploits must have made their way across the pond too, it seemed. "The one time Crispin was on his way to a Jungmann sisters bash and he gave Florence a lift, she was going to Lady Montfort's, she told me. He hasn't mentioned meeting her while he's been out running around with his friends."

They usually met right here at the Essex House Mansions when they met at all, usually in the lift... although it was perhaps best not to mention those encounters to Flossie's mother. If she had been shocked to learn of her daughter's new cosmopolitan wardrobe and bobbed hair, she would be appalled to hear about Florence's exploits with young men—or at least her exploits vis-à-vis St George, which were the only ones I had witnessed.

No, much better to let Flossie breach that subject herself when she came home.

"Hasn't she told you what she's been up to?" I ventured instead.

"We hear from her once in a while," Sarah Schlomsky said. "Not as often as we expected."

"Or we were afraid of," her husband added, *sotto voce*.

Sarah gave him a look before turning back to me. "We'd feared Florence would have a difficult time acclimating. You're all so reserved compared to what we're used to."

She gave me a disgruntled look. I opened my mouth to apologize, but before I could, she had gone on. "But it seems as if she's settled in all right. I'm glad."

"For what it's worth, Florence has always seemed happy whenever I've seen her," I said. And added, a bit grudgingly, "She's very personable."

A bit too much so, especially where certain members of the opposite gender are concerned.

"We're a friendly bunch in Toledo," Hiram Schlomsky said, preening, even as his wife gave him a jaundiced look.

"Well," I said, "I'm certain Florence will turn up today, or if not, at least she'll be here tomorrow morning. Perhaps she got her dates mixed up and thought you weren't going to be in London until today."

They glanced at each other, but didn't respond.

"If there's anything I can do in the meantime, please don't hesitate to let me know. I live just down the hall." I gave them the number of our flat, and added, "We're not on the telephone, but you can always ask Evans to knock us up."

They exchanged a glance, and Sarah Schlomsky's lips

twitched. "If you wouldn't mind, Miss Sweetling—" her husband began.

"Darling."

"—Miss Darling. If you see Florence, would you contact us at the Savoy to let us know that she's back?"

"Of course," I said. "I'd be delighted."

Evans was much more likely to see her than I was, of course. He'd catch her coming in, as long as she did so before eleven o'clock. Although I supposed it wouldn't be all that much of an inconvenience to stop by a few times tonight and knock on Flossie's door...

"We'll leave word with the doorman on our way out," Sarah Schlomsky said, "but we would appreciate it very much if you would keep an eye out too, Miss Darling. As a friend of Florence's."

"Of course." I smiled politely. "It was lovely to meet you both. I'll look forward to seeing you both again soon."

They murmured something in response, and I withdrew, down the hall to my own flat and to Christopher's company.

CHAPTER SEVEN

"THAT'S STRANGE," Christopher mused later, after I had gone over everything that had happened.

I glanced at him across the tea service. "Which part?"

He placed his cup and saucer on the table and sat back against the Chesterfield and crossed one leg over the other, languidly. "All of it, I suppose. Strange that they wouldn't let her know they were coming in the first place, but stranger still that she wouldn't immediately run to meet them, if she hadn't seen them in almost a year."

I nodded. Although— "I don't know that I think it's all that strange that they didn't give her advance notice that they were coming. They said they wanted to surprise her. And they did let her know at least a day in advance. They arrived in Southampton two days ago. If they had truly wanted to take her off guard, they could have appeared downstairs with no warning the way Uncle Harold did two months ago."

"Uncle Harold was trying to catch you and Crispin in *flagrante delicto*," Christopher said with a twitch of his lips, "so he'd hardly give you advance notice that he was coming."

I made a face. "Well, perhaps that was what the Schlomskys were trying to do, too. See what their daughter was up to in their absence."

"But they didn't," Christopher said. "They did give her notice. Enough to know that they were coming, at least. Enough to get rid of anything incriminating. And if they were suspicious, wouldn't they have acted differently, instead of being surprised by everything they saw?"

Perhaps so. The Schlomsky parents seemed to have expected to find a much subdued Flossie compared to what we —Christopher and I, and Crispin—were used to seeing. If they had been suspicious of their daughter's behavior here in London, they wouldn't simultaneously have been surprised by it.

"What's strange to me," I said, "is that Flossie didn't show up at the Savoy, either last night or this morning. If they were my parents and I hadn't seen them for the best part of a year..."

Christopher nodded. "Perhaps she was worried about her parents' reaction to... shall we say 'the new Flossie'?"

"I suppose she might have been. They did seem quite surprised about everything I said."

"And they expected there to be a maid," Christopher said, half question and half statement, "and there wasn't one."

I nodded. "That's what they said. Have you seen a maid around, Christopher?"

He shook his head. "It's a service flat, so no need for a maid, really."

Not really.

"Flossie was here before us. Perhaps she got rid of the maid before we took the flat. The senior Schlomskys were adamant that they wouldn't have sent her across to England without one. So there must have been a maid at some point."

Christopher nodded. "What else?"

"Her mother looked appalled at the state of Flossie's second bedroom, which is essentially her closet, but I was appalled, too. So many clothes, Christopher! You would have been in heaven, or at least you would have been if any of them had fit you. But—"

He nodded. "I know, Pippa. Flossie and I look nothing alike. Her frocks would come to mid-thigh on me."

Yes, they would. And in every other respect, they'd hang off him. He's much slimmer around the hips than Flossie.

"Apparently she didn't dress like that in Toledo. Or she was much less interested in clothes, or something like that."

"Are we certain it's the same girl?" Christopher wanted to know.

I huffed. "How many Florence Schlomskys do you suppose there are in London? Besides, I described her, and her parents said yes, that sounded like their daughter."

Christopher nodded.

"They said she came to London for her health."

"That has to be a joke," Christopher said. "Who comes to England for their health? The weather is hardly ever sunny here."

"That's what I said."

"What's wrong with her health?"

"I have no idea," I said. "The conversation moved on to something else, and I forgot to ask. But whenever we've seen her, she's always looked blooming, hasn't she? Perhaps she was languishing under her parents' thumbs at home, and getting out on her own made all the difference."

Christopher nodded. "It's amazing what a bit of independence can do."

Yes, it was. "Perhaps that's why she didn't rush to meet her parents when they arrived. Perhaps there's resentment there. She left home because she was unhappy, and she ditched the maid because her parents had sent the maid along to spy on her, or to keep her in line or something of that nature, and now she has built her own life here in London, and she didn't like her parents showing up to upset it."

"Might be," Christopher agreed. "It makes as much sense as anything else."

It did. "She can't hope to avoid them forever, though. I mean, she should have known they'd turn up sooner or later, shouldn't she? Here, I mean. At the Essex House Mansions. Once the telegram arrived, and she knew they were in England, she must have known that they'd come here. Surely they're the ones paying for the flat, so they'd know where to find it."

"One would assume so," Christopher agreed. "I can't imagine why she didn't just face the music—and her parents—right away. If it were me, and I didn't want my parents to see where, or how, I lived, I would have gone to them first, before they could come and find me."

I nodded. So would I have. "You don't suppose anything has happened to her, do you?"

"I can't imagine what," Christopher said. "She was alive and well last night, you said."

"That's what Crispin told me." I shrugged. "He mentioned that she seemed distracted—although she did try to have her way with him in the lift, as usual, so I don't know how distracted she could have been—but it was probably just about her parents being in London, you know? I didn't get the impression that he thought anything of it one way or the other."

Christopher nodded. "If something had been wrong, I'm sure he would have noticed. He's not stupid. Or unobservant, really."

No, he wasn't. "Evans said they went off together."

"Flossie and Crispin?"

I nodded. "It makes sense, if they were both going to the Savoy."

"Indeed," Christopher nodded. "But if he took her to the Savoy, why didn't her parents see her there? Do we know that they're telling the truth?"

We didn't. "Perhaps he dropped her somewhere else along the way."

"Why would he do that if they were both going to the Savoy?"

I had no idea, and said so. "We could phone him and ask. She might have said something to him that he didn't bother to convey to me. It's not as if we knew it would turn out to be important."

Christopher lifted a shoulder in semi-agreement. "It can't hurt to ring up the Hall, I suppose. If nothing else, I can assure Crispin that you haven't heard from Natterdorff again since yesterday."

I rolled my eyes. "I can't imagine why you think he would be interested, Christopher."

"Of course you can't," Christopher said, and went on without giving me an explanation. "On our way out, we can knock on Flossie's door again, and see if she's come back."

"Or we could simply ask Evans on our way through the lobby."

"We can do that, too," Christopher said and pushed to his feet.

THERE WAS no answer when we knocked on Flossie's door, and no indication that she had returned home in the time I had been inside our own flat with Christopher. Her parents were gone by now, too, clearly, and the flat was empty. When I reached out my hand to try the knob, Christopher hissed at me.

I rolled my eyes but did it anyway. It didn't turn and the door didn't budge, and when I put my ear to it, there were no sounds from inside the flat.

"No, Mr. Astley," Evans said a minute later, after we had taken the lift down to the lobby and Christopher had inquired as to whether Flossie had come back home.

"No correspondence?" I asked. "No visitors?"

"No, Miss Darling," Evans said. And changed it to, "Not aside from her parents."

"Do inform us when she comes back, will you, Evans?" Christopher took my arm and headed for the outside.

"Of course, Mr. Astley," Evans said, and swung the door open.

"Useless," I said to Christopher as we walked up the pavement towards the call box on the corner. "Utterly useless. And you know, Christopher, I suspect he wouldn't tell us even if he did know something."

He glanced down at me. "Likely not, Pippa. Flossie's doings are none of our concern, are they, any more than our doings are any of Flossie's concern. If I found out that Evans was telling Flossie—or anyone else, for that matter—what I get up to every month, I would have his hide, and so would you."

"Yes," I said, "of course, but—"

He shook his head. "No buts, Pippa. Goose, gander, and all of that. If you don't want him to give away your secrets, or mine, you can't expect him to give away other people's secrets to us."

I grumbled. "I suppose that makes sense. I'm just trying to help, though, Christopher. If something's wrong..."

"I'm sure everything is fine," Christopher said and came to a stop outside the call box. "We'll ask Crispin what happened. Perhaps he took Flossie to the Savoy and it's the elder Schlomskys who are lying."

"Why would they do that?"

Christopher pulled open the door to the red box. "Why does anyone do anything? I assume you want inside with me?"

Of course I wanted inside with him. The London public call boxes are narrow, but we're both young and slender. We'd make it work. I stepped inside, and Christopher followed. The door closed, and we maneuvered around one another, arms and hips brushing, as we got into position in front of the telephone. "Would you like to do the honors?" Christopher inquired.

I shook my head. "No, thank you. I don't imagine Uncle Harold would like it much if I were the one to ring up Crispin. You know how little he likes me."

"It's not as if Uncle Harold would answer his own telephone," Christopher said, "It would be Tidwell, or perhaps Mrs. Mason, and it would make Crispin's evening."

"St George doesn't need any more pandering to his insecurities. He's already egocentric enough."

Christopher shrugged. "Suit yourself."

He fed the telephone the appropriate coins and dealt with the exchange. Time passed, then... "Tidwell? Christopher Astley. Is my cousin in?"

Tidwell, Sutherland Hall's butler, took himself off to hunt down his lordship somewhere in the vast hall, and we waited. Christopher repositioned the earpiece between us so I could hear, too. Several minutes passed, before—

"Kit? What's wrong?"

"Nothing," Christopher said, and amended it to, "Nothing you need worry about."

"Then why are you interrupting my pining and plotting?"

Plotting?

"What are you plotting, St George?" I wanted to know. "Is it murder? Is it Lady Laetitia? Oh, please say it is! I'll help you dispose of the body!"

A moment of silence hung in the air before he said, cautiously, "Darling?"

"Of course."

It took less than a second for my brain to catch up to my mouth, but by then it was too late. Christopher chuckled, and I made a face. "Drat."

Crispin smirked. I could hear it all the way from Wiltshire. "Good evening, Darling."

"Yes," I said, "you too, St George. Damn you."

"Now, now, Darling. We both knew it was only a matter of time before you accepted my pet-name for you. Two years is long enough, don't you think?"

That statement truly didn't deserve a response, so I didn't give it one. Instead I stuck my nose in the air—Christopher saw it, even if Crispin didn't—and told him, "Never mind that, St George. We have a question for you."

"Do you, really?"

"Don't play coy," I said severely, "it doesn't suit you."

"Does it not? What behavior do you think suits me, Darling?"

"Stop flirting," Christopher ordered, and I sniffed. "Serious question, Crispin."

"Of course, old bean."

"Evans said you left with Flossie Schlomsky yesterday evening, after we spoke."

"Yes," Crispin said, after a moment. "I told Philippa that. Didn't I, Darling?"

"You told me that you'd seen her," I said, "not that you'd gone off together."

"Does it matter? We were going the same way, so I offered her a lift. What of it?"

"You were going to the Savoy," Christopher said, and Crispin hummed in agreement. "Where was she going?"

"The Savoy, as well. She told me her parents were staying there, from America."

"So you took her to the Savoy?"

"No," Crispin said. "She asked to be left off down the road a bit. Didn't want to risk her parents seeing her arrive in my motorcar, she said."

He sounded disgruntled. Especially when he added, after a second's pause, "Or perhaps it was my company she said her parents would object to."

"Difficult to blame them for that," I told him sweetly. "Most mothers wouldn't want their daughters going about in your company, you know. You're a terrible cad."

"By all means, Darling," Crispin said coolly. "It's a good thing Lady Euphemia Marsden feels differently, isn't it?"

I made a face. "Touché, St George. You win that round."

His voice brightened. "Do I, really? Good of you to concede, Darling."

"Don't expect it to happen again," I warned him. "Seriously, though... Flossie didn't want to be seen in your company —or in your motorcar—in front of her parents?"

"That's what she said," Crispin confirmed. "It was a surprise, I'll admit. It's not as if I'm interested in Flossie Schlomsky, so it didn't matter to me on a personal level, but it did come as a bit of a shock."

I could well imagine. Given Flossie's flat-out pursuit of him before, having her suddenly treat him like *persona non grata* must have... well, grated.

The thing is, one can't really hope to find a more eligible bachelor in England these days than the Viscount St George. Crispin has a title and a fortune, not to mention good looks and nice manners. He would have charmed the bloomers right off of Mrs. Schlomsky given half a chance. If the Schlomskys wanted a son-in-law from the British aristocracy, they couldn't have wished for better than St George. (Personality aside, of course.) So it made no sense why Flossie would have wanted to distance herself from him, especially when it would have been so easy not to.

But mine was not to reason why, so I left that whole wrinkle alone and went back to what we did know.

"So you set her down on the Strand."

"As I said, Darling. Across the street from the Eleanor Cross, to be specific. It's a five-minute walk to the Savoy, if that. And plenty of people out and about."

"I wasn't disparaging your behavior," I said mildly. "If the lady wanted out of the motorcar, of course you set her down. And proceeded directly to the Savoy to ruin my dinner date, I presume?"

"Of course, Darling."

"Did you see her again?" Christopher wanted to know.

"Florence, do you mean? No, I didn't."

"For how long did you loiter outside the entrance to the hotel before you tried to run me down? You would have seen her go in, wouldn't you?"

"Not long, Darling," Crispin said, blandly, with no evidence of a guilty conscience in his tone, "but certainly longer than five minutes. I imagine I would have done, had she used the Savoy Court entrance."

"How do you know that she didn't?"

"Because I didn't see her," Crispin said. "There are lots of ways into the Savoy, Darling. Savoy Hill, Savoy Street, Savoy Place, Carting Lane... Perhaps she used one of those."

She must have done, if he hadn't seen her. "So you put her down across from Charing Cross, and that was the last time you saw her."

"That's correct. I drove to the Savoy, without once looking in the rearview mirror, because between you, me and Kit, I couldn't care less about Florence Schlomsky and what she was doing—and there I proceeded to lurk outside in the lane until you came out with His Highness and I could carry out my plan of sweeping you off your feet."

"Is that what you'd call it?"

"My apologies, Darling." The tone of voice was accompanied by a mock bow. I knew it as well as if I'd been able to see it with my own eyes. "Did I say 'sweep'? I meant 'knock.' I lay in wait until you appeared, and then I attempted to take you out at the knees."

"Of course you did, you—"

"Stop," Christopher said and pulled the earpiece away from me. "If you can't behave yourself, I'm not letting you listen."

"I'm behaving myself perfectly well. He's the one—"

I dragged the earpiece back towards myself as Christopher leaned in to speak into the mouthpiece. "Listen, Crispin. The elder Schlomskys came to the flat this afternoon. Flossie didn't show up at the Savoy, not last night nor this morning. Are you certain you didn't bring her to Wiltshire with you?"

"Of course I'm certain, Kit," Crispin's voice said. "I think I would know if I'd had Florence Schlomsky in the boot of my motorcar, don't you? Darling can attest that there was no one else in the H6 when I took her home last evening."

I nodded. I hadn't checked the boot, admittedly, but I was inclined to believe Crispin when he said that Flossie hadn't been in it.

Christopher didn't respond, and Crispin continued, "I set her down at Charing Cross. The last thing I saw as I drove away was her waiting to cross the street."

"She didn't go into the Underground, did she?"

"No," Crispin said. "There'd be no point in her taking the Tube, Kit. Charing Cross is the closest stop to the Savoy. She might flag down a cab if she didn't want to walk, I suppose, but it's only a handful of blocks, and hardly worth the fare. I don't see why she'd bother."

I didn't, either. "And you have no idea where she is?"

He sighed. "Why would I? If she were going anywhere but to the Savoy, she didn't mention it to me."

So that was that, then. "Thank you," I said.

"Anytime, Darling. Kit. Anything else?"

"I think that's it," Christopher said. "Get in touch if you think of anything else, would you, old chap? Or if you hear from her?"

"I hardly think I'm likely to receive a missive from Florence Schlomsky," Crispin told him, "but if it'll help, of course I will."

"Thanks, old bean. Pippa?"

"Yes, St George," I said grudgingly. "Thank you."

"Delighted to be of service, Darling. Do let me know when Miss Schlomsky turns up, won't you?"

"Of course. We'll be sure to give you a ring."

"Much obliged, Darling. Sweet dreams. Kit?" His voice became businesslike. "A word?"

"Of course, Crispin."

He nudged me out of the box. I went, but grudgingly, and only because it was obvious that nothing more would be said until I was out of range of hearing.

I POSITIONED myself with my back against the door and my ears peeled, of course. But I might as well not have bothered.

Oh, I could hear what was said. Or I could hear Christopher's end of the conversation perfectly well. He just didn't say anything interesting. It was all a list of "Yes," and "No," and "Not yet," and "Of course," and "I know that," and "Don't be stupid," and finally, "You, too. Good night, Crispin."

I stepped away from the door to the box to let Christopher out. He smirked. "One of these days, that curiosity is going to be the death of you, Pippa."

"But not today," I said. "You didn't say anything worth killing someone over."

"Did you think I would?"

He took my arm and tugged me back down the pavement towards the Essex House.

"I thought you might," I told him as we walked. "He clearly didn't want to say whatever it was where I could hear it. So I thought it might be something I'd want to hear."

"Would it please you to hear that he wondered whether we had heard from Natterdorff again since yesterday?"

"No," I said with a scowl. "Not when we haven't. It would have pleased me a lot more to be able to tell him that we had."

"Of course it would." He squeezed my arm companionably. "I'm sure the dashing *Graf* will be back in touch in a day or two, Pippa. As soon as he gets past Crispin snatching you out from under his nose yesterday. He'll want to try again, I'm sure."

"Do you really think so?"

"Do you doubt it?" He squinted at me. "You said you got on well, didn't you?"

"I thought we did. Until St George showed up and nearly knee-capped me, and then tried to be rude to him." And was put in his place.

"Then I'm sure you did," Christopher said.

I wished I could be as sure. It hadn't been my first time dining with a young man, of course, nor had it been my first time flirting with one. I had had the impression that things had progressed well, at least until the moment when the Hispano-Suiza rolled up behind me. But I was doubting myself now. It had been a full twenty-four hours, and I hadn't heard from Wolfgang again. So perhaps I wasn't the best judge of success in the field of supping with young men, and the date really hadn't gone well. If he liked me, shouldn't he have contacted us by now?

Then again, Christopher was a young man, and while he had very little experience wining and dining the fairer sex, he probably knew the proper etiquette for the beginnings of courtship. If he told me that Wolfgang would be in touch, perhaps I should trust that he knew whereof he spoke.

I shook my head. "No matter. Is that all St George wanted? To find out whether we had heard from Wolfgang?"

"That was the gist of it," Christopher confirmed.

"Onwards, then. He drove Florence to the Strand but left her off a couple of blocks from the Savoy last night."

Christopher nodded. "That's what he said."

I squinted at him. "Do you have reason to think it wasn't what he did?"

He gave me a glance back. "Of course not. If that's what he said he did, I'm certain it's exactly what he did. And she might have had reasons of her own for why she didn't want to arrive at the Savoy in his company. All Americans are puritans, aren't they?"

"I'm fairly certain that was only true several hundred years ago," I said, "although I'll admit that the Schlomskys Senior did seem a bit set in their ways. They thought Flossie was a teetotaler, can you imagine?"

"If that's the case," Christopher said, "it would certainly explain why she wouldn't want to turn up with Crispin. His reputation has probably preceded him to the other side of the Atlantic, too, don't you think?"

Perhaps it had. Or if not, all the Schlomskys would have had to have done, was peek at an old copy of the *Tatler* or the *Daily Yell* since they arrived here, and all would have been made clear.

"So he set her down on the Strand, two or three blocks from the Savoy. What do you think happened after that, Christopher?"

"There's only one of two things that could have happened," Christopher said. "Or perhaps one of three."

"Elucidate me, please."

He held up a finger of his free hand. "She told Crispin that she was going to the Savoy, but she was really going somewhere else instead."

"Why would she do that, if her parents were at the Savoy?"

"I don't know, Pippa. For now, we're talking about the

options for what could have happened, not why Flossie may or mayn't have actually done them. We'll get to that later."

"Fine," I said. "Proceed, please."

He held up another finger. "She planned to go to the Savoy, but was prevented from getting there."

"In the couple of blocks between Charing Cross and the Savoy? On the Strand? How do you imagine that might have happened? A motorcar accident? Surely we would have heard about it, if it had been something like that, don't you think? I mean, Crispin and I were both right there. Surely one of us would have noticed the upheaval."

"Perhaps," Christopher said, "perhaps not. For now, it's option two. She either wanted to go to the Savoy, but something prevented her, or she didn't want to go to the Savoy, and went somewhere else instead."

"If she wasn't planning to go to the Savoy in the first place, why tell Crispin that she was going there? It would make no difference to him whether she was going there or elsewhere."

"No idea," Christopher said. "Also a discussion for later."

I nodded. "What's option three, then?"

"She went to the Savoy," Christopher said, "and her parents are lying about it."

I squinted at him. "Why would they do that?"

"Who knows?" He gave a languid shrug. "You said yourself that her parents seemed surprised by the changes in her. Perhaps she showed up and they were appalled. Maybe things were said and they ran her off."

Or perhaps things had escalated and she had ended up dead. I pictured the hefty silver knob at the head of Hiram Schlomsky's walking stick, and imagined it whistling through the air and meeting Flossie's head. I had seen a young woman with her head bashed in by a trench club less than a month ago. This would probably look very much the same.

I made a gagging noise and Christopher squeezed my arm. "I'm sure she's fine. She'll turn up tomorrow, I'm sure."

"If she doesn't," I said, "I'm phoning Tom."

Christopher hummed agreement. "It can't hurt. If nothing else, he'll be able to tell us whether she's lying on a slab somewhere, and the news just hasn't made it back to the Essex House and the Savoy yet."

Yes, he would. Not that that was the outcome I was hoping for.

"I don't believe it'll come to that," Christopher added, with more optimism than I, frankly, thought the situation warranted. "I'm sure she'll turn up tomorrow and everything will be fine."

"I hope you're right." I let him open the door into the lobby for me, where Evans informed us that no, Flossie had not come home in the twenty minutes we had been out, and there had been no word from her.

"MESSAGE FOR YOU, MISS DARLING," Evans's voice said from the lobby.

It was the next morning, at the unfashionably early hour of eight thirty. Not that I wasn't awake—it hadn't been a late night —but who contacts someone before nine in the morning?

"Who?" Christopher mouthed from over in the kitchen doorway, where he was lounging with a cup of coffee in his hand and his hair sticking up every which way. His eyes were heavy and, I thought, a bit bloodshot. Perhaps he had spent part of the night worrying, too. I knew I had.

"I'll be down in a minute," I told Evans, and turned to Christopher. "If it's Wolfgang, I don't want Evans reading the missive to me."

Christopher's lips twitched. "Would there be sweet nothings, do you suppose?"

"I'd hardly think so." But even without that, I still didn't want Evans reading my note before I could. "I'll be back in two minutes."

I headed for the lobby, where Evans handed me an envelope with my name scribbled across it in elegant script and—yes!—the logo of the Savoy Hotel in the corner. I thanked him nicely and ripped the flap open as soon as the lift door had closed behind me.

Inside was a single sheet of paper, also with the hotel logo in the corner and a few lines of script in the same elegant handwriting.

Miss Darling, it began, with no warmer greeting than that—with no greeting at all, in fact. I lowered my brows. That certainly didn't bode well.

PLEASE COME *to the Savoy Hotel at your first convenience.*
   Sarah Schlomsky.

"THAT DOESN'T SOUND GOOD," Christopher opined when I showed it to him a minute later.

I shook my head. "How long before you can be ready to go?"

"You want me to accompany you? I'm not included in the invitation."

"You went with me when I was meeting Wolfgang," I said. "You can come with me now."

"That was different. That was supper with a foreigner we didn't know."

"This is a meeting with two foreigners we don't know. How do we even know for certain that they're the Schlomskys? They said they were, but we have no proof. Maybe they're planning to kidnap me and sell me into white slavery."

Christopher squinted at me. "Surely you're not serious?"

"Of course not. I'm sure they are exactly who they say they are. Why wouldn't they be? But we don't know anything more about them than we do about Wolfgang von Natterdorff, really."

"Do the parents look like Flossie?" Christopher wanted to know. "Or I guess a more accurate question would be, does Flossie look like her parents?"

I thought back. "Not appreciably, I'd say. It's not a case where you'd look at either of them and say, oh yes, that's definitely Flossie's mama or Flossie's papa. Not the way you would with Lady Laetitia and the Countess of Marsden, for instance. The countess is the very image of what Laetitia will look like in twenty-five years."

And she would still be lovely at fifty-plus. At least St George would have that to look forward to. A wife who kept her good looks well into middle age.

"But it's not as if Florence's parents didn't look like her," I added. "No more than you don't look like your mother, at least."

"Even if they looked completely different, it wouldn't prove anything," Christopher agreed. "Not all children are of their parents' heritage. Some are adopted. Some belong to one spouse and not the other. Or some simply favor one parent more than the other. Francis and I don't look much like Mum at all. Crispin, at least, got Aunt Charlotte's hair and eyes, even if the rest of him is all Sutherland."

I nodded. "So how long before we can go?"

He put the cup down on the counter. "I'm more awake than I was. Let me change and shave and deal with the hair. Fifteen minutes?"

"I'll go get ready," I said, and headed for my room while Christopher made for the shared washroom in the hallway.

IT TOOK MORE than fifteen minutes, but we were underway in less than thirty, and at the Savoy thirty minutes after that. The lobby looked exactly as it had two evenings before, when I had been there. Same checkerboard marble floor, same wood-paneled walls, same gold topped columns, and the same high, coffered ceiling. It's quite beautiful, in case I neglected to mention that, and of course it all practically oozes wealth and privilege. The concierge gave our approach the fishy stare it deserved, but then he did a double-take when we got close enough that he could recognize—or thought he did —Christopher.

His eyes widened. "Lord St George. Welcome back to the Savoy. How may I assist you today?"

Christopher opened his mouth, presumably to deny that he was his cousin, and I elbowed him in the ribs. Gently, of course. (I wouldn't have held back with the real St George.) "We're here to see Mr. and Mrs. Hiram Schlomsky."

The concierge eyed me, and then eyed Christopher, and then eyed me again, before he reached for the telephone and rang upstairs to inform the Schlomskys that we had arrived.

Two minutes later, we were welcomed into the most expensive suite the Savoy had to offer. Or at least I assumed that Hiram Schlomsky would not have been willing to settle for anything less. Unless, perhaps, His Grace the *Graf* von Natterdorff had taken up residence in the best suite before Hiram had had a chance to do so, and had relegated the Schlomskys to sloppy seconds. Crispin had interrupted the proceedings before Wolfgang had had the chance to invite me upstairs the other day, always assuming that that had been his plan, so I didn't actually know where the *Graf* was staying.

The suite was lovely, in any case. The Schlomskys were not. When we knocked on the door, Sarah Schlomsky peered out at us through the crack with wide, terror-filled eyes, as if she had expected to see something horrible outside, instead of the two people she had been reliably told were on their way up. And even as she swung the door open, and closed it again—after peering up and down the hallway behind us—Hiram Schlomsky paced back and forth in front of the big windows with the view of the Thames and the South Bank on the opposite side rapidly enough that I was honestly surprised there was no path carved in the sumptuous rug covering the floor.

"Mrs. Schlomsky," I said when the door was closed. "Mr. Schlomsky. May I present my cousin, Mr. Christopher Astley?"

The Schlomskys had met in the middle of the floor, halfway between the door and the window, and now they looked from me to Christopher and back again. "The fellow downstairs said he was a viscount," Hiram Schlomsky said.

"The chap downstairs mistook me for my other cousin," Christopher answered calmly. It wasn't the first time he'd had to explain this, after all. "Crispin is the heir. I'm His Grace's youngest nephew."

They both blinked without saying anything, and I decided I might as well carry the conversation forward. There was no point in going into the intricacies of the Sutherland succession. "What's wrong?"

Sarah Schlomsky pulled herself together with what was an obvious effort. "Thank you for coming, Miss Darling. And so quickly, too."

Her hair was falling down on one side, and her lips looked pale and pinched. Her husband's complexion was florid.

"What's happened?" I asked, looking from one to the other of them.

"A note," Hiram Schlomsky said. "Delivered with the food this morning."

He nodded towards the small table in front of the window. The remains of breakfast were gone, but the note was still there. I walked over to it and bent, with Christopher next to me.

The words were printed in capital letters, with a heavy dark pen. They slanted across the paper in a rather ominous way, and I don't think it was only the words themselves.

IF YOU WANT TO SEE YOUR DAUGHTER AGAIN, BRING FIFTY THOUSAND DOLLARS TO ST OLAVE'S CHURCH ON TOOLEY STREET AT ELEVEN TOMORROW NIGHT. DON'T INVOLVE THE POLICE OR THE GIRL DIES.

CHAPTER NINE

"WE SHOULD CONTACT TOM," I said.

Both Schlomskys looked politely inquiring, and Christopher explained, "We've a friend who's a detective sergeant at Scotland Yard."

"The note says not to involve the police," Sarah Schlomsky protested, and Hiram nodded vigorously. "Now listen here, young man..."

I looked from one to the other of them. "How will they know?"

"They?"

"The kidnappers. How will they know if you've contacted the police?"

"If someone is watching..." Sarah Schlomsky said, with a nervous glance at the window.

"Do you think someone is watching?" If someone was out there with a pair of binoculars, there was no way to know. The sun glinted on glass and church spires all over the place. One of the latter might have been St. Olave's, for all I knew. This was the first I had heard of it—I hadn't ever spent much time on the other side of the Thames—although that was about to change, I imagined.

Although even if someone was out there with a pair of binocs trained on the Savoy, how would they know which window belonged to the Schlomskys? There are a lot of guests, and a lot of rooms, at the Savoy.

Besides, if anyone was keeping an eye on the Schlomskys, it was more likely that they were camped out in the lobby or restaurant, or in the street outside, rather than watching the windows with binoculars.

Had anyone paid more than the usual attention when Christopher and I had approached the concierge earlier? I tried to bring to mind the surrounding area, but came up with nothing out of the ordinary. And I had kept an eye out, since I had thought there was a chance I might spot Wolfgang. So if anyone had been there, they probably hadn't been close enough to hear me mention the Schlomskys.

Sarah shrugged, somewhat helplessly, and I exchanged a glance with Christopher. "If you don't want to involve the police," he asked, "what do you want to do?"

"Pay the ransom and get our daughter back," Hiram boomed.

"Is this..." I rethought what I'd been about to say and tried again. "This is the first time your daughter has been kidnapped, isn't it?"

Kidnapping for ransom is not a common occurrence in Britain, but I had heard about a few cases in other parts of the world. Several of them in America, I thought, including the abduction of a business magnate's teenage son not too long before I'd been born.

"There was an attempt to snatch her away from university a year and a half or so ago," Hiram said. "That's when we decided to send her abroad. You're more civilized here, it seems."

Not in light of recent events, clearly, although I was loath to say that. Although it certainly put a different complexion on the Schlomskys' statement that Florence had come to England for her health. If she'd been in danger of being abducted at home, London must have seemed like a safer bet, even with its less than desirable climate.

"That's terrible," I said. "What happened?"

Two men had driven up in a motorcar, it seemed, and one had attempted to pull Flossie inside while the other had stayed behind the wheel, ready to take off the second the heiress was inside the vehicle. But somehow Florence had kept her head, and when the kidnapper shoved her into the backseat and tried to squeeze in behind her, Flossie kicked him in the teeth and scrambled out the other side of the car. She had apparently caused such a ruckus that the kidnappers had decided that retreat was the better part of valor, and had taken off with a squeal of tires.

"Were they caught?" Christopher wanted to know. His eyes were bright and interested.

Hiram Schlomsky shook his head. "It's a deserted kind of area, up there north of New York City. Lots and lots of trees. They were long gone before the police could be notified."

"That's awful." It occurred to me to wonder whether that event was related to what had happened now. Two kidnappings—or kidnapping attempts—of the same girl: surely there had to be a connection?

Then again, two kidnapping attempts almost two years apart, on two different continents... perhaps there wasn't a connection after all.

"At any rate," I said, "I don't see how anyone is going to know that you've contacted Scotland Yard. If someone is keeping an eye on the hotel, and suddenly constables start swarming, then of course they'll know that something is going on. But Christopher and I can go and talk to Tom, and no one will be the wiser. It's not as if anyone's keeping an eye on *us.*"

Hiram and Sarah exchanged a glance. It was a long one, communicating thoughts back and forth along an invisible line.

"No police," Hiram said eventually, turning back to us. "I won't risk anything happening to my little girl."

I opened my mouth to argue, but Christopher elbowed me in the ribs. "That's your prerogative," he told Hiram, smoothly. "What can we do to help?"

Sarah shook her head. "Nothing." Her voice was firm. "We'll spend the day today and tomorrow arranging for the money. Then we'll take it to the church tomorrow night, and by Sunday morning, Florence will be restored to us."

I opened my mouth again, but closed it on my own this time. The Schlomskys had made up their minds, and there was nothing I could say that would change them. Nor was it my place to try. It was their money and their daughter—and for that matter their ransom note—and the whole thing was out of my hands. If they didn't want my help, I couldn't force it on them.

Although it did beg the question of why they had involved me, or us, in the first place.

I thought about asking, and then I thought better of it. I glanced at Christopher. "We'll just be on our way, then."

He nodded, and so did the Schlomskys. "Thank you for stopping by," Sarah said politely, as if we hadn't shown up here by direct request.

"Nice to meet you, young man," Hiram added. "Nephew of the Duke of Sutherland, was it?"

Christopher nodded. "Nice to make your acquaintance as well, Mr. Schlomsky. Please let us know how it goes."

"If there's anything we can do to help..." I added, leaving it open-ended.

The Schlomskys smiled pleasantly, but didn't come out with anything they wanted us to do, and on that note, we left.

THE HALLWAY outside the suite was empty, and so was the lift once it arrived, but even so, Christopher shook his head when I opened my mouth. "It's a nice day," he said instead, blandly. "Do you fancy a walk before luncheon?"

I didn't, particularly, as it was in fact somewhat warm, and we would likely work up a sweat making our way to Southwark. (That we were going there was unspoken but obvious to both of us.) I did fancy a look at Tooley Street and St Olave's Church, which I assumed was the point of what he was suggesting, so I nodded anyway. "Certainly."

Perhaps the wind blowing across London Bridge would be nice once we made it that far.

"This way, then." As the lift doors opened into the lobby, he put a hand against my lower back and nudged me forward, towards the doors into the Strand.

I slowed my pace, just enough that I could take a surreptitious look around the lobby. Not blatantly enough that it would be noticeable, but just in case I happened to see anything interesting.

I didn't. There was no Wolfgang von Natterdorff, for one thing. There were also no other familiar faces. Not that I had expected there to be. The only person I had ever seen in connection with Flossie Schlomsky was a young woman with a somewhat plain face, wearing blue chiffon with polka dots, and although she hadn't been terribly memorable—I remembered the frock and hat better than I did the face—I saw her nowhere in the lobby. Nor did I see anyone else who looked particularly nefarious, although admittedly it can be hard to tell.

Then we were outside on Savoy Court, and a few seconds later, took a left onto the Strand.

"This isn't—" I began, since—if we were walking to Southwark, London Bridge was in the opposite direction—and Christopher shook his head.

"Let's just get on the train, and then we can talk."

The train. Of course. He was headed for Charing Cross, and the train to London Bridge.

"I assumed you meant to walk," I said, trotting to keep up along the pavement.

He slanted me a look. "In this weather?"

"It is a lovely day."

"Hot, though. And it's at least a forty-five minute walk, perhaps more."

"It's not as if we don't have the time to spare," I pointed out, and Christopher shook his head.

"I'm not walking to Southwark. Not when there's a train every half hour."

"Is there?"

"I imagine there must be."

We walked in silence another minute before he glanced around. "Hard to imagine anyone being able to drag someone else, kicking and screaming, into a motorcar in this."

'This' being the usual pedestrian and vehicle traffic going on all along the Strand. It's one of the busier thoroughfares in London, between Trafalgar Square and Waterloo Bridge. There were people and motorcars everywhere, as well as cab drivers and constables and the like. Christopher tugged me out of the way of a bobby in full uniform who was ambling down the pavement with no regard for anyone coming in the opposite direction, and I made a face. "That's true."

Especially so if Flossie had been a victim of an attempted kidnapping in the past, and had thwarted the evil-doers on that occasion. She wouldn't have become placid and tractable suddenly.

The constable moved past, and I took a step to the side again. "Perhaps she didn't kick and scream. Perhaps it was someone she knew. Or knew well enough not to be concerned about."

"She was on her way to see her parents," Christopher pointed out. "She made Crispin drop her off on the corner two blocks away because she didn't want to be seen arriving with him. I can't imagine that she'd want to be seen arriving with anyone else, either."

Likely not. If the Viscount St George, heir to the Sutherlands, wasn't exalted enough for Mummy and Daddy Schlomsky, it was hard to imagine who might have been.

"None of this makes sense," I grumbled, as we made our way up the pavement towards Charing Cross station. "If she didn't want Crispin to drive her to the Savoy, she isn't likely to have accepted anyone else's offer of a lift, either. Especially since she only had about two blocks to go. But unless she got into the motorcar willingly, there would have been a ruckus, and someone would have noticed that."

Christopher nodded. "Unless there were two of them—like last time—and one of them... bear with me here, Pippa—"

He snagged me by the waist and moved me in front of him, and then poked me in the back with a finger, "—one of them walked behind her with a syringe that he jabbed into her, and then, when she got woozy, he maneuvered her into a waiting car."

He quick-stepped up to walk beside me again, and I tucked my hand through his elbow as I thought about what he'd just suggested.

It was a more likely scenario than some of the others we had batted about, certainly. "That might have done it. If they were the same two people who tried to grab her in New York, they may have learned something from the last time they tried it on, and decided to do better this time."

"And if they were somewhat circumspect about it," Christopher said before turning onto the cobbles in front of the Clermont, "no one may have noticed what was going on. If it happened fast enough."

"It's possible." Perhaps even likely.

I glanced around. "There are plenty of Hackneys and motorcars around here, picking up and dropping off passengers. Lots of people coming and going. Lots of noise and confusion. If it was quick and easy, no one may have noticed."

We stepped off the cobbles in front of the Clermont and onto the ones lining the parking area in front of Charing Cross, where we headed for one of the arched openings into the station.

"It at least makes more sense than that no one noticed a woman being shoved into a motor against her will," Christopher said.

I nodded. Yes, it did.

"THERE'S ANOTHER EXPLANATION, YOU KNOW," Christopher said a few minutes later, after we had boarded the train and it was picking up speed across the Hungerford Bridge.

I took my eyes off the view—to the left we could see Waterloo Bridge, and to the right the Westminster ditto, while below us, the Thames rippled, murky even in the bright sunshine of a hot August day. The South Bank loomed ahead, closer with every second that passed. "What's that?"

He shot me a look. "Nobody snatched her on the walk from Charing Cross to the Savoy. She made it up to her parents' room, and something happened to her there. Then they wrote the note and pretended it had been delivered with breakfast, when really, they'd just written it themselves to hide the fact that they killed their own daughter."

I thought about it. "I suppose that's possible. We didn't ask the staff whether they'd actually delivered the note."

Christopher shook his head. "I thought about it, but for one thing, I'm not sure they would have told us if we had asked—*we're* not the police—and for another, if she truly was kidnapped, I didn't want to draw any attention to it."

I nodded. "It would explain a few things."

"Such as, why no one saw her being shoved, kicking and screaming, into a waiting car on a busy street with lots of people around."

"Precisely. And why the note asked for American dollars instead of British pounds."

"I hadn't thought about that," Christopher said, and looked like he was thinking about it now, blue eyes distant. "If I had, I suppose I would have assumed that it was because the Schlomskys, and their fortune, is in American dollars."

"Of course. And that's possible, too."

I leaned back in the seat and added, "I can't imagine how they'll gather fifty thousand dollars in London in a day and a half, to be honest. I suppose they'll have to calculate how many pounds fifty thousand dollars is, and bring that instead. I doubt even the Bank of London keeps fifty thousand American dollars sitting in their vaults."

Christopher nodded. "So if the Schlomskys didn't write the note, perhaps the kidnappers are American."

"Or perhaps the Schlomskys wrote the note."

"Or," Christopher said, "if they didn't and the kidnappers

are English, perhaps they thought it would be better to ask for a ransom amount the Schlomskys would immediately understand."

Yes. This didn't really prove anything one way or the other. Although for what it was worth, if it had been me writing the note, I would have asked for the currency I was familiar with, which would have been British pounds. I wasn't even sure exactly how much fifty thousand American dollars was.

"If the Schlomskys wrote the note themselves, do you suppose they would have involved us?"

"I'm not sure why they involved us either way," Christopher said, as the bridge gave way to the docklands on the South Bank. "They didn't actually ask us to do anything. We weren't able to contribute anything useful."

No, we hadn't been. "Do you think they may have done it to establish some sort of an alibi? Or an impression of goodwill or innocence or something, when inevitably Florence turns up dead?"

That was if they had killed her, of course. But if they hadn't, why would they bother with the kidnapping ruse in the first place?

"I'm not certain what kind of goodwill or innocence you and I would be able to provide," Christopher said, "when they won't let us contact the police. Innocence and goodwill to whom, exactly?"

I shook my head. "I wonder if we shouldn't ring up Tom anyway. Unofficially, you know. You see him regularly; what do you think?"

Christopher flushed, a dusting of pink on his cheekbones. "I haven't seen him since he stopped by the other night."

"Two days ago? That's regularly, isn't it?"

"He was only there to tell us about Hughes," Christopher muttered.

"And that's another thing. Strangely coincidental, isn't it, how people we know—or somewhat know—turn up dead?" Or in Flossie's case, missing.

Christopher nodded. He looked relieved to be able to stop talking about Tom Gardiner, and I let him get away with it without comment. Instead, I added, "Although I don't see what that could have had to do with this. Hughes died in Bristol, not Southampton, and there's simply no way that she could have been the maid the Schlomskys sent from America last year. Not when Hughes had been with Aunt Charlotte since Crispin was a baby."

"Not to mention that she's one hundred percent English," Christopher agreed. He shook his head. "Sometimes a coincidence is just a coincidence, Pippa. I don't see how Hughes being mugged in a dark alley in Bristol can have anything to do with Florence Schlomsky going missing in London, or her parents landing in Southampton. Those things didn't even happen at the same time."

No, they hadn't. The Schlomskys had been at sea when Hughes had been killed, and Hughes had been dead when Flossie had disappeared. Any connection was in my own mind, and only there.

"At any rate," I said, as the train continued on, "you haven't seen Tom in a few days. Perhaps you'd like to change that once we're done here."

Christopher muttered something, his blush intensifying.

"And while you're doing it," I continued, "you could casually drop into conversation the fact that our neighbor seems to have been kidnapped."

"Are you certain that's wise, Pippa? The Schlomskys were adamant that they didn't want to involve the police."

"But that's just it," I said. "We wouldn't have to involve them, per se."

He tilted his head to look at me. "How do you reckon that?"

"Well, Tom didn't insist on involving the full force of Scotland Yard when he found us driving around London with Freddie Montrose's dead body in the back of Crispin's motorcar two months ago. I think he'd be willing to keep this on the down-low too, if you asked. Don't you?"

In fact, if the Schlomskys went to Scotland Yard themselves, the powers that be would surely keep things very quiet in an effort to smoke out the kidnappers and rescue Florence.

In my opinion, the Schlomskys could do worse than letting us contact Tom. But if they weren't going to, at least they couldn't stop us from doing it on our own. Flossie may have been their daughter, but she was my friend—or at least she was an acquaintance, and a neighbor, and someone I wasn't willing to give up on without making an effort to rescue her. Let the Schlomskys play along with the kidnappers, and gather the ransom. Christopher and I could handle the investigative part, even if Mr. and Mrs. Schlomsky didn't know we were doing it.

CHAPTER TEN

TEN MINUTES LATER, we were standing in the shadow of London Bridge looking at St Olave's Church across the street. Or rather, we were looking at what was left of St Olave's Church, which wasn't much. Just the transept and a rather squat and square bell tower. Everything else was a mound of dirt with the occasional block of dressed stone that whoever had demolished the thing had left behind.

I opened my mouth and closed it again.

"Well, that's rather a shame," Christopher said distantly, "isn't it?" After a second or two he added, "John Deval built this church, you know."

I squinted at the mess on the other side of the street, and then back at him. "Should that mean something to me?"

He glanced down at me. Not very far down; he's only a few inches taller than me. "He was the King's mason a few hundred years ago, and so was his son. Same name for both of them. This chap built Newgate Prison and several of the London hospitals. His son built Argyll House and King's Bench Prison."

All rather lovely buildings, if antiquated. Still— "Talented family. Although we didn't all study history at Oxford, you know." Some of us studied literature, as it happened.

"This church is mentioned in the Domesday Book," Christopher said with chagrin. "It's been here—or a St Olave's Church has been here—for more than a thousand years."

"Has it really?"

He nodded. "Since just after the sieges of London in 1014 and 1016."

"That's a long time." Even in England, a country with quite a long history.

Christopher nodded. "Olave was a prince of Norway, who helped Æthelred rout the Danes in 1014. The story goes that when the Danes were crossing London Bridge, Olave tied his longboats to the piers and pulled the bridge down into the Thames."

"And Æthelred won?"

"Then," Christopher said, "although it didn't last long. Two years later, Prince Cnut of Denmark came back and took London."

"And the church?"

"Belonged to the Earl of Wessex," Christopher said. "Since 1018."

"And he's the one who named it? The Earl of Wessex?"

"Godwin," Christopher nodded.

"Do you suppose he might have known Olave? The Norwegian prince?" If the church had been built only four years after the incident with the bridge and the longboats.

"Probably did do," Christopher confirmed. "Contemporaries, weren't they? It was nice of him to name his private chapel after a bloke he knew in the war."

We eyed the church, or what was left of it, in silence.

"I wonder what happened to make them decide to tear it down," I said. "Or do you suppose it happened on its own?"

"I would guess one of two things happened," Christopher said, with a wrinkle of his nose. "Either it was built too close to the river, and was damaged in some of the floods—"

The river did have a fairly ripe odor, and yes, the water was quite close by. "Or?"

He glanced around. "This area is more industrial than it used to be. Less need for a church in a location where so few people live."

Indubitably. Which made for a good drop location for the ransom, I assumed. Fewer people around to see what was going on. Safer that way, for the kidnappers.

"Shall we take a closer look?" Christopher suggested.

"There's not much left to look at, but I suppose we might as well. We're here. And I can't see a sign telling us to stay out."

"Out of where, precisely?" He headed across the cobblestones at a diagonal, and I followed. "It's all very accessible, isn't it?"

"Out of what's left, I assume. The tower."

Christopher shook his head. "No, no sign, and no notice on the door. Of course, it might be locked."

He put both hands to the old wood and pushed. The door moved sluggishly and with a groan of hinges.

"Not locked," Christopher said, a bit breathlessly, and slipped through.

"Nothing to protect inside," I added, as I followed, "I would guess. Anything valuable that was here, must have been removed before they tore the nave down."

I looked around at four unadorned stone walls and a staircase winding upwards to the tower.

"After you," Christopher said, and gestured to it.

I shot him a look over my shoulder even as I started up. "Are you quite certain you don't want to go first in case something jumps out at me?"

"That's precisely why I'm behind you," Christopher said, following, "so I can catch you if you fall."

I sniffed, but continued to climb. "You just don't want to face whatever it is first."

"That's true," Christopher agreed, "but I would also do a better job of catching you than you would of catching me if I fell."

Since that was also true, I didn't say any more about it, just kept climbing until I reached the top of the bell tower. The bell itself was gone, to scrap I assumed, but we could see where it had hung, and we could also see out across the roofs of Southwark, and—from the opening on the other side of the tower—across the Thames to the steeple of St Magnus the Martyr, the fish market, and in the distance, the top of the Tower of London as well as the bulk of Tower Bridge.

"Nice view from up here," Christopher commented. He was staring out the south-facing window at the brick of London Bridge and below, Tooley Street.

"Nicer from this side, I'd say."

He glanced at me across the tower, and beyond me to what lay on the other side of the river, before he nodded. "Of course. Scenically speaking. But I meant that this would be a good place for someone to stand and watch fifty thousand American dollars arrive. Nice and private."

I tore myself from the ripples of the river and the buildings beyond to arrive next to him on the other side of the tower, where I peered down as he had done. "You're right."

"I'm usually right," Christopher said.

"If it were me, though, I wouldn't want to be stuck in a tower with only one ingress and egress. If the Schlomskys do end up informing the police, and they do surround the place, this would be the last place I'd want to be. Stuck up here with no way out."

Christopher nodded. "I wasn't thinking of them. I was thinking of us. I'm sure, if the kidnappers are planning to keep watch—and if it were me, I would…"

I nodded.

"—they'll be doing it from somewhere on the ground, and possibly from inside a motorcar, for a quick getaway. I meant for us."

"You want us to hide here tomorrow night?"

He glanced at me. "Do you have a better idea? You did want to be present for the ransom drop, I assumed."

Of course I did, but I hadn't thought about the details beyond that. "What if the kidnappers really are stupid and they do decide to hide up here? And we walk in on them?" Or they on us.

"We'll pretend to be idiot Bright Young People on a scavenger hunt," Christopher said. Clearly he had already thought of a solution to that hypothetical issue. "This is the type of place for it. Or we'll be a couple of lovebirds looking for somewhere private to snog each other stupid, or something like that."

I shot him a look. "If you think I'm going to kiss you, Christopher, you'd better think again."

"I don't," Christopher said, "thank you very much. I don't want to kiss you, either. I'll phone Crispin, and you can kiss him instead."

Ewww. "Don't you dare. There's absolutely no reason to drag him all the way up here from Wiltshire for this."

"You know he'd want to be around for the excitement," Christopher said. "Especially if there's snogging."

"There will not," I told him severely, "be any snogging. Even if we pretend to be a stupid couple looking for somewhere to snog—and I'm talking about you and me, Christopher, not Crispin—even then, we won't have to prove it by kissing in front of them. They'll have to take our word for it."

His lips twitched. "If you say so."

"I do say so. And I am not letting you involve St George. I'll kiss you before I kiss him."

"He'd be devastated to hear it," Christopher said.

I snorted. "He would not. He's well aware of how I feel about him, thank you very much. Besides, he gets more than enough kisses from other people."

"More than enough, is it?" He smirked.

I rolled my eyes. "You know what I mean. If I had a pound for every time—"

And then a mental image dropped, of St George in a corner of the lift at the Essex House, lipstick on his face and Flossie in front of him with a palm against his chest and a look of triumph on her face. All the laughter fled my soul and I winced. "Oh, God. You don't think they're going to kill her, do you, Christopher?"

"I'm sure I don't know," Christopher said, and added, pensively, "I don't see why they would, really, if they get their money. And the Schlomskys seemed to lean in that direction, didn't they?"

They had. "I guess, if you're an American millionaire, fifty thousand dollars more or less won't make a difference to you."

"I'm sure Mother and Father would gladly pay that for either of us," Christopher agreed, and took my elbow to tug me away from the window towards the stairs. "You or me or Francis, or Crispin or Constance, for that matter. Anyone in the family. If they could pay fifty thousand dollars and get Robbie back, I know neither of them would hesitate. I'll go first."

He headed down the stairs.

"Should we tell him, do you suppose?" I asked when we

had reached the bottom and were back outside on Tooley Street, in the sweltering shade of the London Bridge.

Christopher glanced at me. "Tell who what?"

"St George. Tell him about Flossie."

He gave me another look, longer and more intent this time. "I thought you said we shouldn't involve him."

"I said we shouldn't drag him here from Wiltshire just so he can look for kidnappers with us." Or, God forbid, pretend to kiss me.

He took my elbow and started moving in the direction of the train station. I fell into step beside him. "But he and Florence are... well, they've been..."

He arched his brows at me. "I hope you're not suggesting that there are any finer feelings on Crispin's part for Flossie Schlomsky."

I shuddered. "Of course not. But they have been... close."

"By which you mean she has kissed him."

"I suppose," I said grudgingly.

"You suppose?"

I made a face. "Yes, that's what I meant. They've been... not intimate, but close enough to it that perhaps he ought to be told what's going on. I mean, surely he can't be entirely indifferent to a woman he has kissed?"

"I don't imagine he is entirely indifferent," Christopher said as we approached the station doors. "Don't get me wrong, I don't think there are any romantic feelings there at all. With the way he carries on, how could there be? And that's aside from—"

"The girl he says he's in love with." I grimaced. "Whom one would think would be enough to stop him from seducing anything that walks, but what do I know?"

Christopher muttered something, but didn't elucidate. I didn't ask him to. Instead, I pushed the issue with a bit of plain speaking. "Do you think he would want to know? Are we doing him a disservice by not letting him know what has happened to Flossie?"

"I imagine he'll use it as a handy excuse for a trip to Town if we do tell him," Christopher said and headed for the ticket window, "but you make a point. If we don't tell him, he might be upset when he finds out later. If he does."

He approached the ticket window to ask for two tickets back to Charing Cross and pushed the coins across the counter.

"We could run the idea by Tom," I suggested, "and see what he thinks about it."

Christopher accepted the tickets with a nod of thanks and turned away from the window to hand me one of them. "Fine by me. Let's go see Scotland Yard."

Behind him, the ticket clerk's eyes widened.

SEEING Scotland Yard was easier said than done, however. Or rather, of course we could see Scotland Yard. It's quite visible, right there on Whitehall, just a few minutes' walk from Charing Cross. The problem was seeing Tom. In that we couldn't.

"Chief Inspector Pendennis and his team are off-site," the guard at the gate informed us.

"Where did they go?"

He shot me a look. "I'm not at liberty to say, miss."

"Bristol?"

His eyes sharpened, but the answer didn't change. "I'm not at liberty to say, miss."

I made a face. Christopher's lips twitched. "Any idea when they'll be back?"

The guard eyed him up and down. "No, sir."

"We'll leave a note for Tom at home." Christopher turned me towards Chelsea. "Come on, Pippa."

"Are you certain? If we leave the note here, he might get it sooner."

He waited until we were safely away from the gatehouse before he answered. "If we're trying to keep the Schlomskys' confidence, I don't think we ought leave a note detailing a kidnapping and ransom at the gate at Scotland Yard, do you? Even if it's a private note. I wouldn't put it past someone to read it."

"Surely it's illegal to read someone else's post?"

"Perhaps not if you're the police," Christopher said, tugging on my arm. "Come along. It isn't far."

It was far enough that the distance required another train journey, this time on the Underground. By the time it was all said and done, with a note tucked safely into Tom's postbox asking him to please stop by our flat at his earliest convenience, we had whiled away half the day in chasing after things that had ended in nothing useful, and it was well past time for luncheon and close to time for tea.

"Back to the Savoy?" Christopher suggested. "Perhaps there is news."

I supposed it was possible. Flossie had escaped kidnappers once already; perhaps she had been able to do it again, and had turned up, healthy and hale, at her parents' hotel.

So back we went, to Charing Cross via Tube this time, and along the Strand to the Savoy. But this time, when we asked at the front desk about Mr. and Mrs. Schlomsky, the concierge informed us that the American couple had gone out.

"Would you have any idea where?"

"Mr. Schlomsky inquired after a car to take him and the missus to Grosvenor Square," the concierge said, "but that was hours ago."

"What about the *Graf* von Natterdorff? Is he in this afternoon?"

The look I got this time was blank. "Who?"

"The *Graf* von..."

Christopher's hand on my sleeve made me stop talking. "Don't get distracted, Pippa."

"I'm not distracted," I grumbled. "I'm simply inquiring."

"Later. One thing at a time. So the Schlomskys left this morning and haven't been back?"

The concierge nodded, looking from one to the other of us.

"We could leave another note," I suggested, but Christopher shook his head.

"We don't know any more now than we did when we left them earlier. We'll just come back later. Or tomorrow morning."

He nodded to the concierge and tugged me behind him across the lobby.

"I don't see why I can't ask a simple question about Wolfgang," I grumbled, dragging my feet on purpose. "He still hasn't contacted me after St George showed up the other evening, you know."

Christopher flicked me a look as he chivvied me across the lobby. "There might be a note from him at home. Although we have more important things to worry about right now than your love life, Pippa. For instance, since we're on the subject of Crispin, we still haven't rung him up, remember?"

"Why are we on the subject of St George? If it was the mention of my love life, I'll have you know—"

"It wasn't. You brought him up by name." He huffed and pushed me through the revolving doors and back out onto the Strand.

"What do you suppose the Schlomskys are doing at

Grosvenor Square?" I inquired as we made our way back up towards Charing Cross for the second time that day.

I've been there, naturally. To Grosvenor Square, I mean. It's quite a prestigious address, and a pretty place, with trees and buildings, most of them residential, and people and motor-cars. All the usual aspects of London. But unless someone's specifically interested in Oscar Wilde, or perhaps in racecar driving, it isn't a tourist spot.

"I imagine they've gone to confer with the American ambassador," Christopher said.

"He lives at Grosvenor Square?"

Christopher nodded. "Has done since shortly after the American War of Independence."

"Well, we can't go to him. He's not going to tell us anything." And he wasn't likely to be involved in the kidnapping in any other way.

"Wouldn't if he could," Christopher agreed, "and I doubt he can anyway, since all he'd know is what the Schlomskys told him, and we've already spoken with them."

"And if they did anything to Flossie, they aren't any more likely to admit it to him than they were to us."

"No." Christopher tucked his hand through my elbow. "Let's find a telephone box and contact Crispin, and then I wouldn't say no to a spot of tea."

I wouldn't, either. We had missed luncheon in our dash to and from St Olave's and then to Scotland Yard and Chelsea and back to the Savoy. "There's a Lyons a block down."

"That'll suit me fine," Christopher said.

Me, as well. "St George can wait until we've had our fill of tea and buns."

"What he doesn't know won't hurt him," Christopher agreed, and led the way.

. . .

WE FOUND a table by the window and ordered tea and cream cakes. And then, looking out at the hustle and bustle of the Strand, we settled in to have a serious conversation about what we had discovered in our wanderings.

"Whoever took Flossie," I said, "do you suppose they live in Southwark, if they know about the church?"

"I know about it," Christopher answered, "and I don't live in Southwark."

"You only know about it because you studied history at Oxford. It's not likely that whoever snatched Flossie did that."

Individuals with university degrees from Oxford don't have to kidnap young American women for money, one would assume.

Christopher shrugged elegantly. "It's hard to say. But it's easy to speculate that they do. Know about it because they're familiar with that area, I mean. While I've heard of it, I hadn't seen it before today. Now that I know it isn't there anymore, I wish I had gone sooner."

"At least you got to see the tower," I said unsympathetically. "Fewer people live in Southwark than used to, I suppose."

Christopher nodded. "It was all residential at one time. Now it's turning more industrial every day. Which makes it a good place to keep someone you've kidnapped, I suppose. Fewer people around to notice what you're doing."

Of course. "And they do have to keep her somewhere, don't they?"

It wasn't really a question, but Christopher answered it anyway. "Unless they have already disposed of her."

"Killed her, do you mean?" I made a face. "You don't think they have done, do you?"

"It's not for me to say," Christopher said, "but let's hope not."

Definitely let's hope so.

"As long as they've kept their faces covered, she wouldn't know who they are. And if she can't identify them, there would be no reason to kill her."

"One would think," Christopher said and took a sip of tea.

I peered out the window at the hustle and bustle of the Strand. Pedestrians flowed past the Lyons at a steady clip, while motorcars rolled by beyond them. Just a few evenings ago, Flossie might have passed this window on her way to the Savoy. "It's quite an easy trip from here to Southwark. Just five minutes, and one could be on the other side of the river. Although I still find it hard to believe that they managed to snatch a fully grown woman off the street in view of everyone."

"You and me both," Christopher agreed. "But as we discussed, she might have gone with them willingly, if they were people she knew. I don't know how they could have managed it otherwise."

We sat in silence a moment while the cream cakes arrived. When the Nippy walked away, black skirt swinging around her calves, we got back to it.

"I don't suppose a door-to-door search of all of Southwark is in the cards."

"It isn't somewhere where I'd be comfortable going door to door," Christopher admitted. "The police could do it, of course, but if the Schlomskys don't want to involve them..."

"Do you suppose the American ambassador will insist?"

"I don't see how he can. She's the Schlomskys' daughter. It's their decision, surely?"

"Then..." I hesitated. "If it's their decision, are we wrong to involve Tom?"

"Not if it helps us—or them—get Flossie back in one piece," Christopher said firmly.

"And if we don't?"

He eyed me. "Then I think I would rather have tried and failed than not have tried at all."

"Even if it's our trying that pushes the thing over and makes it fail?"

He didn't answer, and we finished our cream cakes and tea in silence.

CHAPTER ELEVEN

"KIT?"

Crispin's voice was tinny through the earpiece of the telephone. "What's wrong? Is the bloody bastard back again?"

"Hullo, St George," I said smoothly, and had the pleasure of hearing what I was fairly certain was a snap of teeth from the other end of the line when he closed his mouth. "What a pleasure to hear your dulcet tones. To which bloody bastard are you referring?"

"Darling." His voice was flat. "I was unaware you were listening. Tidwell informed me Kit was on the telephone."

"Oh, he's here, too." I smiled at him. "And I'm sure he'd be just as interested as I am to know who the bloody bastard is, if you'd just refrain from changing the subject."

"Never mind that," Crispin said. "Kit already knows what I'm on about. Are you there, old bean?"

"Right here," Christopher assured him. "You'll have to excuse Pippa. I'm sure she suspects you of referring to the illustrious *Graf von und zu* Natterdorff."

Crispin scoffed. "As if I would spend any of my precious time thinking about him."

I rolled my eyes. "Naturally. I doubt you ever spare a thought for anyone but yourself."

He didn't respond, and I added, "For your information, you seem to have successfully scared him off. I haven't seen or heard from him since you took me away from him two evenings ago."

"What a shame." His voice was perfectly flat, and it was impossible to guess whether he was pleased by that bit of information or not. "To what do I owe the pleasure of your call?"

"A situation has arisen," Christopher said, "that we thought might be of interest to you."

"Let me guess. Another drag ball?"

I snorted, and Christopher made a face. "I'm afraid not. Since the raids in April and June, Lady Austin has lain low. I have hopes for September."

Crispin hummed. "If not that, then what?"

"Flossie's missing," I said.

There was a beat of silence that vibrated loudly down the line. Then— "Pardon me? Did you just say that Florence Schlomsky is missing? And you think I have her?"

I scoffed. Christopher didn't, because he's much nicer than me. "Of course not, Crispin. Not unless your father's keeping you so short you have to resort to kidnapping and extortion for pocket change."

"Kidnapping?"

"No one's seen her since you dropped her off on the Strand two nights ago," I told him bluntly. "This morning, her parents received a ransom note demanding fifty thousand American dollars for her safe return."

"And naturally you thought of me."

His tone was as dry as the Sahara.

"Pippa thought you might like to know," Christopher told him, and it was Crispin's turn to snort.

"Oh, I'm certain Philippa was acting purely out of the goodness of her heart. Weren't you, Darling?"

"Don't be absurd, St George," I told him severely. "Of course I don't suspect you of having had anything to do with it."

He made a disbelieving sort of noise, and I added, "Back when we thought there was a chance she might have eloped or simply decided to waste her time in someone's bed for a few days, yes. You were high on the list then. Naturally."

"Naturally," Crispin echoed.

"But neither of us thinks you'd commit abduction for money. Whatever else is wrong with you, you're too much of a gentleman for that."

"Charmed," Crispin said, sounding anything but.

"Knock it off, Crispin," Christopher told him. He must have gotten tired of the bickering. "This is a serious matter. They want fifty thousand dollars by eleven o'clock tomorrow night, or they'll kill her."

"That *is* serious." Crispin waited a moment and then he added, "What do you expect me to do about it?"

"Nothing at all," I told him. "There's nothing any of us can do. Just..."

"Yes?"

"You were telling the truth, weren't you? When you said you dropped her off on the Strand?"

"Yes, Darling. I was. The last time I saw her she was standing on the corner waiting to cross the esseet. Besides, you were in my motorcar after that. You'd know if I hadn't left her off. Unless you think I somehow managed to stuff her in the boot in the middle of the Strand?"

I sniffed. "Of course not. That would be impossible."

"Quite."

"Although we don't know that she didn't go into Charing Cross and meet you in Salisbury later that night."

"If she had done," Crispin said coolly, "she wouldn't have ended up in Salisbury. I would have taken her to Waterloo instead. The Charing Cross trains run on the South Eastern line. Salisbury is on the South Western."

Of course. I knew that. I just hadn't been thinking straight.

"But if you'd like," Crispin continued, "I'd be happy to put Tidwell or Mrs. Mason on the telephone, and they can assure you that she isn't here. Or my father, if you prefer."

"No, thank you," I said with a grimace. "Nothing against Tidwell or Mrs. Mason, of course. Under no circumstances do I wish to talk to your father."

I'm sure Uncle Harold has his own reasons for disliking me. I'm half German, I'm poor, his brother has had to take care of me since I was eleven years old because my own parents are dead and unable to do so; I honestly don't know what Uncle Harold's reasons may be, because he's never admitted that he feels that way, not out loud. But as for me, I dislike him because he's a right bastard to his son much of the time, and I don't appreciate it. I've earned the right to torment Crispin. He has tormented me enough to deserve retaliation. But Uncle Harold has no business meting out punishment. Crispin is his son and heir and should be treated with love and care by his father.

The scion of the Sutherlands sighed. "Then what would you have me do, Darling?"

"Nothing," Christopher said firmly. "It's nothing to do with you, Crispin. We both know that you don't have Flossie stashed away in your bed chamber at home."

Christopher glared at me over the mouthpiece, expectantly. I made a face but said obediently, "Yes, St George. We know that."

The latter huffed. "What do you want, then?"

"We don't want anything," Christopher told him. "Really, Crispin. Pippa asked if I thought we ought to tell you, and I said yes. You know Flossie, and you deserve to know what has happened to her. We didn't ring up because we suspect you of having had anything to do with it, or because we think there's anything you can do. It's truly just because we thought you should know. Flossie is... the two of you... well, she isn't—"

"Don't you dare, Kit."

"Right," Christopher said, biting back whatever words he had foolishly thought of saying. "Flossie's gone, kidnapped and held for ransom. You know Flossie, so we thought you would want to know. That's all."

There was silence on the line. "Fifty thousand American dollars?" Crispin asked.

"Her father can spare it," I told him. "Florence has told me he's a millionaire."

The Sutherland money was unnecessary, if that was what Crispin was thinking. Not that I imagined that Uncle Harold would be willing to part with any of it, for Florence Schlomsky.

"Of course he is," Crispin said. "And is he going to pay the ransom?"

"They've spent the day collecting it," Christopher confirmed, "we think. We haven't spoken to them since this morning. They went to Grosvenor Square, we assume to talk to the American ambassador, but we don't know how else they may have been spending their time. Mr. Schlomsky was adamant about not involving the police, though."

"So naturally the two of you went directly to Thomas Gardiner." It wasn't a question, or didn't sound like one.

"We tried," I said. "He's away on a case. We left a note."

There was a moment of silence.

"What do you want me to do?"

"Nothing, Crispin," Christopher said again, and I added,

"We meant it, St George. We really just wanted you to know. Because... Well, it seemed as if you should have the information, that's all."

He hummed. "Thank you, I suppose. When and where does the transfer of money take place?"

"Tomorrow evening at eleven," Christopher said, "just across the Thames in Southwark."

"It would be Southwark." I could hear the eyeroll all the way from Wiltshire. "You're planning to go, I assume?"

"We thought we might," Christopher said.

"I'll see if I can get away."

I made a face. "That's really not necessary, St George."

"I don't doubt that you would much rather have His Grace, the *Graf* von Natterdorff, by your side, Darling. But as you said, Flossie and I were..." He paused for a second, "close."

My eyes narrowed. "I had no intention of inviting Wolfgang, you prat. I won't need protection, and if I do, I trust Christopher to provide it."

"As you should." His voice was smooth and colorless. "Nonetheless, I'll do my best to be there. Thank you for letting me know."

He disconnected before either Christopher or I had the time to come up with anything to say.

"You upset him," Christopher told me as he replaced the earpiece on the telephone.

I resisted the temptation to roll my eyes, because if I had, they would have rolled so hard that they might disappear into the back of my head. "I did not. I said nothing to upset him. And I think you overestimate how easy he is to upset, anyway."

"You don't think finding out that a girl he has dallied with has been kidnapped and is being held for ransom might be upsetting?"

"He never dallied with her," I protested. "She kissed him a few times when she was able to corner him in the lift, that's all. Hardly a dalliance. Not considering the way he has of carrying on with other women. All those girls he brought back to Sutherland House for the night, not to mention Lady Laetitia Marsden..."

"So you don't think he was upset?"

I scowled. "He might have been upset. But if he was, he hid it well."

"Not well enough for me," Christopher said. "I do wish you wouldn't go out of your way to be disagreeable, Pippa."

"I don't go out of my way to be disagreeable," I said—disagreeably—as we headed down the Strand. "He just brings out the worst in me."

"And you in him."

There was no arguing with that, so I didn't try. Instead, I asked, "What now?"

He slanted me a look, but accepted the change of topic. "What do you suggest?"

"I'm not sure what else we can do," I admitted. "We've tried the Schlomskys, and they're gone. Tom's gone. Flossie's gone, obviously. We looked at the church, or what's left of it. Nobody can have noticed anything amiss on Wednesday night, or I'm sure we or the Schlomskys would have already heard about it. There would have been a notice in the newspaper, if nothing else, about a woman being forced into a motorcar on the Strand."

"Unless she went willingly."

Yes, unless that. "I suppose we could take another look at Flossie's flat, if Evans will let us in. Just in case she did go willingly and there's a clue there."

"Or just in case her parents killed her," Christopher agreed, ignoring the startled look he received from a woman passing by in the other direction, who caught what he was saying, "and there's a clue about that."

I nodded. "Certainly. We can't discount infanticide."

He flicked me a look. "She's hardly a baby."

"Of course she isn't. But there's no word for killing your adult child, is there? There's matricide, when you kill your mother, and patricide, when you kill your father." I held up two fingers. "Sororicide and fratricide when you kill your siblings." Two more. "Infanticide when you kill your child who is a child." The whole hand. "But no word for killing your child who is an adult."

"Homicide?" Christopher suggested, only half in jest.

I rolled my eyes and dropped my hand again. "I know *that*, Christopher. Also murder and manslaughter and a few others. But no specific word for killing your own child once they've reached maturity."

"You think the Schlomskys may have done that, then?"

"I should certainly hate to think so," I told him, "and they did seem quite frantic this morning, about the kidnapping and ransom. You saw them. Did they appear to be hiding guilt?"

Christopher shook his head. "That's assuming they'd feel guilty about it, of course, and not everyone would. But no, I didn't get the impression that they were trying to cover up a murder. Then again, we don't know them well enough to know what they're usually like, do we?"

I supposed we didn't. If it came down to it, we didn't even know that they *were* the Schlomskys. No one had asked them to prove it. Not that I really thought they weren't, of course. They had known where to find Flossie, so really, they had to be her parents, didn't they? No one else would know that, in this teeming metropolis of Englishmen.

"Let's see if we can't talk Evans into letting us into Flossie's flat," I said. "There's likely to be nothing there, but I wouldn't mind another look around."

"I wouldn't mind a first look," Christopher said, "Especially at that closet. How do you suppose we convince Evans?"

"We lie," I told him.

EVANS REQUIRED VERY little in the way of convincing when it came right down to it. All I had to do was tell him that Mrs. Schlomsky had wanted me to retrieve the pair of gloves she had left behind in Flossie's flat yesterday, and bring them to her—and by the way, here was the ten shillings she had given me to pass on to Evans for his trouble—before he gave me the key and told me I had five minutes to bring it back downstairs. Whereupon Christopher and I opened Flossie's flat, retrieved a pair of likely-looking gloves from Flossie's ostentatious second bedroom/closet, and then I took care that Evans should see them when I brought the key back. "Thank you, Evans. I'll bring them to her in the morning. I'll be sure to mention how helpful you were."

Evans nodded and tucked the key away tidily. "Note for you, Miss Darling." He lifted it out of the cubby and held it out. I took it between two fingers and peered at the envelope. It had the Savoy Hotel logo—a circle with the letters S and H inside—in the corner.

"Why didn't you give this to me earlier?"

"It just now arrived," Evans said blandly, which may or may not have been the truth.

There was nothing I could say, though—not when I didn't know any better, and besides, I wanted to stay on the right side of Evans. So I simply thanked him and took my letter and buzzed off towards the lift, heart knocking excitedly. The German *Kurrentschrift* was easily recognizable, and when I ripped the envelope open, the note invited me to have supper with *Graf* Wolfgang again, tomorrow night, back at the Savoy.

"What have you got there?" Christopher asked when the door was shut behind me and it was just the two of us in Flossie's flat. "Another note from the Schlomskys?"

I shook my head. "Wolfgang."

"The *Graf?*" He held out a hand, and it didn't even occur to me not to hand over the envelope. Christopher fished out the note, perused it, and sniffed.

"The nerve."

I slanted a look at him. "Whatever do you mean?"

He handed the envelope back. "It's a bit petulant, isn't it? If you 'can spare the time' he would like to treat you to supper and try to make a better impression than last time. Crispin must have given his *amour propre* a knock." He grinned.

I tucked the envelope into my reticule. "St George does have a way of doing that, although I won't say that Wolfgang seemed particularly wounded at the time. I don't think it was his self-esteem that took the knock so much as his vanity."

"One and the same for some people," Christopher said. "Do you want to go?"

"Of course I want to go. But whether I'm able to depends on how early you want to get to Southwark tomorrow evening, doesn't it? I wouldn't want it to interfere with our looking for kidnappers."

One must have one's priorities in order, after all.

"We'd have to be there at least an hour ahead of time," Christopher said, "don't you think? Just in case they've had the same idea and are there early to keep an eye on things."

I thought about it. "If that's the case, wouldn't it be better if we're late? If two people go into the tower at ten, and they still haven't come out by eleven, surely that's somewhat suspicious?"

"For that location," Christopher agreed, "perhaps."

"It's something we can discuss later." I glanced around Flossie's foyer. "We shouldn't waste the time we have here on things that we can talk about in our own flat."

Christopher nodded. "I took a closer look while you were downstairs, and as you said, that's quite an ostentatious wardrobe."

"Isn't it? I can't imagine that much of it has been worn more than once or maybe twice. And some of the frocks are so much alike it's hard to imagine why she wouldn't just wear the same one instead of buying another."

"Hiram Schlomsky can afford it," Christopher said, which was certainly true, but no excuse for being a wastrel. He looked around vaguely. "Any idea what we're looking for? Other than accessories?"

"I think we'll probably know it when we see it, don't you?" I looked around, too, with no idea where to start the search for something we didn't even know what was. "Anything that doesn't belong, I suppose. Anything that strikes you as being strange or out of place. Anything dodgy?"

"Not sure what you'd consider dodgy," Christopher said, "but I suppose we'll just take a look around and see what we can see. Chances are there's nothing here, anyway."

Chances were that he was right. But we were here now, with an opportunity to explore, and I'm nothing if not inquisitive, so I wasn't about to let the opportunity pass.

"You can start in the closet," I told him, magnanimously, "if you would like. Admire the frocks while you check pockets and inside handbags."

He gave me a dubious sort of look. "I'll do my best, I suppose."

"I'll start with the other bedroom," I told him, "the one she actually seems to sleep in, and we'll meet in the sitting room?"

Christopher nodded, and headed for the closet. I left him there, standing in the middle of the floor with his hands on his hips, looking around at the plethora of pockets and bags and toes of shoes with a calculating expression on his face, before I headed down the hallway towards the back of the flat.

While I had told him I would start with Flossie's bedroom, I made a detour into the lavatory on my way past.

It looked precisely like the one in our flat, all white tiles with black trim, a toilet, a sink, and a claw-footed tub. Flossie's towels were pink—I don't know why I was surprised by that, although I've never used anything but a white towel myself—and the medicine cabinet held a toothbrush, toothpaste, a twist of headache powder, some plasters, eyewash... all the usual things. No prescriptions, so at least we didn't have to worry about Flossie succumbing to illness while in captivity, due to lack of access to her medicine.

The toilet tank was mounted at the top of the wall, so there was no way to hide anything inside it, and I wasn't about to climb on top of the toilet and risk having the water pour all over me if I made a mistake in trying to open it up. So I considered the job well done, and moved on.

Flossie's bedroom was next. There was another closet here, chock full of... night clothes, as it happened. Gowns, and negligees, and pyjamas in silky colors. Some of them—most of them—were in shades of pink, from shell to raspberry, but a few were green and blue and lilac, as well.

One set was black, and put me in mind of Laetitia Marsden, who had worn the same sort of slinky see-through thing at the Dower House back in May. It wasn't the type of nightclothes that you sleep in; it was the type you'd wear to impel susceptible people of the opposite gender to notice you. Laetitia had worn hers for Crispin's benefit. I wondered who Flossie wore hers for.

After that, I moved on to the night table. There was only one, from which I deduced that Flossie slept alone, at least most of the time, fancy nightclothes notwithstanding.

Of course, I had already known that she lived alone. In the time we had lived here at the Essex House Mansions, I had never seen Florence with a man other than Crispin, and to my knowledge, she had never managed to finagle him into her flat, let alone into her bed. She might be misbehaving in other people's bedrooms—there was always that possibility, in which case she would have had to travel with her negligees—but she had never, to my knowledge, brought a young man, or for that matter a young woman, back here. At least not that I had noticed.

The night table yielded a water glass—half full or half empty, depending on your definition; I sniffed it, and it seemed to be simple water—along with a notepad and a pencil, an alarm clock—silent and stopped at 11:37, since Florence hadn't been here to wind it for a few days—a handkerchief (good quality cotton, embroidered with roses but no monogram), and a copy of the *Daily Yell* with Crispin on the cover, from the week back in April when Duke Henry, Lady Charlotte, and Grimsby the valet had died. There was no image of Simon Grimsby, of course, but there were photos of everyone else: the late Duke Henry, the new Duke Harold, the new Viscount St George, and the lady responsible for it all. I flipped through the pages to see whether anything was hidden inside, or whether Flossie had made any notations anywhere, but there was nothing. Not even the crossword was filled out. She must have kept the paper for Crispin's picture and no other reason.

The night table drawer contained a small stack of airmail letters, all of them sporting American stamps and the same handwriting that had appeared on the note Evans had handed me this morning. They started with *Dearest Florence*, and ended with *Your Loving Mama*. News from home, I assumed, and since it felt a bit intrusive to start reading them, I left them on top of the counterpane and moved on. They weren't likely to shine any light whatsoever on what was going on right now, unless Mama Schlomsky was indeed a rabid murderess who had killed her only child, and the letters indicated it.

The makeup table looked like mine, and Christopher's.

When Christopher puts on his alter-ego Kitty Dupree, he does it in my room. Kitty's evening gowns hang in my wardrobe and Kitty's black wig sits on my dressing table. If someone were to look closely, he or she would see that a few of the gowns are not in my size nor in my best colors, but my wardrobe is a better place for them than Christopher's. In mine, they can mostly be overlooked, and we're still not clear on what the current duke might do if he realizes that his youngest nephew goes to drag balls and cavorts with men. Nor do we know how Uncle Herbert and Aunt Roz might react, really. They have a better idea of how Christopher's feelings run than his uncle does, and so far they seem mostly all right with it, but they don't know about the drag balls.

At any rate, I was going through Flossie's makeup table. It was full of tubes and pots and brushes, expensive creams and cosmetics. There was nothing there that shouldn't be there, as far as I could tell. A small, white card was stuck behind the edge of the mirror, but when I lifted it down, it was just a ticket stub for a West End musical that was taking London by storm this season. The date matched the day last month when I had first laid eyes on the Girl with the Baby, so Flossie must have been on her way to the Prince of Wales theatre when we took the lift down to the lobby together that evening. She must have been attending the performance with the friend who had met her in the lobby: the plain-looking girl in the too-fancy outfit of chiffon and polka dots.

The ticket stub held no secrets other than simply being there, so I left it alone and turned at Christopher's approach.

He stopped inside the door and looked around. "Nothing?"

"Nothing worth mentioning. You?"

He shook his head, and his eyes landed on the small stack of letters on the bed.

"Letters from America," I told him. "I haven't read them yet. Not sure that I should, honestly. They're private, and it's not as if we'll learn anything about Flossie's disappearance from what her mother writes."

"We might learn something about her mother, though." He headed towards the bed with a glance at me out of the corner of his eye. "I know that it isn't likely to be Mr. and Mrs. Schlomsky behind Flossie's kidnapping, but I don't think we ought to disregard them entirely, either. She was so close to the Savoy when Crispin set her down, and it's so unlikely that anyone could have taken her against her will on the Strand between Charing Cross and the hotel, that I think we need to consider that she might have made it there."

"Perhaps we should have inquired of the concierge this morning," I said.

"That would have been rather a dead giveaway of our suspicions," Christopher answered, picking the top letter off the stack with delicate fingertips, "but perhaps we ought to have done."

"The Schlomskys have enough money to pay for silence, though." I watched as he extracted the flimsy airmail paper from the equally flimsy airmail envelope.

He nodded. "Indeed they do. Cheap at twice the price, if she did arrive at the Savoy and they did something to her."

He unfolded the letter and cleared his throat. *"Dearest Florence. Thank you for your letter dated May 2nd..."*

CHAPTER TWELVE

I AM glad you are enjoying London and making new friends. Ruth tells me that everything is more expensive there, so we have increased your monthly allowance by one hundred pounds, and are giving Ruth another hundred for household expenses, as well. Here in Toledo, everything is well. Your father...

CHRISTOPHER'S VOICE trailed off as he skimmed the rest of the letter before folding it and sliding it back into the envelope again. "Nothing else of interest there. Just how things are at home and how so-and-so sends their regards."

I nodded. "It makes sense that London would be more expensive than Toledo, but two hundred extra pounds a month? What on earth did she do with it all?"

"Frocks?" Christopher suggested with a grimace. "I don't know, Pippa. It's a lot of money, even for someone with no self-control."

It was. "How much do you suppose St George goes through a month? Just for comparison?"

"Less than that," Christopher said, "but then he spends most of his time in the country. If he lived in Town, I suppose he might fritter away that much on frivolities, although for all his fun and games, he's never been a spendthrift. But no matter. I'm more interested in the other hundred to Ruth for household expenses. Ruth is the maid, I assume? The one you said they sent over with Flossie?"

"That's what Mrs. Schlomsky called her," I nodded. I could still hear her voice in my head. *Ruth, Hiram! Where is Ruth?* "She was adamant that Ruth had to be around. And if they've been sending her money for household expenses, it makes sense that she would be."

"But she's not. I've never seen her."

I hadn't, either. "Perhaps she made it to England and then left Flossie's employ?"

"If so, why would Sarah Schlomsky continue to send her money?"

She wouldn't, of course. Not unless Flossie had kept Ruth's defection silent. "Perhaps Flossie let her go, because she didn't want Ruth to report on her to her parents, and the money is hush-money so Ruth won't spill the beans."

Christopher thought about it. "That makes more sense than a lot of other things."

It did. Although it didn't explain the kidnapping.

"No," Christopher agreed when I said as much. "If it was a matter of fooling the elder Schlomskys, all Ruth would have to do was come back for a week while Hiram and Sarah are in London, and pretend to be working here, and then leave again once they're gone."

Yes, it would. They would have to clear out Flossie's 'closet' and make it look like a proper bedroom for Ruth, but they had had enough time to do that, had they wanted to. So why hadn't they?

"For the money Flossie's paying her," I said, "an extra hundred pounds per month, on top of how much to begin with, I wonder?—it would certainly have been worth it to her."

Christopher nodded. "So why not simply do that? It would be in Ruth's best interest to keep the charade up and the money coming."

"And in Flossie's best interest to convince her parents that everything was copacetic and Ruth was still on the job," I agreed. "She left the Essex House just after the telegram arrived that night. You saw her leave. That might have been to contact Ruth and tell her what was going on."

Christopher nodded. "Ruth never came back, though. And it's hard to imagine why she wouldn't."

Yes, it was. "Should we take the letters with us and read the rest of them?"

"I can't imagine what else we might learn," Christopher said with a glance at the stack. "The one I read was mostly just updates on what was going on in Toledo and greetings from people I assume Flossie must have known. If they thought Ruth was still here as late as three months ago, I don't see what the earlier letters might tell us that's different. That was the most recent one, I assume?"

"It was the one on top of the stack, but I suppose I can check." I did so, and nodded. "Yes. Five letters, the first postmarked November last year, the last postmarked early June. No mention of a trip to visit England in the part you didn't read out loud, I assume?"

Christopher shook his head. "So if we estimate two weeks for a letter to travel from England to the US, and then a few days to write a response, and another two weeks for the response to travel from the US back to England... I would assume Flossie posted a response sometime in mid-to-late-June, which arrived in Toledo around the first week of July, and the

Schlomskys sent a response in mid-July, which would have gotten here early this month... except perhaps not, if they were planning a surprise trip and didn't want to give the surprise away."

I nodded. ""That's logical. So as far as Mama Schlomsky knew, the last time she communicated with her daughter, Ruth was still here, taking care of Florence."

"So it seems," Christopher agreed. "But we've been here six months or so now, and as far as we know, there's never been a Ruth."

I looked around, vaguely. "I wonder if Flossie has the contact information for Ruth written down somewhere."

"If she had, I imagine she would have tidied it away before her parents arrived, don't you?" But he was looking around, too, vaguely.

"She didn't know she was going to be kidnapped," I said, "did she? Although it isn't anywhere in this room, if she had it. I looked everywhere. There's nothing but jewelry in the jewelry box—a few very nice pieces, a couple of strings of real pearls, something I would swear are real diamonds—but no contact information for anyone."

"False bottom?"

I shook my head. "If there was, I didn't find it."

Christopher nodded. "Let's check the sitting room, then. And the kitchenette. Nothing's likely to be there, I guess, but we should look."

Of course we should.

"I'll take the escritoire," Christopher said, "if you'll take the table and chairs. Be sure to check the cushions."

"I hardly think Ruth's direction is going to be hidden behind a sofa pillow," I told him as I headed towards the seating area, "but I'll certainly check. It will be a formality, I'm sure. If there's anything, it'll be in the desk."

"If it is, I'll find it. But look carefully anyway."

Of course I would. I flipped sofa pillows and slid my hands below and under cushions and found nothing for my trouble except a few coins, a misplaced lighter—no distinguishing marks, but it looked more dainty than masculine, so was probably one of Flossie's own—and several Kirbigrips that must have made their way out of her—or someone else's—hair.

"Have you noticed the gaps?" Christopher wanted to know, and I turned to him with a wrinkle between my brows.

"Noticed what?"

He threw out a hand, and I looked around. And now that he had mentioned it, I did notice a few gaps. The mantel had a vase in the middle, with pink flowers in it, and to the right, a few small trinkets. To the left there was nothing.

"You've never been here before, have you, Pippa?"

I shook my head. "We're not close, Christopher. You know that. You've never been in Flossie's flat before either, have you?"

He shuddered. "No. You were here yesterday, with the Schlomskys."

I glanced around again. "Yes, but nothing has changed since then. How could it? She was already gone yesterday afternoon."

"The kidnappers would have had her key," Christopher said.

"I hardly think they would risk coming back here, do you? Besides, Evans would have mentioned anyone coming in and going up to Flossie's flat."

He hummed. "It's more likely that Flossie herself removed whatever was there. But if so, where did she put it?" He looked around, pensively.

"And why remove it in the first place?" I glanced over at the mantel again. "Photographs?"

"That would be my guess," Christopher said.

"Someone she didn't want her parents to see, then, most likely. So she tidied it away in advance of their arrival."

Like an unsuitable gentleman—or less than a gentleman—friend.

Although if she had an unsuitable boyfriend, what was she doing, kissing Crispin at every opportunity?

"Or perhaps it was a photo of herself doing something she didn't want her parents to see," Christopher suggested. "Smoking, drinking, dancing. The same reason we don't have any photographs of Kitty in our flat, really."

"I didn't realize there were photographs of Kitty."

"Certainly there are. But I'm not about to put them on display in places where our family might see them."

No, that was probably best. "I don't think Flossie gets up to those kinds of shenanigans," I said, "do you? The first time Crispin met her, she said she was on her way to Lady Montfort's soiree, and those are as staid as they come."

"Where was *he* going?" Christopher wanted to know. "Some Bright Young party, wasn't it? The Jungman sisters, or something like that? Perhaps he took her there instead, and corrupted her, and now she's deeply into the Bright Young Set, and drinking cocktails and doping herself and having sex and all the rest of it. Her parents would be appalled."

They certainly would. Or I had gathered the impression that it wouldn't be what they'd expect from their darling Florence, at any rate.

"I suppose that's possible." I looked around again. "Would she get rid of the evidence entirely, do you suppose, or just hide it away somewhere less visible?"

"There weren't any framed photographs in the closet," Christopher said. "Or the second bedroom, I guess I should say."

"None in the actual bedroom, either. Or the bathroom."

"So where would she have put them? Behind the tea leaves in the kitchen?" He eyed the sitting room. "There are no bookshelves to speak of, so she couldn't have taken them out of the frames and hidden them there."

"They're not in the desk?"

He shook his head. "I'll go look through the kitchen. Leaf through those magazines, if you would, and see if there's anything hidden between the pages."

He headed towards the other side of the sitting room while I reached for one of the magazines on the coffee table. Flossie might not be much of a reader—he was right; there were no bookshelves anywhere, and no books, either—but she must like gossip, or perhaps pictures of pretty people in pretty clothes, because there were plenty of *Tatlers* and *Daily Yells*.

I leafed through them all, making faces at pictures of Crispin and Lady Laetitia Marsden, and Crispin and other young ladies of the aristocracy. I turned them over and shook them to see whether anything would fall out, I looked for notations... and eventually, I came up empty.

"Nothing?" Christopher asked when he appeared in the doorway to the kitchenette. I shook my head. "No, not here either. She must have taken the photographs with her when she left. Perhaps she took them somewhere to dispose of them. Or hide them until her parents were gone."

"Much easier just to take them out of the frames and put them on the fire if she wanted them gone," I said.

We both eyed the fireplace. It was clean and tidy with no ashes. Not surprising, since it was August, and we had no need of extra heat.

"Perhaps she took them to a friend to hold for her until her parents left again," Christopher suggested.

I looked around again, disgruntled. "I suppose she must

have. Although it seems like a lot of trouble to go to when she could have just stuffed them in a drawer for a week. Surely her mother wouldn't snoop through her unmentionables to see if anything was hidden underneath."

"We did," Christopher said.

"But only because she has been kidnapped. And she couldn't have known that that would happen."

There was a pause. "Maybe I was right," Christopher said, "and the kidnappers did come here after they grabbed Flossie. Perhaps she was taken by someone she knows, someone who had struck up a friendship with her, and they were in the photograph with her. And after they got Flossie, they had to get rid of the photograph because it was a clue."

Perhaps. It would explain the gone-in-almost-broad-daylight-from-the-Strand, and it made more sense than that Flossie would want to hide her own face from her parents, too.

"I'd like to know how they made it past Evans," I said, "although I suppose he might have been asleep, or in the loo, or they lured him outside and then sneaked in while he had his back turned, or something."

"Or they came in during the night, when he was off duty," Christopher said. He looked around. "Anything else we can learn from this place, do you think? Or is it time to go?"

I did the same, and couldn't see anywhere we hadn't already inspected. Nothing I looked at gave me any ideas for something we might do that we hadn't already done. "I think it is."

"Then let's go back to our own flat," Christopher said and headed for the front door. "You have a supper invitation to consider." He waited for me to go past him into the hallway, and then he shut the door behind us and made sure it was locked.

. . .

THERE WAS NOTHING TO CONSIDER, of course. I accepted the invitation from Wolfgang, with the caveat—made between Christopher and me—that if supper went late, he'd fetch me, straight from the table if he had to. While I liked Wolfgang, and looked forward to spending more time with him, I wanted even more to be on time to catch the money drop in Southwark.

There was no response from the note we had left for Tom the next morning, and because we'd be going to the Savoy anyway come early evening, and because the Schlomskys had not been in touch to request our presence again, we didn't go near the Strand until it was almost time for me to meet Wolfgang for supper.

By then, Christopher had tweaked and polished me in front of the mirror for an hour. I was wearing the new evening frock I had purchased for Cousin Francis and Constance Peckham's engagement party in July, the frock I hadn't had the chance to wear at the time, because of the murder.

It was a rather stunning salmon pink confection with a very simple cut—V-neck, straight arms, slightly uneven hem, just enough for some movement. It ended right below the knee. There were no variations in fabric, no different top and bottom, nothing like that. It was all of a piece and all very simple. What made it special was the decoration: tiny beads the same color as the fabric over most of the dress, making the whole thing sparkle with depth in the light, but with a pattern in warmish brown along the neckline, the arm holes, and the hem. The same darker color was used to make patterns of reeds here and there: from the shoulder down toward the middle, and in both directions from the beaded 'belt' that circled my hips.

"Stunning," Christopher told me when I was standing in front of him after he had finished putting on my face. "He won't know what hit him."

I smirked, somewhat complacently, as I looked at myself in the mirror. "I'd like to see St George come up with anything derogative to say about this."

He had likened my apple green evening frock to a Bramley and made snide comments about my banana yellow frock, as well. That had been deliberate, admittedly. Christopher had asked him to, but he had been able to come up with something nasty to say, so the thought must have been there in his head all along, or he would have been stumped. And he had managed the Bramley comment all on his own. But this, this was beyond his nastiness.

"So would I," Christopher agreed, looking me down and up again.

I tilted my head. "You haven't heard from him, have you?"

"Crispin? Not since we spoke on the telephone yesterday afternoon."

"He doesn't know that I'm going out again with Wolfgang?"

"I haven't told him," Christopher said.

"Good." Then I wouldn't have to worry about Crispin taking a hand in removing me from Wolfgang's company later tonight. Christopher at least would be polite when he did it. With Crispin, all bets were off. "So you don't know if he's planning to show up in London tonight, or not."

"I haven't heard," Christopher said. "But you spoke to him yourself yesterday. I wouldn't be surprised if he showed up, after that. But he hasn't said one way or the other."

"Uncle Harold might be successful in keeping him in Wiltshire."

"Might," Christopher agreed, and was kind enough not to comment on my wistful tone. "I wouldn't count on it. Crispin usually manages to do what he wants to do."

"He didn't really know Flossie well."

Christopher shook his head. "But he knows us well. And

how likely is it that he'll let you and me go to Southwark on our own—without Tom's backup—to look for a ransom drop and a blackmailer?"

Not very likely, I supposed. Although— "He's younger than both of us. If anyone should stay home, it's him. He's the baby."

"Better not let him hear you say that," Christopher advised with a quirk of the lips. "He's more used to taking care of himself than either of us, I daresay. He gets up to a lot more trouble than we do. And he usually does it alone. We have each other."

"You go to drag balls alone."

"And when there's been trouble, I have had Tom there to pull me out," Christopher said. "So far."

"It was St George and I who got you out of the drag ball in June before the raid started."

"And dragged me straight into a murder," Christopher answered. "Besides, I don't think you can take credit for that, Pippa. It was a coincidence. You had no idea that there was going to be a raid that night. We just happened to leave early."

I shrugged. He was right, so there was no point in persisting. "Perhaps we'll just hope that Uncle Harold has St George under lock and key tonight, then."

"Perhaps we won't," Christopher said. "I'd much rather take the Hispano-Suiza to London Bridge at eleven, than the train. I'd feel much safer in Crispin's motorcar. The docks district at midnight isn't a place I'd like to linger with no way home."

"We can always run across the bridge."

"And be thrown into the water by the kidnappers," Christopher said. After a moment he sighed, "I know how you feel about him, Pippa. But I'd rather have him—and the H6—in London tonight than in Wiltshire. And if that means that you have to put up with him, then so be it."

I made a face. "Have it your way." He had a point, after all. About the motorcar and all that, and why we'd rather have the H6 here with us tonight. If Crispin came along, too—as he would have to—then that was just something I would have to deal with.

"Off to see the Schlomskys, then," Christopher suggested, "before supper?"

"We may as well," I told him, and let him escort me out.

THE SCHLOMSKYS, luckily, had not gone anywhere for supper yet. And although they seemed less than thrilled to see us, they did allow us inside the suite and consented to answer the handful of questions we had.

"Yes," Hiram Schlomsky said, "the money's all taken care of. Or as much of it as I could get on short notice."

He gestured to a valise on top of one of the beds. I eyed it a little longer than perhaps I should have, since it was frankly a lot smaller than I had expected it to be. I would have believed fifty thousand American dollars to take up more space than that. But perhaps he had gathered very large bills, hundreds or thousands, even...

Hiram cleared his throat significantly. I flushed and dragged my attention away from the bag, and Christopher wiped a smirk off his face.

"You look nice, Miss Darling," Sarah Schlomsky said, with an up-and-down look that was, frankly, less flattering than you might think from the words. There was a tiny wrinkle between her brows. Perhaps she thought my skirt was too short—her own was longer—or perhaps she thought the color of my frock was too bright. They were both dressed in shades of black and gray with some white. Mourning, I would say, if they were Brits, but perhaps the colonies held other traditions.

Although it wasn't as if Flossie was dead, was it? Unless they knew something we didn't, of course.

"Thank you," I said. "I'm having supper with the *Graf* von Natterdorff later. Christopher escorted me here."

"The *Graf* von Natterdorff?"

"A German nobleman," Christopher said. "The equivalent of a British earl."

"And he's staying here, is he? At the Savoy?"

"We assume he is," I said, with a glance at Christopher. "The first time we met him, we were taking tea in the tearoom. Last time he invited me to supper, it was in the restaurant downstairs."

It was the Schlomskys' turn to exchange a glance. Years of silent communication was wrapped up in it, and we didn't stand a chance of understanding what they were tacitly saying to one another.

"How pleasant for you, Miss Darling," Mrs. Schlomsky said blandly. "And you, Mr. Astley? You're just going back home? Alone?"

"I'm expecting my cousin up from the country later," Christopher explained. "The two of us will be picking up Pippa after her date. Can I assume that you've already familiarized yourselves with St Olave's? If not, we'd be happy to tell you what we know."

The Schlomskys exchanged another look. "Are you familiar with it?" Hiram asked.

"We took the train out yesterday morning," I explained, "to see the terrain. You're planning to travel by Hackney, I assume? Unless you would like Lord St George to—?"

"The doorman will arrange for a taxi," Sarah said.

I nodded. "That's probably best. Charing Cross isn't far, but the docks district can be a bit questionable at night. Best if you have him wait while you leave the valise, I think."

"I'm sure you're right," Sarah said and exchanged another glance with Hiram. I exchanged one with Christopher, who looked as if he found something about the whole situation humorous.

"If there's nothing we can do to help," he said, "I suppose we'll leave you to it. All that's left of St Olave's, for your information, is the bell tower. The rest of the church looks as though it was demolished quite recently. It's just a mound of dirt with some blocks of worked stone left behind. But the money ought to be safe in the tower. I'm sure it won't be there long. The kidnappers will be keeping an eye out, I'm certain."

"Ready to snatch up the valise as soon as it gets there," I nodded. "I certainly wouldn't linger."

Christopher's lips curved further. "No, Pippa. You've never been one to let the grass grow under your feet."

"Precisely." I nodded, and turned to the Schlomskys, who were standing side by side presenting a united front while watching us carefully. "If you will excuse me, I should go downstairs and find the *Graf*. We'll be in the dining room for the next two hours, if you think of anything I can do to help you. And Christopher will be back here by nine-thirty, as well. Please let us know if there's anything we can do."

"Yes," Christopher nodded. "Please do let us know if we can be of any further assistance. Come along, Pippa."

He took my arm and tugged me towards the door, lips twitching. I smiled apologetically at the Schlomskys over my shoulder. "So nice to see you again, even under the circumstances."

"Out you go, Pippa." Christopher shoved me through the door and into the hallway before I could say anything else, and ducked out behind me before he shut the door behind us. The last thing I saw was the Schlomskys' partly baffled, partly suspicious countenances.

CHAPTER THIRTEEN

"GOOD GRIEF, CHRISTOPHER," I said, as I let myself be pulled down the hallway towards the lift. "What on earth was that all about?"

His shoulders were shaking inside the tailored cut of his evening jacket, and I added, suspiciously, "Are you laughing?"

It was that or crying, and I didn't see how it could be the latter. Flossie's kidnapping was distressing, but not to that degree.

He shot me a look over his shoulder, and yes, his cheeks were pink and his eyes were dancing. "You realize they're suspicious of us, Pippa?"

"Suspicious?" I repeated, and for a moment the word, and the concept, didn't make any sense. Then— "Christopher!" I hurried so I could look up at him. "They suspect us? How?"

"We must sound guilty as hell," Christopher said with another gurgle of laughter. He stabbed the button to summon the lift and turned back to me. "It makes sense if you think about it. We knew Flossie, and they have only our word for it that we were on friendly terms with her. We keep turning up with no warning, like bad pennies. Your excuse of having dinner with someone sounds extremely transparent, and so does my excuse of escorting you."

"But it's true!"

He smirked. "I know it is, Pippa. But then we tell them that we're familiar with the church from the ransom note, and we advise them on the safest way to drop off the money. And we mention that Crispin—the person we told them was the last to see Flossie before she was kidnapped—is on his way back to Town." He shook his head. "Truly, it's difficult to blame them. What are they supposed to think?"

"Not that we have their daughter stashed in our flat," I said, offended, as the lift arrived on our floor and Christopher pulled the grille aside. "That's appalling. We'd never!"

"Of course we'd never." He stepped into the lift behind me and slid the grille closed again. "But they don't know that. They don't know *us*. For all they know, we're a pair of evil knaves who have kidnapped their daughter and are after their money, and everything we've done so far has been an attempt to get close to them to see whether they suspect us."

Well, yes. But— "If I had kidnapped Flossie Schlomsky, I would never be so stupid as to draw attention to myself," I said crossly. "Certainly not by sidling up to her parents, for God's sake!"

"Of course not." His lips twitched.

I crossed my arms over my chest and stuck my bottom lip out. "I wouldn't! I'd stay far away from them and ensure that they had no idea who I was. I would never offer to help out!"

"Naturally." He smirked.

The lift arrived on the ground floor, and Christopher got busy with the grille again. "You can see how it looks, though," he said as he held the door open for me. "From their point of view, we look quite suspicious."

"I'm sure we do. That's no excuse for letting us know that they think so." I sniffed. "How very uncouth."

"Well, they're American," Christopher said, as if that explained it. "It's the Wild West on the other side of the pond, isn't it?"

"Is it? I rather thought it was mostly civilized these days. Apart from the jazz and the gangsters and all that."

"Perhaps it is," Christopher said, and put a hand on my back. "Who knows, really? There's His Grace, ready and waiting for you."

I looked around and spotted Wolfgang standing a few feet from the entrance to the restaurant, scanning the lobby and the area just outside the doors. He wouldn't have expected us to come from the direction of the lift, and that gave me a moment to admire his form, tall and handsome in black tie, while he was unaware that I was staring.

"He really is fabulously good-looking," I said, "isn't he?"

"I wouldn't kick him out of bed," Christopher answered with a shrug, and I lost my breath at the audacity.

"Christopher!"

He shot me an unrepentant look. "He doesn't swing my way, Pippa. But if he did..."

"You just like a pretty face," I told him, half accusing and half amused.

"Who doesn't?" Christopher asked with a shrug. He nudged me forward. "Go on, then. While you're having supper, I'm going to check in on Tom one more time, just in case he has made it back to Town by now, and then I'll fetch Crispin and come back for you."

"I thought we agreed that it wasn't a certainty he'd show up," I said.

Christopher agreed that we had, indeed, agreed on that. But— "There was never a chance that he wouldn't be here,

Pippa. Surely you knew that? As soon as you told him what's taking place tonight, it was a sure bet that he'd come." He inclined his head to Wolfgang. "*Graf* von Natterdorff. Good evening."

"*Herr* Astley." Wolfgang made a polite little bow from the waist before his eyes moved on to me. Like last time, they were a fabulously dark blue. "*Freulein* Darling."

He snatched my hand and hovered his lips above it for a little longer than strictly necessary. I could feel his breath moisten my skin before he deposited a kiss on the back of it and gave it back to me. His eyes smoldered. "You look beautiful."

I simpered. "Thank you."

"That's a lovely dress. Very becoming." He offered his arm. "Shall we?"

I put my hand upon it. "Please. I'll see you later, Christopher."

"I'll be back." He gave Wolfgang another nod, less formal this time. "Have a nice time. Don't do anything I wouldn't do."

Wolfgang nodded solemnly, but I'm sure he had no idea what he had agreed to. Not only is Christopher not interested in girls in general, and so not inclined to misbehave around them, but he considers me to be the next thing to a sister, and wouldn't do anything untoward in my presence whatsoever. It didn't leave Wolfgang with very many options for flirtation.

Naturally I didn't say so, just let him escort me into the dining room, where he deposited me tenderly in a chair. The waiter snagged the serviette from the table and flicked it open with a snap before draping it across my lap. He stood at attention while Wolfgang seated himself, and then put a leather-bound menu in front of each of us.

After we had made our selections and the waiter had withdrawn, Wolfgang gave me a soulful look across the table. "I'm happy you consented to have supper with me again."

Why wouldn't I? "I had a lovely time in your company last time. I'm happy to do it again." I simpered.

"I thought perhaps your cousin..." He trailed off.

"Christopher?" Why would he think Christopher would mind my going to supper with a wealthy and titled suitor? Especially after he had delivered me straight into Wolfgang's hands a minute ago?

"Your other cousin," Wolfgang said, lowering his brows. "The annoying popinjay in the flashy car."

Oh, him. "He's not my cousin," I said. "And while I agree that he's annoying, he's hardly a concern. He has no sway over what I do or don't do."

"He would like to have," Wolfgang said.

"He's just trying to prevent me from having any fun," I answered. As if Crispin had any room to complain about what I do. With the shenanigans he gets up to, he's in no position to lecture me on proper behavior, the cad.

"He wants you for himself," Wolfgang said sullenly.

As if. "No, he doesn't. He doesn't like me any better than I like him. It's always been that way."

Wolfgang scowled. "Then why—?"

"He's Christopher's cousin, and we did grow up together." And he had had to take me away from a gentleman who had me crowded into the corner of a Chesterfield a few months ago. "It would be surprising if there wasn't some level of protective instinct there."

Wolfgang stuck out his bottom lip.

"He's not something you need worry about," I told him. "He's harmless, and no threat whatsoever to... I mean..."

I stopped myself before I went any further, both with the babbling and the possibly rash statements. I had no real evidence that he was interested in me romantically, after all, and probably oughtn't to assume. Yes, he had invited me to supper twice. That's usually a good sign of a man's interest in a young lady. But beyond that, he hadn't made his feelings clear in any verbal or physical way. Everything between us had been quite prim and proper.

Wolfgang smiled, a bit like the cat with the saucer of cream. But before either of us could say any more, the waiter arrived with the bottle of wine Wolfgang had chosen—German and red —and he got busy sniffing the cork and swirling the wine around the glass to let it breathe. Once he had declared it acceptable and the waiter had withdrawn after filling both our glasses, the moment had passed.

"I hope you like a robust red," Wolfgang said, fingers around the stem of the glass. "This is a *Spätburgunder* from Baden. The best Germany has to offer."

He sounded proud, as if he had fermented the grapes personally. I smiled politely. "It's lovely, thank you."

I'm fonder of cocktails than I am of wine, but I wanted to upset him less than I wanted my drink of choice, so I kept my preferences to myself and sipped on the *Spätburgunder*. As wines go, it was quite tasty, so it could have been worse.

"What have you been up to in the past two days?" I asked next, on the assumption that most men like to talk about themselves.

Wolfgang seemed to be the exception. He said something vague about business interests and meetings, and then he turned the question around. "And you?"

I thought about it. The past few days had been taken up by very little except worry about Flossie Schlomsky and attempts to find out what had happened to her. It was difficult to imagine that Wolfgang wouldn't be interested—kidnappings and ransom demands would excite most people, I imagine—but a crime had been committed, involving someone else's family, and it wasn't really my place to tell total strangers about it.

So I told him about Tom's visit to Bristol instead, and how my late aunt's lady's maid had been found dead in an alley with her head bashed in. Wolfgang found that interesting too. As would I, honestly, if I hadn't had other, nearer, things to worry about.

"How appalling," he said, but with the ghoulish interest of any normal person.

I nodded. "Tom—our detective friend—said they thought it was a robbery gone bad. Her purse had been searched, it seemed."

Wolfgang nodded. "That makes sense. Unless she was—how would one say it in polite company...?"

One wouldn't, but I let him finish anyway, since I assumed I already knew what he was going to say.

"*Eine Nutte?*" he articulated delicately. "*Ein Flittchen?*"

"A prostitute?" I suggested, since there is no point in not calling a spade by its proper name.

Wolfgang nodded, looking relieved. "Yes. *Eine Proztituerte.*"

"I hardly think so," I said. "She was forty-five if she was a day—"

Wolfgang opened his mouth, presumably to tell me that hookers come in all sizes and ages, but he didn't actively interrupt me, so I went on.

"—and furthermore, I happen to know that she was flush when she left Wiltshire." Flush with a thousand pounds of Uncle Herbert's hush money. "I'm sure it was as they said. A robbery. Such a shame."

Not that I had many fond feelings for Hughes. She had blackmailed Uncle Herbert, after all. Although I certainly hadn't wanted her to die for it. I'm not that bloodthirsty.

"Indeed," Wolfgang nodded. "And your friend, the detective..."

"Tom? He went to Eton with my cousin Robbie, and with Francis and Christopher." And Crispin, of course, but there was no point in mentioning that.

"Francis is your elder cousin?"

I nodded. "Christopher is my younger. Robert was in-between. But he died in the war."

"Many bad things happened in the war," Wolfgang said, as a shadow crossed his countenance.

Yes, indeed. And it was probably best if we didn't go too deeply into those weeds, given that Wolfgang was German, and so was I, technically speaking.

"Tom went to Cambridge after he came Home," I said, "and then he joined Scotland Yard. He's a photographer."

Wolfgang nodded politely. "And the two of you..."

I shook my head. "We are not involved at all."

I honestly didn't know whether Tom liked men or women in the romantic sense. I did know that he didn't like me. There'd never been anything even remotely flirtatious about our interactions. I suspected he was rather fond of Christopher, although I wasn't sure whether that was because Tom had been Robbie's friend, and with Robbie gone, he had taken over some of Robbie's responsibility towards Robbie's youngest brother, or whether it had to do with Christopher himself. He's eminently loveable, after all.

I was fairly certain Christopher's feelings towards Tom were anything but brotherly, though. And I suspected there might be something going on, but I had no proof of it. If they were romantically involved, they'd been quite circumspect about the whole thing.

And none of this was any of Wolfgang's concern, so I kept it to myself. "What about you?" I asked instead, fluttering my eyelashes and dimpling. "Is there someone in Germany who's waiting for you to come home?"

Wolfgang disavowed this idea in strong terms. But of course he would, whether it was true or not. He seemed to have designs on me, so whether there was another girl in Germany or not, he wasn't going to mention her to me.

"For how long are you in London?" I wanted to know. It seemed like a safe question to ask.

Not that I got a straight answer. "Until my business is done," Wolfgang told me. And then he smiled indulgently. "Don't worry your pretty head about it."

I simpered back. "I'm not. I'm just wondering for how long I'll have the pleasure of your company."

Wolfgang drew in breath, but before he could utter whatever was on the tip of his tongue—I suspected some sort of bromide about my ability to have the pleasure of his company for as long as I wanted—the waiter appeared with the first course. Wolfgang let the breath out again as I sat back in my chair and smiled politely at the waiter.

We fell into small-talk after that. I asked him how he liked England, and he extolled the beauties of Bavaria. I had memories of growing up in Germany, but the older I got, the farther away that time seemed—which of course it was.

"You should come back for a visit," Wolfgang said.

I smiled politely. "I'm afraid that would be rather difficult."

"Nonsense." He beamed as he dismissed my concerns. "You'd stay with me at *Schloss* Natterdorff, of course."

Oh, of course. "That would be somewhat unconventional, surely?"

He smirked, but didn't say anything, leaving me to wonder whether I'd be expected to stay as his mistress or his intended. Instead he said, "We're distant cousins, you know."

"Are we really?" A bit strange to wait until now to mention that, wasn't it?

Where I would stay in Germany wasn't the kind of difficulty I'd been concerned about, however. I wasn't sure I wanted to go back to where I'd had a happy childhood, when my mother and father were both gone. It was one thing to live here in England and know I was an orphan. It was quite another to go back to where we'd lived together as a happy family, and confront the loss there.

Although if I still had family in Germany, that might make a difference to my feelings about visiting my homeland.

"How are we related?" I wanted to know. "Is that why you visited us on the occasion you told me about? When we were both children?"

Wolfgang nodded. "Do you still not remember?"

"I'm afraid I don't," I said apologetically, since no man wants to be told he isn't memorable, even when he was a tyke of seven or eight. "But there's a lot I don't remember. And I forget more every day. Germany seems like a different life."

"But you have been happy here?"

I nodded. "My Aunt Roslyn and Uncle Herbert have treated me like their own. Christopher is like the brother I never had. So is Francis. And if St George is a bit of an acquired taste... well, there's a black sheep in every family, I suppose."

Wolfgang's lips twitched, but he didn't comment. "Can I expect to see the Viscount this evening?"

"I'm not sure," I said honestly. "I'm hopeful that he'll decide to stay in Wiltshire—or that his father will take away the key to the Hispano-Suiza and keep him there that way—although I have a feeling he'll find a way around it even if Uncle Harold does do..."

Wolfgang kept watching me with a halfway patient, halfway amused look, and I nodded. "Yes, I think you can probably expect him to turn up. If we're very lucky, he won't try to take us out at the knees this time."

"He's very protective," Wolfgang said, "isn't he?"

"They all are," I told him. "It's as if I have three older brothers, except two of them are younger than me, and none of them is actually my brother. My Uncle Herbert is fairly protective, too."

Crispin's father is the only man in the family who isn't protective of me. While Crispin normally has all the sensitivity of a cheese grater, and isn't opposed to letting me feel the sharp edge of his personality, he'd most likely put his life on the line for mine if he had to. His father would watch me burn without a flicker of compassion.

Then again, I rather suspect Uncle Harold would watch his own son and heir burn without a flicker of compassion, either. He'd most likely step in to save him, at least if it didn't involve the risk of harm to himself, but it wouldn't be out of compassion for Crispin's suffering, but merely because if Crispin died, Uncle Harold would be on the hook to make another heir, unless he wanted Uncle Herbert and Francis to carry on the line.

"Tell me about our family," I asked Wolfgang. "How are we related? Are you an only-child, as well?"

Wolfgang said he was. The last of the Albrechts *von und zu* Natterdorff. "I shall have to marry soon, to secure the succession."

He gave me a soulful look. I smiled politely, and wondered whether he was opening up negotiations for me to marry him, or whether he was simply trying to get under my skirt before he had to marry someone else—someone whose father hadn't been a commoner—to bear the son and heir he required.

When I didn't snap up the bait one way or the other, Wolfgang backed off a bit, and we settled into a conversation about his experiences at Heidelberg University, and mine at Oxford ditto. He had studied political science, and had received his *Schmisse* in a Mensur duel with a classmate named Stefan, he told me. When I feigned interest, he proceeded to describe the duel in detail. When I informed him that Mensur dueling wasn't something undertaken in English institutions, and that a facial scar wasn't considered a badge of honor in Britain, he sneered at me.

"The British prefer a man with a pretty face to a man with a brave heart?"

"I don't know that one precludes the other," I said mildly. "Surely it's possible to be both handsome and brave?"

I accompanied the rhetorical question with a lingering glance, and he preened.

He was still in a good mood when we left the table after dessert, as we made our way back to the Savoy lobby, with its checkerboard floor and tall columns. That only lasted until he spied Christopher and Crispin lounging in one of the seating areas near the front doors.

I know I have rather gone on about how handsome Wolfgang is, but the truth is, neither Christopher nor Crispin is exactly hard on the eyes, either, especially in evening kit and in their element. Which they so clearly were: two beautiful young men-about-town at their leisure, with no worries beyond which cocktail to order with dinner. Christopher was draped over the arm of the chair with his chin propped on his hand and one leg folded elegantly over the other, while Crispin leaned back insolently, feet kicked up on the low table in front of him and hands folded across his stomach, with no concern for the Savoy's table or the people who shot him sideways glances. But unlike Christopher, who appeared for all the world like he was half a moment from falling asleep, Crispin's eyes were sharp under the lowered lids, and he caught sight of Wolfgang and me the moment we came through the doors from the restaurant.

Not that one could tell from his demeanor. He didn't sit up, didn't stiffen or show with so much as a twitch of an eyelash that he had noticed us, but his eyes nonetheless watched us come closer with all the attention of a snake eyeing an approaching fieldmouse.

"Darling," he uttered when we got close enough that I could hear him over the other conversations taking place in the lobby.

Christopher straightened and turned towards us. Unlike Crispin, I assumed this was the first he had noticed we were there.

"St George," I responded coolly. If he wasn't going to grace me with an actual greeting beyond just my name, he couldn't expect anything better himself, either. "Hello, Christopher. Have you been waiting long?"

"Just a few minutes," Christopher said and stretched. "*Graf* von Natterdorff." He nodded politely to Wolfgang, who nodded back.

"*Herr* Astley. Lord St George." He clicked his heels and bowed in Crispin's direction. Not too deeply, but enough to be courteous. The latter, of course, couldn't even be bothered to sit up.

"*Graf.*" He gave the barest of nods before he turned his attention back to me, with an insolent up-and-down motion of his eyes along the length of his nose. "Is that a new frock, Darling?"

Beside me, Wolfgang growled.

I ignored it, just as I ignored what I knew was going to be some sort of snide remark about it. "As a matter of fact it is."

Crispin nodded. And said nothing.

"What?" I demanded.

His lips twitched. "I didn't say anything, Darling."

I removed my hand from Wolfgang's arm and put it on my

hip, along with my other hand on the other side. "I know you didn't. What I want to know is why."

"Why what, Darling?"

"Why didn't you? Don't you have anything to say? Don't you want to tell me that I look like a peach, or a salmon, or an apricot, or something?"

His lips twitched again. "I don't know why you would assume that, Darling."

"You never have anything nice to say," I told him.

"Is that so?" This time the lips twitched into a smirk, and he took his feet off the table and unwound, sinuously, into a sitting position, without ever taking his eyes off me. "Would you like me to tell you that you look lovely, Darling?"

His voice was so smooth it was practically a caress, or would have been without the distinctly malicious undertone.

"No," I said petulantly. "I just don't want you to tell me that I look like a vegetable."

His eyebrow rose. "Vegetable?"

"You know what I mean. You always tell me that I look like a fruit or vegetable. Like a... a..." I cast about for something else that was vaguely salmon-colored. "A stalk of rhubarb or something."

The smirk widened. "If you think you look like a stalk of rhubarb, I don't know why you'd buy the frock, Darling."

"I don't think I look like a stalk of rhubarb," I growled, while my hands clenched into fists. It was only the fact that we were standing—and sitting—in the Savoy lobby that kept me from smacking the smug expression right off his face. "You always find something less than complimentary to say about what I wear."

Or something that sounds like a compliment but is, indeed, the opposite. Like the next thing that came out of his mouth.

"Not this time, Darling. The frock is very becoming. And that color looks good on you."

His eyes flicked from the dress up to my flaming cheeks and back.

I narrowed my eyes. "I hate you, St George."

He nodded. "I know, Darling. The feeling is mutual, I assure you. Are you ready to go?"

"I suppose so." I turned to Wolfgang with the best smile I could muster while I was still vibrating with anger. "Thank you for supper. It was delightful to see you again."

"We will do it again soon."

He snatched up my hand and bowed over it, for far longer than necessary. This time, I'm fairly certain I heard a growl from Crispin, although it might have been just a scraping of the chair legs as he got to his feet.

"I will contact you," Wolfgang told me, after he finally took his lips off the back of my hand and could use them to speak again.

I simpered. "I'll look forward to it."

And because I knew it would annoy Crispin, I held the hand Wolfgang had kissed against my breast while he turned to click his heels and bow to the others. "*Herr* Astley. Lord St George."

"Good evening," Christopher said politely, while Crispin said something I couldn't make out, although it certainly wasn't wishes for a good night.

Wolfgang withdrew with a smirk and a final lingering glance at me, and I dropped my hand and turned to Christopher. "No Tom?"

He shook his head. "Still not back yet, it seems. I left another note."

"We should go, then." I glanced around the lobby. Wolfgang was almost to the lifts by now, but I didn't see anyone else

I recognized. "I don't suppose you've seen the Schlomskys come through while you've been sitting here?"

"Not that I noticed," Christopher said. "But it's still early. Unlike us, I don't think they're planning to lie in wait."

No, they would most likely get to St Olave's as close to eleven as they could, drop the money, and hurry away, the sooner to see their daughter again.

"No sense in waiting," I said, and headed for the front doors with them both picking up the rear behind me.

CHAPTER FOURTEEN

THE OTHER END of London Bridge was quiet on a Saturday night in August. There was some noise from the docks down the river, winches grinding and heavy loads dropping, but just below the bridge, where St Olave's—or what was left of it—was waiting, it was dark and silent.

"The H6 is likely to draw attention," Christopher said, looking at it, and I nodded. There are only so many blue Hispano-Suiza racing cars in London at any given time, and most of the constabulary, at least, recognize this one.

Crispin gave him a scowl. "Thanks a lot, Kit. Shouldn't you have thought of that before you asked me to drive you here?"

"As if I could have kept you away," Christopher sniffed. "As soon as you found out that—"

"Yes, yes." Crispin waved him off. "Never mind that. What do you want me to do with it?"

"I'm sure we can find somewhere to tuck it away," I said, looking around. "And you along with it."

He opened his mouth to protest, but Christopher nodded.

"That's a good idea, Pippa. Someone should stay with the motorcar."

Crispin had his lower lip stuck out petulantly. "Why does it have to be me?"

"It doesn't," I told him, "but whoever stays with the motorcar will have to follow the kidnappers and the ransom, and I assumed you would rather keep your precious out of my hands."

He gave me a look down the length of his nose. "Indeed."

"So you'll do it?"

He made a face. "I suppose. I'd rather not have *you* take off in my motorcar, at any rate."

"No," Christopher agreed. "We can't have Pippa go off alone. What if something happened?"

"I'm perfectly capable of taking care of myself," I said, "thank you very much."

"Of course you are. But Mum and Dad would kill me if they knew I had left you to fend for yourself, and in Southwark of all places. So unless you want me to be killed the next time we visit Beckwith Place, I'm going to request that you stay with one of us, and the other stays with the Hispano-Suiza."

"Fine," I said. "It's all set, then. You and I go inside the tower, while Crispin lies in wait in the shadows. And when the kidnappers pick up the ransom," I told him, "you follow them."

He didn't say anything, and I added, coaxingly, the way I would have done with a recalcitrant five-year-old, "It's a very important job. They may take you to the place where Flossie is kept."

Which was true. It *was* an important job. And I wanted to do it myself, but I knew that the chances of me being allowed to go off by myself in the Hispano-Suiza, trailing a kidnapper, were below nil. I accepted it with as much grace as I could.

"But don't go inside," Christopher added, for Crispin's benefit. "Not alone. Come back for us first. Mum and Dad would kill me if anything happened to either of you."

Crispin nodded, but he still looked unhappy.

"Or you can stay here and protect Pippa," Christopher added, "and I'll follow the kidnappers."

There was a moment's pause. Crispin looked at his beloved, and then at me, and then back at the beloved again. Indecision was writ all over his face. I was about to make a snide comment about my value or desirability vis-à-vis the automobile when Christopher went on.

"I'm capable of handling your motorcar, you know, and I'm also capable of protecting Pippa should she need it—"

I opened my mouth to tell him that no one needed to protect me, but I shut it again when he went on, "but if you don't trust me—"

"Of course I trust you, Kit." Crispin's voice was irritated.

"It's settled, then." Christopher sounded cheerful. "You'll stay with Pippa and I'll stay with the Hispano-Suiza. Well done, Crispin. I know it must have been a difficult decision for you, your love for the motorcar at war with your—"

"Enough," Crispin growled. "Knock it off, Kit, or I'll change my mind."

"Too late," Christopher told him brightly. "You get Pippa and I get the motorcar."

"Nobody gets Pippa," I said irritably. "Pippa doesn't need either of you. Pippa can take care of herself."

"Of course you can, Darling," Crispin said. "Just open your mouth, and that sharp tongue will leave them bleeding out on the floor in no time."

"Oh, poor baby," I cooed. "Did I hurt your feelings?"

"I don't have feelings," Crispin said, with an air of someone who thought they were beneath him. "Certainly none you are capable of affecting."

"Off you go, then," Christopher said. "Into the tower with you."

"Not so fast," I told him. "We have lots of time before it's eleven. Shouldn't we find a safe spot for you and the motorcar, and then St George and I will make our way into what's left of the church once we know you're safe and situated? I don't suppose it's likely that anyone's watching already, but just in case someone is, shouldn't we be approaching on foot?"

"Here's a likely spot," Crispin said, pointing the nose of the H6 into a dark area between two buildings: one the dark red brick of Denmark House, and the other the tall, yellow brick of a wharf warehouse on the waterfront. "Tuck in here, nose out, and you'll be able to see everyone who comes and goes."

He suited action to words and then turned the motor off. Silence descended, only broken by the winches and calls from the wharfs.

"Time?" Christopher asked.

Crispin pulled his watch out of his waistcoat pocket and flicked it open. "Just after ten."

"You two should go," Christopher said. "Just in case they— or he, or she—come early."

"The kidnappers, or the Schlomskys?" I scooted towards the side of the seat.

"They could be one and the same," Christopher said, but he reached for his door handle and wrenched it down. "Come along." He reached a hand into the back and pulled me out, similar to the way one pulled a cork from a bottle.

"What's that supposed to mean?" Crispin wanted to know, as he extricated himself from his own side of the motorcar. "The parents?"

"Pippa will explain." Christopher shut the door after me

and then proceeded to tug me after him around the car to where Crispin was holding open the driver's side door. Christopher let go of my hand and slid behind the wheel. "Ah!" He looked around, delighted.

"If you break anything, I'll break your kneecaps," Crispin informed him, as he shut the door.

Christopher grinned up at him. "If I break anything, I'll pay for it, Crispin."

"You know what you're doing?"

Christopher nodded. "Clutch. Hand brake. Steering wheel." He pointed to them. "Lights, but it might be better if I do without those. Less chance of being seen."

"More chance of getting fined," I said.

"I really don't think the constabulary is going to be patrolling for speed demons in Southwark at eleven on a Saturday night, do you?"

"I have no idea," I said, putting my nose in the air. "I don't break the law. St George would be the one to ask."

"I don't imagine you'll be moving beyond a crawl," Crispin told Christopher. "Whoever picks up the money won't want to risk being stopped by going too fast away from here, and you'll be dawdling along behind. So I don't think you'll have to worry."

"That's a good point." Christopher flicked his fingers at us. "Off you go, then, children. To the tower."

He added an evil laugh. I rolled my eyes and tucked my hand through Crispin's elbow. "Come along, St George. And attempt to look amorous."

There was a beat of silence. Then—

"Why?" Crispin wanted to know, apprehensively.

"We have to try to look natural in case anyone's watching. That was the idea we came up with."

"Just two lovebirds looking for a spot of privacy for some

slap and tickle," Christopher said cheerfully. "Don't say I never gave you anything, Crispin."

"Yes," Crispin said, sounding murderous, "I'll definitely remember this."

I sniffed. "So sorry to put you out, St George. Just close your eyes and think of Lady Laetitia."

"While you close yours and imagine the handsome Count, I assume?"

He slapped a hand over mine on his arm, and pulled me alongside him towards the remains of the church. Behind us, everything was quiet as Christopher settled into the H6.

"Stop manhandling me, you brute," I told him, and dragged my feet as best I could to slow him down. "The last thing I need is bruises."

He scoffed. "You're the one holding on to me, Darling. If anyone's going to end up with bruises, I'm the one."

I scoffed back. "Don't be ridiculous, St George. I'm only holding on so tight because you're dragging me along too fast for me to keep up. Eager, are you?"

That, as I had surmised, slowed him down. And while it was hard to tell in the dark, I think his cheekbones might have darkened a bit, too.

"That's preposterous, Darling."

I sniggered. "Oh, is it?"

He shot me a look. "It's not as if anything is actually going to happen, is it?"

It didn't sound like a question, more like a challenge, and I snorted. "Of course not."

"So what would I be eager for, precisely? The pleasure of your company?"

I smirked. "Now, now, St George. Don't you like me?"

He made a little noise that might have been irritation or

perhaps exasperation. Or perhaps it was simple amusement. "About as much as you like me, Darling."

The church tower loomed ahead, and I pointed to it. "In there."

Crispin glanced around, surreptitiously, before he ducked through the door and pulled me in after him. I giggled a little, since—if someone were in hearing distance—they might expect that.

Of course, if someone was in hearing distance, they would have heard the rest of the conversation, too.

Then again, everyone was forever accusing us of flirting, so maybe it wouldn't matter.

"Over there," I pointed, before my eyes had adjusted to the gloom inside the windowless tower. "Stairs going up."

He pulled me after him across the floor until we practically ran into the bottom step. The floor was more uneven than I had realized when I'd been able to see it. "Oops." Crispin sniggered and regained his balance by holding on to me. "Up you go, Darling."

I started up, and heard him stumble along behind me. After a few steps, the gloom lifted as the ambient light from above bled down the stairs. By the time we reached the top, I felt like I could breathe again.

I could also look around the platform and see that we were alone. The kidnappers had not decided to take a leaf out of our book, it seemed, and hide themselves at the top of the tower until the ransom was paid. It had crossed my mind that they might. I might have, had it been me. But we were alone on the tower, peering past the balustrade at the bricks of Tower Bridge in one direction, and the lights of the north embankment on the other.

"Nice," Crispin commented, for once not sounding like he was being snide or sarcastic or anything else.

I nodded. It was nice. Romantic, even. The moon was a waxing crescent, a thin scythe low in the sky, and the lighted windows across the Thames reflected in the ripples of water. In the dark, we couldn't tell that the river was murky and disgusting. The scene looked beautiful and peaceful as I leaned on the balustrade and enjoyed the view.

Of course, that was only until Crispin came up behind me and slid an arm around me to prop himself against the balustrade, in a way that left me boxed in, with his body on one side of me and his arm on the other.

I stiffened—who wouldn't?—and he leaned closer and put his mouth close to my ear. "Relax, Darling. We want to look authentic, don't we? In case someone's watching."

"No one is watching us from this direction," I pointed out. There was nothing down below but wharfs and warehouses and the water. It was the other side of the church tower, with the street, and the train station, not to mention the bridge, where there would be people possibly watching.

Where Hiram Schlomsky would arrive to drop off the ransom, and where the kidnappers, presumably, would arrive to pick it up.

"But a pair of turtledoves," Crispin said smoothly, "would be looking this way, admiring the ripples on the water. Romantic, isn't it?"

His arm tightened on my waist, and his breath tickled the hair at my ear. I shivered and nudged him back a step with my elbow. "Stop breathing on me."

"That's going to be difficult when I'm supposed to look like I'm making love to you, Darling." His voice was amused.

I rolled my eyes. "There's nobody up here. You don't have to pretend."

"Perhaps I enjoy pretending."

Perhaps he did. Or perhaps he just liked to see how far he

could push me before I snapped. If that was the case, I had better nip this in the bud before it went any further.

"I mean it, St George," I said, "you had better not think you can take advantage of the situation to—"

He rolled his eyes. "We have an hour to kill before anything is likely to happen downstairs, Darling. How do you suggest we spend the time?"

"Not by you breathing on me and making suggestive remarks," I said.

He huffed. "What's it going to be, then? A game of pinochle, perhaps? Did you bring a deck of cards?"

"Of course I didn't," I said. "I was on a date when you picked me up, wasn't I?"

"Of course you were." His tone was sour. "And I'm sure His Highness kept you well occupied, didn't he?"

"He certainly did," I said pleasantly. "He told me all about his bragging scar and where he got it, for one thing. They're a sign of bravery, you know."

My tone indicated, as best I could, that he wouldn't know bravery if he fell over it.

He rolled his eyes. "Let me guess. Skirmish in the trenches? Saving fair maidens from fleeing bandits? Jealous husband?"

I snorted. "Hardly. Just a standard Mensur duel at Heidelberg."

"Probably leaned into it," Crispin said, "just so he could brag about having it later."

Quite so. "He's not such a bad bloke, you know."

"I'm certain he's perfectly lovely," Crispin said, "and we'd be fast friends and drinking companions in other circumstances. But as it is..."

"Which circumstances are those?"

He glanced at me, and I continued. "Under which circumstances would you be fast friends and drinking companions?

Or rather, which are the circumstances under which you can't?"

"He's either trying to get under your skirt, or trying to take you back to Germany with him," Crispin said. "You can't imagine that any of us are all right with that."

"He's made no move to get under my skirt. And he hasn't proposed, either."

He *had* suggested that I pay Germany a visit, and that I stay with him at Schloss Natterdorff when I did, but it would perhaps be better if I didn't mention that right now.

"Biding his time," Crispin said. "Besides, it's hard to get under someone's skirt in the Savoy dining room."

"I suppose you'd know, wouldn't you?"

"Don't be insulting, Darling." He grinned. "I'm far too well bred to try that sort of thing in that sort of setting. That's what grotty nightclubs in Soho are for."

Of course. "And if it hadn't been for this little excursion, I suppose that's where you'd be tonight?"

"I'd be in Wiltshire," Crispin said. "I'm not surprised you haven't noticed, Darling—you rarely think about me when I'm not right in front of you, do you?" He flicked me a look, "—but I haven't actually been spending much time in London over the past few months. Father has had me nursing my broken heart at Sutherland instead."

I snorted. "Your father doesn't care about your broken heart."

Although Crispin might be right about the rest of it. Now that I thought back, he really hadn't been in London much over the summer. Uncle Harold had kept a tight rein on him immediately after Duke Henry's and Lady Charlotte's deaths the last weekend in April. It wouldn't do for the scion of the Sutherlands to appear on the front cover of the *Tatler* or the *Daily Yell* before his mother and grandfather were even in the ground, of course.

After that, there had been his birthday in June, which had culminated in us driving around London in drag, with a dead body in the back of the Hispano-Suiza. But no tabloid reporters had caught us that night, luckily. And he had driven up for the inquest, of course, the week after, but there hadn't been any carousing on that occasion. Supper with Christopher and me and back to the inquest the following day. And that was it, as far as I knew. We were now into August. Had he truly only been in London two or three times in the past three months?

"See," he told me, because of course he knew exactly what I'd been thinking. "You've misjudged me, Darling. I'm not the philandering playboy you think I am. I spend all my time in my bower in Sutherland, pining."

"Only because your father keeps you under lock and key," I answered with a snort. "I should start calling you Rapunzel."

He shook his head. "Rapunzel didn't pine, Darling. It was the prince who pined, after the evil stepmother took Rapunzel away and cut her hair and hid her in the desert."

"Good for him," I said. "You, on the other hand, would probably just go off and find yourself another princess. You're not a playboy, you're a cad. Ready to throw in the towel at the first sign of trouble. It's no wonder your lady-love doesn't want you. She could never trust that you would stick around if things got tough."

"Which is precisely why I won't declare myself," Crispin said. "I'm not cut out for garret living. I like my creature comforts, and if I don't get them, I'm difficult. I'd rather not inflict myself on someone I care about under those circumstances."

"So you'll marry Laetitia Marsden instead, and inflict yourself on her."

He shrugged. "She wants me. She can put up with the difficulty in exchange for the title and money."

And with her, he wouldn't have to live in squalor on the Continent. As he had expressed once, his father would be only too happy to give him to Lady Laetitia. It was only if he wanted to marry the girl he said he was in love with, that he'd be disinherited.

"Your father's a bastard," I said.

His lips twitched. "Good thing my grandfather didn't hear you say that."

I rolled my eyes. I hadn't meant it that way, which he knew perfectly well. "Have you seen her lately? Or has your father truly kept you secluded from everyone and everything?"

He shot me a look. "Laetitia? Or, as you call her, my lady-love?"

I shrugged. "Either? Both?"

"The Earl and Countess invited Father and me to spend the weekend at Marsden last week. I saw Laetitia then. As for—"

"Are you engaged?"

I hadn't noticed a new ring on his finger at any time this evening, but he might have put one on Laetitia and refused to wear one himself. I wouldn't put it past him.

He shook his head. "Of course not. I would have let Kit and you know if anything momentous had happened."

"That would be momentous, would it? Getting engaged to Lady Laetitia?" I turned my back on the view and folded my arms over my chest to look at him.

"Getting engaged at all would be momentous," Crispin said, stuffing his hands in his trouser pockets. "Father would send notices to all the newspapers, and the church would read the banns for three weeks. There'd be sobbing and gnashing of teeth all over London, as the Bright Young Set learned that I was off the matrimonial market. You couldn't avoid hearing about it, if that were the case."

I harrumphed. "I really don't know why we put up with you and your self-esteem issues, St George."

"Kit loves me," Crispin said.

"I suppose he must. So Laetitia is still going out of her way to try to tie you down."

He hummed agreement.

"What about the girl you say you're in love with? Have you seen her lately?"

There was a moment of silence while Crispin endeavored to look at me, probably to try to ascertain whether I was being mocking or serious or something else. It can't have been easy, in the darkness of the tower and with the lights behind me. Eventually he decided that I must be asking in truth, because he said, cautiously, "We cross paths once in a while. When one of us doesn't go out of our way to avoid the other."

"She avoids you?"

"She doesn't much approve of me," Crispin said. "Thinks I'm a cad and a philanderer and all those other things you accused me of earlier."

Good for her.

"Are you certain you shouldn't damn the torpedoes and propose, and introduce her to the family? Your father may not be happy, but I think the rest of us would like to make her acquaintance. Any girl who doesn't fall flat for your charms seems worth knowing."

"You would say that," Crispin grumbled. "No. I told you. I'm not putting her through squalor on the Continent."

"Squalor on the Continent might not be so bad. My mother seemed happy." In her flat in Heidelberg with her carpenter husband and child. "Of course, that presupposes that this girl likes you enough to want to marry you..."

"Which God knows she doesn't," Crispin said, and then stopped, mouth open. He looked like a goldfish, and I opened my own mouth to comment on it, but he shook his head. "Listen."

I listened, and heard, for the first time, the sound of a motor coming towards the tower. When I looked in that direction, there were the reflections of moving lights in the brick of Tower Bridge.

"Surely it isn't eleven yet?" We couldn't have stood here for a whole hour bickering, could we?

Crispin shook his head. "Shhh. Let's go take a look."

He turned his back to me and moved towards the other side of the clocktower. I left the balustrade and the view over the Thames, and followed. "Stay back from the edge. You don't want him, or them, to look up and see you."

He flicked me a look over his shoulder. "You're the one who needs to stay back, Darling. I'm in black and white. I'll blend with the shadows. You're the one who'll light up like a bonfire when those headlamps hit you."

I grimaced. He was right about that, wasn't he?

"Really," he told me, "you knew you were going adventuring after your supper date. You might have worn something sleek and black for His Highness."

"You must have me confused with Lady Laetitia," I said sourly. "She's the one who wears nothing but black. I like bright colors."

"You certainly do." He turned back to the street. "Looks like a Hackney."

I peered over the parapet and saw what looked like a black Austin Twelve come rolling slowly across the cobblestones towards us, past the place where Christopher and the Hispano-Suiza were tucked away.

I nodded. "Looks very much like one. Perhaps Papa

Schlomsky is early." Sitting around at the Savoy waiting for it to be time to go drop off the ransom couldn't be easy. And it might have been difficult to estimate the time it would take to get here, too, for that matter.

"Or the kidnappers are," Crispin said, as the Austin passed out of sight below the tower.

"Did it stop?"

He shook his head. "It's moving past, going under the bridge now."

"Just doing an initial recce, then?"

"Seems so," Crispin said. "Come on. Let's get into position while they're out of sight."

He headed for a corner of the tower, just beside the opening onto Tooley Street, and melted into the shadows. All I could see of him was the slightly paler triangle of his starched shirt, and the pale hair and skin above. If I hadn't known that he was there, I might not have noticed even that.

I tucked myself into the corner opposite and proceeded to wait.

"Here they come again," Crispin said softly. "Hackney cab on its way back."

"The same one?"

"Who can tell? They all look the same, don't they? It's coming from the direction where the other one disappeared, so I assume so."

He watched it as it came closer. The headlights hit the tower and lit up the area around us for a second—I squeezed myself into the corner, out of the way, so none of my sparkling salmon beads would catch the light and reflect it back like a mirror—before the wheels turned to follow the curve of the bridge and the motorcar rattled across the cobbles away from us.

We stood in silence until the sound of the motor had faded away down Tooley Street.

"Could be the kidnappers," I said, breathing again, "making sure that there aren't coppers crawling all over the ransom drop."

Crispin nodded. At least I think he did. I could hear movement from the opposite corner, and then a scrape as he moved forward, far enough to see the time.

"Fifteen minutes to go."

CHAPTER FIFTEEN

HIRAM SCHLOMSKY'S cab rattled up in front of the church tower at eleven on the nose. I could hear church bells tolling from all over London as the Hackney turned the corner from the bridge. The racket was loud enough to drown out the sound of the tires on the cobblestones, and practically everything else, as well. We did hear the door of the cab open and then Hiram's voice—with his very American accent—tell the driver to wait.

I leaned out and peered over the parapet far enough to see that Hiram had left the Hackney door open while he ducked into the church, valise in hand. It was a smart move, at least if he were afraid that the cab would leave without him. The driver would have to take the time to close the door before he could take off, and that would give Hiram time to come out of the tower again before the cab vanished.

Not that it tried. There was the sound of the door opening downstairs, a few scuffing steps across the stone, and then something soft hitting the floor. A moment's silence, possibly Hiram sending a prayer aloft that he would get his daughter back in one piece, and then he withdrew, back out the door, which he closed carefully behind him—and no wonder, if close to fifty thousand American dollars in cash was sitting below—and into the waiting cab. The Hackney's door slammed shut behind him, and they were off, across the cobbles and under the bridge.

I turned to the other corner, where I knew Crispin was. "There's fifty thousand dollars in a valise below our feet."

"I have fifty thousand dollars of my own," Crispin retorted, "and no desire to spend the next ten to fifteen years in Wormwood Scrubs."

Well, when he put it that way...

"What do we do now?"

"I suppose we wait for someone to come and pick it up?" Crispin said. "It shouldn't take long, I don't think."

Probably not. If I had fifty thousand dollars waiting for me, especially in a place where anyone could wander in and pick it up, I wouldn't tarry, either.

Nor did the kidnappers. They must have been waiting and watching, because no sooner had the Hackney disappeared—no more than two or three minutes; just long enough for someone to get down here from on top of the bridge, say—another motorcar approached, this one from the direction of the bridge.

It was another Hackney, or looked like one. Another Austin Heavy Twelve-Four, anyway, and these days, those aren't used for much beyond cars for hire.

The headlamps lit up the area inside the clocktower again as the car came around the bend—lit up Crispin in his corner, so his hair shone like moonlight against the shadowy brick and his shirt-breast gleamed a bright white—before it passed out of sight below the tower.

"It stopped," Crispin murmured.

I nodded, although I didn't think he could actually see me. Below, there were sounds to indicate that someone had opened the car door, and then there were quick steps across the cobblestones and the door opening again. A movement towards where the valise was waiting, and then the retreat. The door shut downstairs in the tower, and almost simultaneously, the Austin's door did, as well. Crispin darted forwards, and so did I. We met at the parapet, in time to lean out and watch the top of the motorcar move away down the street towards Emblem House. As it disappeared out of sight, the nose of the Hispano-Suiza emerged from behind Denmark House, headlamps dark, and took off in pursuit.

"We might have almost made it," Crispin muttered, watching it go and clearly wishing he was inside it along with Christopher.

"Not without being seen bursting through the door downstairs," I told him. "Hopefully he won't be long."

"What if they're driving to Surrey or Kent? We didn't discuss what we'd do if they keep going for a while."

No, we hadn't. "If Christopher isn't back in a timely manner, I suppose we could walk to the train station and take the train back across the river and go home and wait for him."

"Not that Kit can't think for himself," Crispin said, "because of course he can. But if they do keep going for miles and miles, will he keep going too, or will he think of us and come back?"

I had no idea. "I don't know that I'd want him to stop and come back for us, to be honest. It's more important for him to figure out where the kidnappers are holed up than to rescue us, don't you agree? We're perfectly capable of taking care of ourselves, and while it would be uncomfortable to spend the night here, I don't think we'd be in any danger. We can hear anyone coming up the stairs, and honestly, who would bother?"

"I usually attempt a better showing than this," Crispin said, looking around, "when I spend the night with a girl."

I rolled my eyes. "Let's just sit down and wait. If he's not back in thirty minutes, we can reassess the situation and decide whether to head to the train station. Cigarette?"

"Of course, Darling." He fished his case out of his pocket and opened it. "Shall we perch on the balustrade on the romantic side of the tower?"

"We might as well," I told him, as I picked a cigarette out of the case and waited for him to light it for me.

IT WAS LESS than thirty minutes, but not by much, by the time we heard a motorcar pull up to the bottom of the tower again. By then, we had smoked a number of cigarettes, bickered a lot, watched the moonlight on the water, bickered and smoked some more, and checked Crispin's pocket watch roughly every five minutes. It was almost time to do it again when the car arrived. Crispin looked at me as I looked at him.

"Kit?" he asked.

I shrugged. "Kidnappers? Hiram Schlomsky? Scotland Yard?"

"Scotland Yard?"

"Didn't I mention that?" I blinked innocently. "Christopher and I got the distinct impression that the Schlomskys suspected us of something earlier this evening. Probably of being complicit somehow in Flossie's kidnapping."

"And you think they sent Scotland Yard after you?"

"Not really likely," I admitted, "when they were adamantly opposed to involving the police in the first place. But if they happened to notice us standing up here when they came by to drop off the ransom, and they recognized me and thought you were Christopher, I wouldn't put it past them."

He stubbed out his fag against the balustrade. His movements were languid, in contrast to the snappy irritation in his tone. "You didn't think it might have been courteous of you to tell me this sooner?"

"Would it have made you stay away if I had?" I followed suit, scraped the lit end of my cigarette against the stone and flipped what was left out the opening. He hadn't said anything by the time all that was done, so I twitched a brow at him. "Shall we?"

"I suppose we'd better. Do you need a hand on the stairs?"

"I'll hug the wall," I told him. "Just don't run into me from behind."

"I wouldn't dream of it, Darling." Something about the remark must have amused him, because I could hear the smirk in his voice. "At least not without getting your permission first."

"Well, you don't have it. So stay back a step or two, if you would."

I headed into the gaping maw of the staircase, trailing one hand along the stone wall on my left. The ambient light from above made it possible to see the first couple of steps, but after that it was basically the equivalent of descending into the pits of hell, except without any flames to light the way. Behind me, I could hear Crispin enter the staircase and start down, the smooth soles of his polished shoes whispering across the stone. "Twenty-six steps," he told me. "I counted, going up."

That had been smart of him. I hadn't. It galled me to have to do it, but— "Thank you. That's helpful."

"I aim to please," Crispin said blandly. I would have snorted, but all my attention was fixed on the impenetrable darkness in front of me, and it was hard to catch my breath enough to snort. It's not that I'm afraid of the dark, exactly. But all the same, it was quite unnerving to head down into the stygian blackness of it with my eyes wide open and yet seeing nothing of what was in front of me.

And then the door opened and a lighter square of dark

widened into a view of Tooley Street. A dark figure stood in the aperture, and I would have worried had I not recognized the voice that told us, "Get a move on, will you? I've been waiting forever."

Crispin snorted behind me. "We heard you drive up, Kit. It's been two minutes, no more."

"Well, that's in addition to the ten minutes it took me to get here," Christopher said. "Anything at all might have happened while I've been gone."

"They arrived somewhere?" I moved past him into the street, and started to breathe easier as soon as I could see the familiar sights of ground and sky and air around me.

"Of course they arrived somewhere," Christopher said, turning to watch me. "Are you all right, Pippa?"

"Just glad to be somewhere where I can see my surroundings again." I took another deep breath while Crispin came out of the tower behind me and shut the door on his way out. "We thought there was a chance that they might just keep going, and so you'd be going, too."

"We thought you might end up in Kent," Crispin added. "We were making plans for the night in case you didn't come back."

Christopher snorted. "I bet you did." He headed for the passenger side of the Hispano-Suiza. "I assume you'd like to do the motoring, now that I'm back?"

"It's my motorcar," Crispin confirmed and headed for the driver's side. "Darling?"

He opened the door and gestured for me to crawl into the back.

"Why is it that no one asks me if *I* want to do the motoring?" I grumbled, but I went. Crispin slid behind the wheel and Christopher made himself comfortable in the front passenger seat.

"We know what you're like on the road," he told me over his shoulder.

I sniffed, offended. "I'm no worse than St George."

"Not much better, either," Christopher said.

"I resent that," Crispin told him, as the motor roared to life underneath us. "I'm a very capable driver, I'll have you know."

"So am I," I said.

He flicked me a look, but didn't comment, just continued, "It's the only reason I can drive the way I do. If I were less capable, I'd be dead."

"Tell that to the light pole you had your encounter with last year," I informed him. "I think it would beg to differ."

He shot me another look. "I walked away, didn't I?"

"The Ballot didn't." The motorcar before the Hispano-Suiza. Dead and buried now.

He huffed. "That's the point, Darling. I'm a good enough driver to wrap my motorcar around a light pole and walk away without a scratch."

"Not quite without a scratch." He had a scar above his left eye from the encounter. Really, the hypocrisy of him commenting on Wolfgang's *Schmisse* was astounding.

"Besides," I added crushingly, "that's hardly due to your prowess, is it? A capable driver would have avoided the accident. You only walked away because you got lucky."

Crispin sniffed in offense, but didn't continue the conversation. Instead he turned to Christopher. "A bit of direction might be nice."

"Of course." Christopher looked from him to me and back. "Just go that way—" He indicated the direction in which we had seen the two motorcars disappear earlier, "and I'll tell you where to turn."

Crispin let the clutch out and we rolled off.

"Tell us what you saw," I told Christopher as we proceeded

down Tooley Street into Bermondsey. "We couldn't see much at all from where we were standing."

He nodded. "I didn't see much more from where I was sitting. There was a Hackney cab that passed twice, and then it either came back with Mr. Schlomsky, or a different Hackney did do."

"We noticed that, as well," I nodded. "The first taxi could have been the kidnappers looking the place over, or it could have been Hiram getting the lay of the land before coming back to actually place the money. Unless you could see who was inside?"

Christopher said he hadn't been able to. "Eventually one of the Hackneys stopped, and I saw Hiram duck out and into the tower with the valise. It only took a few seconds for him to drop it, and then he was back in the cab and off they went."

"And then a few minutes later the other Hackney came," I said.

Christopher nodded. "Or the same one. There was no way to tell them apart, really. Especially in the dark. Turn right here, Crispin."

Crispin turned right, and asked, "Am I understanding you right, Kit, that it could all have been the same motorcar?"

"Who can tell?" Christopher said with a shrug. After a moment he added, philosophically, "It's dark, and all black cars look the same."

I snorted. "But you saw Hiram drop the valise, and then the Austin he was in drive away. And a few minutes later another Austin drove up, or the same one, and someone else went inside the tower and picked up the valise."

"A young man in a tweed suit," Christopher nodded. "Definitely not Hiram."

"No sign of Flossie, I suppose?"

"Not that I saw," Christopher said. "She might have been

inside the motorcar, or Hiram might have been, but if so, I didn't see her. Or them. Only the chap driving. Left here, Crispin."

"Did you recognize him?" I asked. "The bloke who picked up the valise?"

He shot me a look over his shoulder. "How would I recognize him, Pippa? There are almost eight million people in London!"

"I thought perhaps he was someone you had seen before," I said.

"Because I regularly spend time around kidnappers?" He shook his head. "No. I've never seen him before. Not to my knowledge."

"Can you describe him, at least?"

"Young," Christopher said. "Over twenty-five, under thirty. He was wearing a cap and he kept his head down, so I didn't get a good look at his face. I think his hair was dark. Slow down, Crispin. The streets are getting rough."

"I can see that," Crispin muttered. "I'm frankly surprised you and my car made it out of here alive."

I looked around and realized he was right. While I had been busy interrogating Christopher, we had entered a part of Southwark that wasn't for the faint of heart. A far cry from either Sutherland House in Mayfair, or the Essex House Mansions, with its slightly less upscale but nonetheless very reputable address. Here, dilapidated tenement buildings rubbed elbows with pockmarked walls and peeling paint. Rubbish clogged the sides of the streets where nobody cared enough to pick it up, and the few people we saw kept their shoulders up and their heads down, even when they cast furtive glances at the H6.

"How much farther?" Crispin wanted to know. His hands

were wrapped tightly around the steering wheel. "I don't like the way people are looking at us."

I didn't either, but I wasn't about to admit it in front of him. "Don't tell me you're afraid, St George?"

He flicked me a look in the mirror. "Cautious, Darling. As you should be. This isn't the sort of neighborhood where we're welcome."

No, it clearly wasn't.

"I don't know what we'll do with the motorcar when we stop," Christopher commented. "Up here on the right, Crispin. See the row of clapboard houses? The second one."

Crispin eyed it. "That's awful."

I nodded. "There's no Austin Twelve outside."

"If it was a Hackney, there wouldn't be," Christopher pointed out. "But that was where it stopped. The man in the cap got out and went into the second clapboard house."

We eyed it in silence from across the street. "No lights in the windows," Crispin said.

I glanced at him. "They're shuttered, can't you see?"

He glanced back. "I can see the shutters, Darling. But no light coming through the slats."

No, there wasn't. "They may not have electric lights down here," I said, looking around. Everything was quite dark, and lit only by the faint light of the moon, which had a difficult time penetrating the narrow street and gloom to reach us.

"I wouldn't bother to electrify that," Crispin said, eyeing the row of clapboard shacks. "It's a slum."

"People in slums deserve lights and heat, too."

He glanced at me. "I didn't say they didn't, Darling. Just that I understand why no one's bothered."

We sat in silence a moment.

"I'm going in," Christopher said and reached for his door.

I grabbed him by the back of his collar. "Not alone you're not."

He glanced at me over his shoulder. "I'm not taking you inside there, Pippa."

"I'm not letting you go alone," I retorted.

"I'll take Crispin."

We both turned to look at him. He shook his head. "That would mean leaving Philippa alone in the motorcar, and I don't think that's safe. She's better off going inside with us."

"That means leaving the motorcar alone," Christopher pointed out. "By the time we come back out, there's likely to be nothing left but the chassis."

"Do we have to go inside at all?" Crispin wanted to know. "Can we not notify the police—or tell the elder Schlomskys— where the kidnappers went, and have them deal with it from here? It isn't our jobs to track down kidnappers."

Christopher looked at me and I looked at him. It was a reasonable suggestion, well-suited for a man who didn't want to leave his luxury motorcar in a slum to be picked over by vultures. I thought about accusing Crispin of being cowardly again, but truthfully, I understood where he was coming from. There was no part of me that wanted to sit here, on this awful street, with an expensive motorcar, while the two of them went into the building without me.

On the other hand, there wasn't really any part of me that wanted to go inside the building, either. Even the air smelled rank here, rancid and leathery from the tanneries, and the boarded-up windows gave the place an unfriendly air.

"We're here," Christopher said. "We should at least take a look before we tell Scotland Yard what we know. Maybe the kidnappers brought a note to the Savoy to let the Schlomskys know where Flossie is, and she's sitting inside, bound and gagged, waiting to be rescued."

It was possible. And he was right: we were here. It seemed a shame to leave without doing at least a little bit of investigating. If Flossie was inside, and we left without looking for her, I would have a hard time forgiving myself.

"We go together, then," Crispin said. "We don't know how many kidnappers there are, and if they're inside, you two may be outnumbered."

"You're prepared to put our safety above that of your girlfriend, then?"

"My...?" He watched me pet the top of the seat, and his face cleared. "Oh. Yes, I am. The car can be replaced. You cannot."

"Dear me," I said. "I'm glad to know I rank above the vehicle in your estimation, at least."

"I was referring to Kit," Crispin said coolly, "but I suppose I might miss you too, if something happened to you."

"Like a prickly rash, no doubt. Let's go, then." I gave his shoulder a nudge. "Out."

"Grab the tire iron," Crispin said as he reached for the door handle. "It's on the floor by your foot."

I reached down and scrabbled along the floor, and yes, there it was. "Taking a leaf out of Wilkins's book?"

"It's a tire iron, Darling," Crispin said, and extended his hand to help me out of the car, "not a trench club. A tire iron is a perfectly natural thing to keep in a motorcar. The fact that it makes a handy weapon is secondary."

"It'll be nice to have, anyway," Christopher said. He was standing beside the door on the other side of the car, watching the house across the way. "There's no telling what we'll find inside."

"Do we trust Philippa with the only weapon we've got between us, or should one of us take it?"

"I need protection more than you do," I said. It was a

galling thing to have to point out, but a fact nonetheless. They are both more capable of defending themselves with their fists than I am. Not that either of them, to my knowledge, has ever been in the habit of getting into fist fights. But as Christopher had pointed out, we had no idea what we'd be walking into, or who may be waiting inside the clapboard house.

"I can swing harder than you," Crispin retorted, "if it comes to that."

That was true. If someone had to swing the tire iron at someone else's head, it might be better to have it in the hands of the one of us who was the most capable of cracking a skull.

Or one of the two: Christopher would be no less capable, I thought, at least physically, but he eyed the tire iron with revulsion, so the idea of having to use it clearly didn't appeal to him the way it did to Crispin.

"There's a torch in the glove box," Crispin told him. "You'd better have that, Kit. And give the tire iron here, Darling."

I handed it to him while Christopher fished the torch out of the glove compartment. He flicked it on to make sure it worked, before hefting it in one hand and swinging it through the air.

"That'll do to crack a kneecap or two, if need be. Let's go."

He started across the narrow street without waiting for an answer. Crispin and I exchanged a look and followed.

CHAPTER SIXTEEN

THE DOOR WAS JUST as old and wooden as the rest of the house, and didn't fit into the frame any too well. Christopher reached for the handle, but stopped halfway there. "Better not. There may be fingerprints."

"Use your handkerchief on the knob before you turn it," I suggested. "At least your fingerprints won't be on it that way, even if you smudge whatever is already there."

Christopher glanced around—there was no one in sight but the three of us; in fact, this end of the street appeared abandoned—before he lifted a foot and kicked the door just beside the handle.

"That's one way to do it," Crispin muttered.

Christopher must have expected more resistance than he got, however, because the door swung in with no problem—it must have been unlatched as well as unlocked—and he stumbled over the threshold and into a dark hallway.

We all froze while we waited to see what would happen: Christopher inside the house, and Crispin and I on the stoop. When a few seconds had passed without anyone appearing to ask us what on earth we thought we were doing, Christopher beckoned. "Come along, then, if you're coming inside."

I cast one last look up and down the narrow street—empty —before following. Crispin did the same, except he shot an apologetic look at his motorcar before he shut the door behind us, plunging us yet again into stygian blackness. There was a *click*, and then Christopher moved the torch slowly from side to side.

Crispin wrinkled his nose. "It smells in here."

It did, a mixture of sweat and rancid food and refuse and a few other things. Eau de Southwark, I supposed.

"Leave the door open a sliver," Christopher said. "It's not as if it was locked when we came."

Crispin cracked the door. "Best be quick about it. I don't fancy leaving the H6 out there any longer than I have to."

No, that was probably for the best.

Taking stock of our surroundings in the beam from the torch, we were standing in a hallway that ended in a door and, beside it, in a set of rickety steps going up. The door was the only one on this level, and it stood halfway open. We all exchanged a look, and then moved towards it in unison. It opened with a creak when Christopher put his elbow to it and pushed. "Hello?" he called. "Anyone here?"

No one answered. Nothing else happened, either. There wasn't even the scurry of small paws across the floor, and I would have expected that in a building like this.

"Florence?" I tried. "Are you here?"

"Let's just take a quick look around," Christopher said, "it doesn't seem very big."

He pushed into the flat—if one could call it that—torch first.

He was right: it wasn't big at all. From what I could gather in the torchlight beam, there were only two rooms: this one, with a shuttered window onto the street, and another behind it, with shutters that probably opened into some sort of courtyard in the back. There was no lavatory, and also no cooking facilities, so whoever had lived here—no one did now; there wasn't a stick of furniture left—must have done their necessary business elsewhere. The courtyard might boast shared facilities, or perhaps some of the odor we had noticed was the lingering scent of a chamber pot.

"Let's go up," Christopher said after we had ascertained that we were alone in the ground floor hovel and that Flossie was not hiding, bound and gagged, in any of the corners.

"Take care on the staircase," I told him. "It doesn't look safe."

He nodded. "I'll go first. If it's safe for me, it's safe for you and Crispin."

"Test each step before you put weight on it," Crispin advised. "The last thing we need is for you to step through something and contract a fatal case of lockjaw."

"I'll be careful. Just be ready to catch me should I pitch over."

Off we went, with Christopher in the lead. He did tread very carefully on the makeshift stairs, and while the rough planks groaned under his feet, they did bear his weight. We made it to the top without stepping on anything worse than what had the consistency (and smell) of the contents of someone's slop jar—"Ewww!" Christopher moaned, dancing out of the way, "that explains the smell; stay to the side, Pippa!"— before we found ourselves in the equivalent hallway to the one downstairs, with the exception that this one ended in a door but not in a set of steps.

The door was shut, and Christopher took a deep breath before he nudged it with his elbow. When it didn't swing open, Crispin handed him the elegant silk square from his breast pocket—as if Christopher didn't have one of his own he could use—and Christopher draped it over his hand before trying the doorknob.

It turned, and the door opened. With a squeal of hinges, of course. It was that sort of place.

"Hello?" Christopher called again, into what was surely the matching room configuration to downstairs. "Anyone here?"

There was no answer, although this level, unlike the ground floor, had a strange sense of expectancy. Downstairs had been empty, and had felt like it. This set of rooms gave the impression that it was waiting.

I pushed the feeling aside and started forward. Only to stop, perforce, when Christopher didn't move out of my way.

I glanced up at his face, close enough to me to make out even in the semi-darkness. "What is it, Christopher?"

"Something doesn't feel right," Christopher said.

I nodded, since I felt that way too. Not something a staid Englishman, or Englishwoman, should admit to—sensations of woowoo—but there was definitely something in the air up here.

Before I could verbalize my agreement, however, Crispin had spoken up. "Are you sure that isn't just the contents of the slop jar on your shoes, Kit?"

Christopher shook his head. "It's not the slop jar. It feels ominous."

"I agree," I said. "Although the smell in here doesn't help, I'll admit. Slop combined with rot combined with... what's that sweet smell?"

"Opium," Crispin said.

I eyed him. "Are you serious?" He certainly sounded knowledgeable, but... "How do you know?"

"I've smelled it before," Crispin said.

"I didn't know you frequented the Limehouse dens, St George," Christopher sniggered.

"I don't," Crispin told him. "But the Bright Young Set will try anything once. Babe Bendir and Lizzie Ponsonby organized an opium party last year sometime. It was a far cry from Limehouse, but I'm sure the opium smelled the same."

No doubt. "Is this an opium den, then? Should we expect dope addicts to attack us?"

"Opium smokers are generally too mellow to attack anyone," Crispin said, "and I don't think anyone's smoking right now. It smells more like someone has smoked opium here for so long that it has permeated the wood in the walls, and now it's residual. I don't notice any actual smoke."

I didn't either, now that he mentioned it. Just the lingering smell of it. "It's probably safe to proceed, then."

"After you, Darling." He nodded to the door.

"You're the one with the weapon," I pointed out.

"Kit's the one with the torch."

Yes, he was, and now he used it to nudge the door to the flat open and walk in. Crispin and I followed, him with the tire iron held aloft as we peered around the room. The torch lit up bare walls and a shuttered window and dusty floors. No furniture, but a lot of—

"Footprints," I said, pointing to them. Coming and going, from the entrance to the door of the other room and back. "Men's heavy boots. Textured soles."

"And two pairs of women's shoes," Christopher added. "One bigger than the other. Both with Cuban heels."

"Flossie and someone else?" Ruth, perchance.

"Might be," Christopher nodded, turning the torch from the impressions in the dust to the door. "Better give the pathway a wide berth. Detectives are very much into footprints, aren't they, Pippa?"

"I'd expect you to know more about that than me," I said. "I'm not the one seeing a Scotland Yard detective on the sly."

He probably flushed, although I couldn't see it in the darkness. "I'm not seeing Tom. I just... see him occasionally."

Crispin sniggered.

"Meanwhile, you're the one cutting your teeth on Agatha Christie and Dorothy L Sayers. You can't tell me footprints don't feature prominently in those stories."

No, I couldn't. Footsteps are always important clues. I gave in, and told him, "You're right. We should walk around them, so that, if Tom wants to, he can take photographs and perhaps match the footprints to the suspects' shoes if he finds them."

"May we just get this over with?" Crispin interrupted irritably. "The longer we stand here, the longer my motorcar is sitting unprotected on the street outside. There won't be anything left by the time we get out of here."

"We'll just poke into this last room," Christopher said, "to make sure Florence isn't there. Although with the way we've been carrying on, I'm sure she would have said something by now."

"Or kicked the wall or something if she's bound and gagged and can't speak," I added. "But St George is right. This is eerie. Let's just get this done so we can go home. It's been a long day and I'm tired."

I headed for the door to the other room, circumventing the footprints in the dust as I moved.

"I'm sure you simply cannot wait to get home to your bed so you can dream about His Highness and the way he wields a steak knife," Crispin said disagreeably as I reached for the knob.

I smiled sweetly. "Quite right. Come here, if you will, and protect me with the tire iron. Just in the event someone dangerous is behind the door."

"You want me to go first?"

"You're the one with the weapon," I repeated, "although if

you would like to hand it to me, I'd be happy to precede you into the room. I had no idea you were such a coward, St George."

"Not a coward," Crispin protested. "Just cautious. I don't see any reason to let anyone destroy my face unless I have to."

"That's probably for the best. You have so few qualities to recommend you, and your face definitely helps. Wouldn't want to harm it. Half of London, the female half—"

"And a fair few of the lads," Christopher said, getting into position with the torch while I prepared to open the door.

I eyed him. "Really?"

"He's quite pretty, isn't he? Even without the makeup and wig."

I snorted. Christopher smirked. Crispin rolled his eyes. "Can we get on with it?"

"Ready to break a few kneecaps?"

"No," Crispin said, hefting the tire iron, "but I'm ready for you to open the door. Stop dilly-dallying. We've been in here long enough."

We had, in fact. The opium smell had probably permeated both my lovely new frock and my hair by now, and it would be difficult to get it out. For that reason alone, I turned the knob and pushed the door open. Christopher turned the beam into the room, and Crispin took a step forward.

Only to stop with a rock-back on his heels, as if he had run into an invisible wall.

Christopher's hand jerked, and he whispered an obscenity, but not before I had gotten a glimpse of a figure in a pink frock, sprawled on a dirty mattress up against the opposite wall.

I recognized the frock. There was no way anyone would recognize anything else. Where the face should have been, there was nothing but blood. Blood and torn flesh and broken bones poking through the skin in jagged ivory shards.

My stomach roiled, and I turned and buried my face in Christopher's shoulder. He put an arm around me. It shook. So did I.

I took a step back, pulling him with me. He pushed Crispin backwards out of the way. Neither of us spoke until we had shut the door on the monstrosity beyond, and were standing in the middle of the floor with no care whatsoever for any footprints or evidence we were trampling underfoot.

"Was that...?" My voice gave out, and I had to clear my throat.

"Who could tell?" Crispin answered. He might have meant it to sound nonchalant, but his voice was shaking, too, and so was the tire iron in his hand.

I eyed it, and he told me, "Don't be ridiculous, Darling. I've been with you, remember?"

Of course he had. I took a breath. And another one. "Should we perhaps check and see whether...?"

"There's nothing we can do for her," Christopher said firmly. "No one could survive that and still be breathing."

"Sometimes amazing things happen. We might just look...?"

"Be my guest, Darling," Crispin said and headed for the door. Not the one that led to the—for lack of a better word—bedroom. The other one, to the hallway and the stairs and the outside. Christopher's torch beam followed him. "I'm going for the police."

That was probably a good idea, actually. "Leave the tire iron," I said.

He shook his head at me over his shoulder. "Better not, Darling. Safer if it's in the back of the motorcar when the police get here. That way they won't get any ideas."

"Unless you've used it on someone at some point—" I began, and then gagged when I got a visual reminder of what exactly 'using it on someone' would look like. "Yes, good idea. Hurry."

Crispin nodded. "If anyone attacks you, Kit can hit them with the torch. But hopefully that won't happen. I won't be long."

No, I imagined he would put all his skills to use to get to where he was going as quickly as was humanly possible. "Be careful," I told him. "You won't be doing anyone any favors if you motor straight into a wall between here and Scotland Yard."

"How lovely to know you care, Darling." He pulled the door to the hallway open. "I'll—"

...be back as soon as I can, I assumed. He didn't say it. Instead, the sentence turned into a high-pitched squeak of surprise as a dark figure materialized in the doorway.

The tire iron rose—I would have done the same thing, admittedly—and Christopher threw himself forward and yanked Crispin back before the weapon could do anything but fall in a whistling arc through the air, narrowly missing the nose of the person standing there.

They both stumbled back a few steps, knocking into me, and for a second or two we huddled in the middle of the room facing the doorway, before—

"What in tarnation is going on here?" Hiram Schlomsky roared.

CHAPTER SEVENTEEN

IT WAS PANDEMONIUM AFTER THAT, of course, with Hiram yelling, and Christopher and Crispin both trying to calm him down, and then Sarah Schlomsky showed up in the doorway, and as soon as that happened, Hiram turned on her instead, because he assumed that her being inside the house instead of outside in the Hackney meant that their driver must have driven away and left them there, which a trip down the stairs to peer out the front door proved to be true—the driver was gone, and so was the Hackney, and furthermore, it was hard to blame him, because it wasn't the kind of neighborhood where anyone would want to linger.

"Why did you pay the fare?" Hiram screamed at his wife, who told him, in quite a cold and cutting manner, that the driver wouldn't let her out of the cab until she had done so.

"Then you should have stayed there!" Hiram insisted, frothing at the mouth. The bottom edge of his mustache was wet with spittle. "Like I told you to do!"

Sarah drew herself up to full height and puffed out her not-inconsiderable bosom. "You're not the boss of me, Hiram Schlomsky!"

"That was the whole point of leaving you there!" Hiram raged. "So he wouldn't drive away and leave us stranded!"

"Don't be silly, Hiram," Sarah said. "We're not stranded."

"The cab is gone!"

"But these nice young people are here with their car." She gestured to us. "They'll give us a ride back to the hotel."

"Capital idea," I said enthusiastically, and had both Christopher and Crispin goggle at me as if they suspected that I had lost my marbles. "We should take you back to the hotel right now."

I looked at Christopher and Crispin, one after the other, significantly, and tried to convey the thought that we should try to get the Schlomskys out of here before they saw what—or rather who—was lying dead on the soiled mattress in the other room.

It took a second, but then they both caught on.

"Yes," Crispin said, turning to beam at both Schlomskys, "of course. I'd be happy to drive you both back to the Savoy. I don't think we've met. I'm Lord St George."

He stuck out a hand in the direction of Hiram, who stopped his rant mid-sentence to eye it with all the enthusiasm of a dead fish.

Sarah, meanwhile, stepped in to grab it and pump it up and down, heartily. Crispin, who had looked ready to lift her hand to his mouth in the proper upper crust manner, appeared taken aback.

"See, Hiram," Sarah said triumphantly, "this young man will see us home."

"You would let a criminal drive you home?"

"I'm not a criminal," Crispin protested, just as I said, indignantly, "We're not criminals!"

"What makes you think that?" Christopher wanted to know. He's the least reactive of us, and the most prone to thinking things through before flying off the handle. I'm quite easily riled, and so is Crispin, at least by me.

"I saw you!" Hiram said, eyes moving between me and both the boys. "Upstairs in the church tower, waiting for me to leave the ransom. Where's my money? Where's our daughter?"

I didn't want to answer the second question—I took care that my eyes shouldn't flicker to the door in the far wall—so I tackled the first one instead. "We don't have your money. We waited for you to put it inside the tower, and for the kidnapper to pick it up, and then we followed him here."

"No, you didn't!" Hiram was practically apoplectic with rage. "We watched you. You waited up there, smoking and talking, for twenty minutes, and then you went downstairs, were picked up, and drove directly here!"

Well, yes. It was easy to see how that might look damning to someone who didn't know us, and didn't know how things had actually happened.

"Christopher stayed with the motorcar," I explained, "while St George... while Lord St George and I went to the upper level of the tower. We saw you drive by, and then come back. And then we watched one of the kidnappers go inside and come out with the valise, and when he drove away, Christopher followed him. He came here."

I gestured to the room we were standing in. "Once Christopher knew where they were hiding, he came back and fetched us. But by the time we got here, the house was empty and the kidnappers—and their motorcar—were gone."

Hiram glanced around. "Empty, you say?"

"Not a living soul," I told him, and was happy to hear that my voice was steady.

It's not that I have a problem lying with a straight face. I'm quite good at fibbing when it doesn't matter. But knowing that the man's daughter was lying dead—and not just dead, but brutally murdered—behind the closed door behind us, made it a bit more difficult than usual to keep my composure.

And I wasn't the one who cracked. To this day, I'm not sure whether it was Christopher's eyes, or Crispin's, that drifted towards the door. (If I had to guess, I'd say it was Christopher's. He's more soft-hearted than Crispin. On the other hand, Crispin was the one with the relationship—if one could call it that—with Flossie, so it was a toss-up, really, who had given the game away.)

Someone did something, at any rate, and Sarah Schlomsky gasped, and then darted around her husband and made for the door to the other room. I took a sideways step to stop her—

"No!"

—but since I didn't move fast enough to actually get in her way, she circumvented me, and made it to the door, and flung it open. And plunged inside.

"Florence! Hiram, bring the light!"

"No," I cried again, "don't!" but neither of them listened to me. Hiram brought his torch to the now-open door, and then we heart a horrible soul-sucking gurgle from Hiram and a high-pitched shriek from the bereaved mother.

"Florence!"

No question who was dead inside, then. I had only gotten a brief glimpse in the unsteady beam of the torch before Christopher moved it away, and I had identified the dress more than the woman inside it. But if Sarah Schlomsky recognized her daughter, I guess there was no doubt that the dead woman in the next room was Florence Schlomsky.

Sarah devolved into wracking sobs—she had fallen to her knees next to the mattress with her daughter's body—and

Hiram came back through the door like a bull at a red cape, head and brow lowered. "What did you do to her?"

His eyes lighted on the tire iron in Crispin's hand, and he raised the cane in his own. "You! You're a murderer!"

The silver-tipped mahogany stick whistled through the air, only missing Crispin because the latter jumped back, eyes wide. "I'm not! I didn't do anything to her! Look..."

He brandished the tire iron, presumably to give Hiram the opportunity to see for himself that there was no blood or brain matter on it. "We only brought it inside for protection, because we didn't know whether there'd be anyone here."

But Hiram was beyond listening to reason, it seemed. "Murderer!" he screamed again, spittle flying, as he raised the cane for another go at Crispin's head. "Murdering bastard!"

I shrieked, and Crispin bellowed. The cane was at the apex of a swing and starting to come down when Christopher reacted. "Go!"

He gave me a push towards the door with the arm holding the torch while the other hand shot out and snagged Crispin by the arm and yanked. All three of us stumbled towards the door to the hallway as Hiram checked the downward chop of the cane and brought it around for a swing instead. By the time it hit the place where Crispin's head would have been, he was halfway to the door and we were almost out of the room.

"Hurry," Christopher told me breathlessly, as he nudged my back. "Down."

I was already headed for the top of the stairs, but didn't waste my breath telling him so. Instead, I simply started down with the two of them scrambling behind me. By now, Hiram was on his way through the door, as well, roaring, and Sarah's raised voice could be heard from the bedroom. "Hiram! Come back here! Hiram!"

I hit the bottom of the stairs and legged it down the dark hallway towards the front door as fast as I could in my elegant, T-strap heels. At least the dress wasn't constricting around the knees: I could move my legs just fine. Behind me, Christopher and Crispin shoved each other down the hall, until we all three tumbled out into the dark and dirty street.

"This way," Christopher said breathlessly, snagging me by the arm and yanking me up the street away from the motorcar. I had made for it like a safe haven, but he was right: Hiram was already pounding down the hallway behind us, and we couldn't take the time to get situated in the Hispano-Suiza and wait for Crispin to get the motor going. By the time any of that happened, Hiram would have caught up, and then all three of us, not to mention Crispin's pride and joy, would be beaten to a pulp by Hiram's silver-tipped cane.

So we pelted up the narrow street, two aristocratic young men in expensive black tie and one poor relation in a salmon-pink evening frock, with an incensed American millionaire in hot pursuit.

On level ground we were younger and faster, though, and by the time we had made it to the corner and out of sight, Hiram had fallen behind. He was huffing and puffing like a bellows, both due to his age and because he was a portly gentleman who enjoyed his food and his leisure in equal measure, from what I could determine.

Nonetheless, we kept going to the next corner, and then to the next. By now, Hiram was long gone, and we had made our way in a circle, or rather a square, back to where we started. When we peered around the final corner, the narrow street where the Hispano-Suiza was parked lay dark and empty. Hiram seemed not to have taken his anger out on the motorcar, because the windshield still gleamed with glass, and the stork emblem stood proudly. I felt as much as I heard Crispin's sigh of relief.

"Go on," I told him, between breaths, with a nudge to the shoulder. "Go fetch the police."

He looked at me, and then at Christopher, and then at me again. "Shouldn't we all go?"

"I thought someone ought to stay behind and keep an eye on the Schlomskys," I said.

He shook his head. "I don't think they're going anywhere, Darling. Their driver left, and this isn't the sort of neighborhood where one can simply flag down another Hackney. If they have any sense at all, they'll stay inside the building."

"And wait for what?" I wanted to know. "They're stuck here, St George. As you said, their driver left. Their daughter is dead. They'll want to fetch the police as quickly as possible."

"But I'm sure they won't start walking the street in the middle of the night," Crispin said. "Not in this neighborhood. It doesn't take great wisdom to see that it would be a bad idea."

No, but— "I'm not sure that would matter to them. Their daughter is dead. They're going to want the police. And Hiram has his cane. Perhaps he thinks he can handle whatever comes his way."

"Then he's a fool," Crispin said, which of course was true as far as it went. I couldn't argue with it.

"You go," Christopher told him. "You'll be safe in the motorcar by yourself. Drive quickly to Scotland Yard, tell them what has happened, and come back for us."

He glanced at me before continuing. "We'll wait for Hiram to calm down—it was you he was trying to kill, anyway, not us, and perhaps if you're not here, he'll be more reasonable."

Crispin muttered something—I couldn't hear what it was, but I was inclined to agree with him anyway, since I could guess what he'd said—and then shot me a look.

"I'll take care of Pippa," Christopher said. "We'll keep the torch. If Hiram attacks us, I'll hit him with it. And if someone else does, between the torch and Hiram's cane, not to mention Pippa's natural inclination towards bloodthirst, we ought to be fine."

"Don't joke about that," I told him. "Not after what we just saw upstairs."

He nodded. "Of course not. My apologies."

"The only person Philippa wants to murder," Crispin added, "is me."

He pulled open the door to the Hispano-Suiza and fitted himself behind the wheel. The tire iron went on the seat beside him. I suppose he might be afraid he'd find trouble along the way, at this time of night and in this neighborhood, and he wanted to keep it handy, just in case. "I'll be as quick as I can."

"We'll go back inside and see if we can hear what Hiram and Sarah are talking about," I said. "It didn't escape my attention that in a city of eight million people, they made their way here, to where their dead daughter was, within an hour of the ransom drop."

Crispin arched a brow. "They followed us, didn't they?"

"So they said," I nodded, "but that doesn't mean that they didn't know about this place already."

"So you think they murdered their own daughter?"

"Stranger things have happened," Christopher said. "He was awfully quick to brandish that cane, for a peaceful man. And it would make for a handy murder weapon."

I nodded. "You would have been dead had it connected, St George."

Crispin grimaced. "In justice to him, he did think we had murdered his child."

"Or else he pretended he thought so," Christopher said, "when, in fact, he knew better."

There was a moment's silence while Crispin and I both chewed on this, and then Christopher added, "But yes, we'll go inside. If they don't notice us, we'll listen to the conversation. If they do, we'll try to stay safe. Worst case scenario, we run away again."

"But do be quick, St George," I told him. "Both for Flossie's sake, and for ours. I don't fancy spending the rest of the night here."

Crispin nodded. "I'll be as fleet as the wind."

"Just stay away from light poles. No accidents on the way. No stopping to chat up comely young ladies."

"Especially not the sort who frequent this area," Christopher added.

Crispin gave us both a crushing look. "If I wanted to trade money for affection, I could find that commodity closer to home, thank you both."

Of course he could. And not in the sense that he'd have to pay for it nightly. He was an eligible peer of the aristocracy, with a title and a fortune and a dukedom in his future. His entire purpose in life, at least according to his father, was to find a woman on whom to bestow that title and money in exchange for the means to make an heir. The affection would come gratis, or at least as an unspoken part of the deal. Most any woman would manage to muster up quite a bit of it for a man who promises to make her a viscountess in the immediate future, and a duchess in due time.

"Just go," I told him. "Stay safe. Hurry."

"Not sure I can do both of those at the same time, Darling. But I'll be back as quickly as I can with reinforcements. You two run back inside the house before I start the motor. That way, maybe he'll think we've all left."

That made sense, so Christopher and I wished him luck one last time before we scurried across the narrow road and back into the dark hallway. From upstairs we could hear Sarah wailing and Hiram try to console her.

"In here," Christopher said, darting towards the empty ground floor flat. "We can stay hidden in the event he comes downstairs when he hears the car."

We ducked behind the door just as the H6 came to life outside. It has a powerful motor, the same one Woolf Bernato used to set the Brooklands record in 1924, and the noise was practically deafening in the narrow street. All noise ceased from upstairs as soon as it happened, and then we heard footsteps overhead as Hiram presumably left Sarah beside the body and walked across the floor above us and into the hallway.

We waited for him to descend the staircase, but that didn't happen. Instead, he stood and listened to the sound of the Hispano-Suiza fading away, before crossing the floor above our heads again to rejoin his wife.

We heard the murmur of voices above, but not what they said.

"We'll have to get closer if we want to hear anything," I murmured.

Christopher looked at me. We were nose to nose in the dark room, and our eyes had adjusted well enough to the lack of light that I could see his face almost clearly. His eyes glittered. "What could they possibly be saying that would make it worth the risk of being brained by Hiram Schlomsky's walking stick if they hear us?"

"You never know," I said, or whispered, rather. "I'm still not a hundred percent certain that it wasn't Hiram and Sarah who killed Florence. They could have staged the whole thing. We could have been looking at a single Hackney cab motoring past St Olave's in both directions all night. Go past twice to get the lay of the land, then go back to let Hiram deposit the money in the church tower. Wait three minutes and go back again. This time, the driver picks up the valise. Everyone drives here. But they notice you following them, so they turn the tables and follow you instead, back to the church tower. And then they follow all three of us back here and pretend to find the place for the first time."

"Convoluted," Christopher opined.

Of course it was. "It's possible, though. Sarah isn't stupid, and it was stupid to allow herself to be stranded here. Unless it was on purpose, to throw us off guard. And Hiram is awfully quick with that cane. He might have been just as quick if his daughter said something he didn't like."

"One would hardly think so, Pippa," Christopher said. "And her mother seems genuinely grief-stricken, if nothing else."

That she did. The loud wailing from earlier had died down by now, but Sarah was still sniffling softly upstairs, and doing it loudly enough that we could hear her one story below.

"That," Christopher said, "is not for our benefit. Not if they don't know that we're still here."

Fine. "So perhaps it's just Hiram," I said. "We don't know anything about this family, other than the fact that Florence left her family and friends and everything else behind to come all the way to London. That could certainly indicate a strained relationship with her parents."

Christopher nodded thoughtfully. "So Florence left the Essex House Mansions on Wednesday evening in Crispin's motorcar. He dropped her on the Strand, and she proceeded to the Savoy, where her father was waiting. Where was her mother?"

"No idea," I said. "A more likely scenario is that Florence was proceeding along the Strand towards the Savoy when her father saw her. Her mother was in the hotel, but Hiram was outside, either in a cab or on foot, and he and Florence went off somewhere together. That would explain why nobody noticed anything amiss in the street. She got into a cab with her own father, so there was no fuss and no kicking and screaming. But then something went wrong, and Hiram killed her. Sarah doesn't know anything about it."

Which would explain her grief, which certainly seemed genuine.

"And Hiram arranged for the ransom note to take attention off himself?" Christopher asked.

"It makes sense," I answered, "doesn't it?"

"I suppose so. The driver saw him do it, I assume, so Hiram paid him off in exchange for keeping quiet about the murder and for driving the motorcar tonight?"

"I wouldn't be surprised. If there's one thing Hiram has a lot of, it's money to throw at problems."

"It's possible," Christopher allowed. "But it's all the more reason why we don't want him to find us here, Pippa."

Yes, it was. I wished I had thought of all this before I let Crispin go off on his own. If I had been just a bit quicker on the uptake, we could have gone with him, instead of being left here with one or two people who may be murderers.

"Then again," Christopher said, "Hiram might not be guilty. I don't think you touched the body, did you?"

I shook my head. No, indeed. There was nothing that would have induced me to do so.

"I did," Christopher said. My eyes widened, and he added, "Someone had to, to make sure there was nothing we could do to help."

"Honestly, Christopher," I said, as I fought back the mental images, "you should have been able to tell by looking at her that she was beyond help."

He nodded. "I know. But I had to check. And the body was

still warmish. If she had been dead since Wednesday, she would have been stone cold."

And not just that, but decomposition would have been well advanced, too. We would have been able to smell the body as soon as we stepped foot inside the building. Maybe even as soon as we stepped foot outside the motorcar.

"In that case," I said, "perhaps Hiram truly did follow us here thinking we were the guilty ones. He left the valise and withdrew, the kidnapper picked it up, and you followed him here. Then you went back to fetch St George and myself, and while you were doing that, the kidnapper dispatched Florence and made tracks. Then Hiram followed us back here because he thought we were the kidnappers."

Christopher nodded. "That makes sense."

It did. Even if it didn't explain some of the minor details, such as how they had managed to snatch Flossie off the Strand on Wednesday night without anyone noticing. Her father being involved made that whole scenario a lot more likely. "I suppose they've kept her here for the past three days, feeding her opium along the way to keep her quiet."

"Feed someone enough opium," Christopher agreed, "and they don't notice, or care, about much. Including the fact that they're sleeping on a soiled mattress in a Southwark slum."

I nodded. "How long before St George comes back with the police, do you suppose?"

"I imagine we have a while to wait yet," Christopher said. "Do you want to sit down and try to get comfortable? Maybe even try to sleep? It's getting late."

"In this house of horrors?" I shuddered. "I think not. Besides, there's no way I'm lowering any part of this dress onto the filth on this floor."

"We'll stand, then?"

"Or we could go upstairs and see if Hiram has calmed

down. If we tell him that Crispin has gone for the police, maybe it'll help."

"Are you certain that's something you want to risk?"

"Just keep the torch ready," I told him, "and whack him over the head with it if he tries anything."

Christopher sighed, but kept a tight grip on the torch as we made our way out of the room and back up the stairs.

CHAPTER EIGHTEEN

THE SCHLOMSKYS HEARD US COMING, of course, and Hiram was ready for us when we walked through the door. But the absence of Crispin, or more likely the absence of the tire iron, seemed to help. Hiram kept a tight grip on the cane, and a keen eye on us, but he didn't attack.

"Lord St George went to fetch the police," I said immediately, and I daresay that may have helped, too.

Hiram grunted something, but he didn't respond. It was Sarah who spoke up from where she was sitting: on the dirty floor beside the mattress with the body, with no care for her own clothes. "Thank you."

"It seemed the least that we could do," Christopher told her. "Hopefully it won't be long before he's back with reinforcements."

He took a step towards her. "We're sorry for your loss."

It was, thankfully, too dark in the room for me to see Flossie's head and the damage that had been done to it. I could see Sarah, could even see the tear tracks on her cheeks, but if I kept my eyes on Sarah and not on Flossie, the darkness of the room allowed me to pretend, when I wasn't paying too much attention, that everything was mostly all right.

Christopher added, gently, "Is there anything we can do?"

"You can tell us everything you know," Sarah said, in a voice that brooked no argument whatsoever.

"We don't know much at all," I told her. "It was as we said. We went to St Olave's this evening to see the kidnappers, and to follow them to see if we could find Florence."

Hiram shifted, and I winced. "Not like this. Of course not like this. We thought they'd have her bound and gagged in a room somewhere, while they went to fetch the money, and that once they had it, they'd let her go." In one piece and none the worse for wear.

Truly, it made no sense that they would have killed her, and still less sense that they had done it in such a brutal way. I hadn't gotten a good look earlier—and I was glad for it—but Flossie's face had been all but obliterated.

A thought struck me and I added, perhaps unwisely, "It *is* your daughter, isn't it?"

There was a moment while they both stared at me, and then Sarah said, in a voice just this side of hysterical, "Do you suppose I wouldn't recognize my own flesh and blood, young lady?"

"Of course not," I said. "I was just trying to think of a reason why—"

I trailed off before I could wonder, out loud, why someone would have bothered to make Florence, for all intents and purposes, unrecognizable. There was no need to belabor that particular point. And after all, it had been the best part of a year since Sarah and Hiram had seen their daughter, hadn't it?

Besides, it was dark in the room. I had recognized Flossie mostly based on the fussy pink frock she was wearing, but the frock couldn't be familiar to her parents. Not if they had been surprised and shocked about her wardrobe in the flat two days ago. So it seemed at least possible that Sarah was mistaken.

Then again, if it wasn't Flossie, who was it? Christopher had trailed the kidnapper straight to this house. It had to be Flossie.

Perhaps she had angered the kidnappers outrageously in the handful of days they had kept her, and that was why they had beaten her so brutally. It isn't hard to murder someone without violence. Crispin's mama had managed just fine when it came to both herself and her father-in-law. Both of them had looked as if they were asleep in bed when we'd found them. Florence had been in no position to reject an injection or any kind of food or drink, so it would have been easy to kill her with no fuss whatsoever. Destroying her face must have meant something to the kidnapper.

Christopher cleared his throat and I came back to myself with a murmured apology.

"What happens now?" Sarah Schlomsky asked. She sounded exhausted, and who could blame her?

"We wait," Christopher answered. "Crispin is a speed demon, so it won't take him long to get across the river to Scotland Yard, especially at this time of night. He'll bring the police here, and they'll tell us what to do."

He hesitated for a moment before he added, "I imagine they'll tell us to go home, and they'll seal off the crime scene and wait until daylight to start working on it."

The Schlomskys nodded. So did I. It's one thing to work through the night when you can see what you're doing. It's another thing entirely to try to get anything done in pitch darkness, and when you're tired anyway, after a long day's work.

"So we wait," Hiram said.

Christopher nodded. "We do."

We waited. Time passed slowly, and it was difficult to stay

awake. Not even the presence of the body prevented my eyelids from becoming heavy. We sat down on the stairs between the ground and first floors, and I leaned my head against Christopher's shoulder and dozed. He leaned his shoulder against the stairway wall and did the same. When the door downstairs opened with a bang, and knocked against the wall in the hallway, we both jumped.

"Upstairs," someone said, and through the adrenaline spike I recognized Crispin's voice. "There are no lights on. Or they don't exist. I'm not sure which."

A dark figure came into view in the hallway below, followed by another. A torch lit up the dusty floorboards. Then the person in the lead turned onto the stairs and aimed the light up. Christopher and I both squinted into the glare.

"There you are," a voice said. "Hullo, Kit. Philippa."

"Tom." Christopher sounded relieved, or perhaps just pleased and happy. The bright light leached all the color out of his skin, but under normal circumstances, I'm certain I would have seen a tell-tale blush on his cheeks.

"St George filled me in on what has happened." Tom moved the torch aside so it wasn't shining directly into our faces anymore, and climbed a few steps towards us with Crispin right behind. He stopped when we were face to face: him standing a few steps below, and us still sitting. "I sent Finch home to get some rest—it's been a long day—but I'll secure the crime scene, and then I brought a bobby along to stand guard for the rest of the night."

"Bristol?" I asked.

He shook his head. "Different case entirely. Jewelry theft in Mayfair. Bristol PD is handling Hughes's death."

I nodded. "Sorry to interrupt. Carry on."

He looked past me to the top of the staircase. "The elder Schlomskys are upstairs?"

"All the Schlomskys are upstairs," Christopher said and pushed to his feet. He extended a hand to me. "Up you come, Pippa."

I let him pull me up and then we both stepped against the wall so Tom could squeeze past on the narrow staircase. "Is there anything we can do to help?" I asked after him, but he shook his head.

"I'll take care of it. The three of you may leave. I'll need statements from all three of you tomorrow."

Crispin opened his mouth, and Tom, without even having looked at him, said, "Yes, you too, St George. Your father will just have to lump it, I'm afraid."

Crispin shut his mouth again, defeated. "I'll let Tidwell know not to expect me."

Yes, let us not bother Uncle Harold in the middle of the night, but it was perfectly fine to drag Tidwell out of slumber after a long day of butlering.

"You can kip with us," Christopher told him. "Or go to Sutherland House, as you please."

"Your father would probably prefer it if you spent the night at Sutherland House," I added, "under the watchful eye of Rogers." And far away from my supposedly distracting presence.

Crispin smirked. "Will you let me sleep in your bed again, Darling?"

"As long as I can stay on the Chesterfield," I said.

"Then how can I resist? Between a cold and lonely bed in the ancestral pile, under the eagle eye of old Rogers, or a delightful few hours in sheets that smell of Chanel No 5, how could anyone make any other decision?"

""It won't make any difference to me," I told him. "I won't be sharing it with you either way. Although you must have me confused with one of your other conquests. I wear Shalimar."

"Of course, Darling." He smirked. "For the record..."

"No, you cannot count me among your conquests. It was a figure of speech only."

"It's settled, then," Christopher said. "You're coming to ours for what's left of the night. Hopefully we won't wake up to your father hammering on the door at the crack of dawn this time."

Yes, indeed. Although in justice to Uncle Harold, I imagine it had been equally distressing for him.

"I know where to find you," Tom said, waving us away. "Go home and get some rest. I'll be by to get your statements tomorrow."

I shot a glance at the door behind which the Schlomskys were no doubt listening. "You don't want any help with them?"

"I've done this job for a long time, Miss Darling." He winked at me. "I'm sure I can manage."

As he's all of twenty-seven, and had been at university until he was twenty-three, courtesy of the war and getting a late start, it hadn't really been all that long. But since he was no doubt saying it for the benefit of the Schlomskys, I declined to make a case out of it.

"Of course you can. We'll be off then. You wouldn't like for us to give the Schlomskys a lift back to the Savoy once you're done speaking to them?" And to give me a chance to hear the conversation he was about to have with them before he let them go?

"I brought a Tender," Tom said, about the fleet of Crossleys the Metropolitan Police had invested in after the war. "I'll take care of it. Off you go. Shoo."

I stuck my lip out, but shooed. Crispin preceded me down the hallway to the front door, while Christopher lingered for long enough to exchange a few soft words with Tom before he followed. They may have been personal, or a warning about what Tom would see on the upper floor; I don't know.

"After you." Crispin held the front door open with a bow, and waited for me to pass through, for all the world like he was ushering me out of a ballroom in Mayfair, and not this rickety shack in a slum in South London.

"Thank you." I entered the narrow street where, between Crispin's H6 and Tom's Tender, there wasn't much room to walk at all. A young constable in uniform stood a few feet away at parade rest. He nodded when we came out, but didn't speak.

"You made good time," I added, when we had reached the Hispano-Suiza, and Crispin was opening the door for me.

"I got lucky." He kept a hand under my elbow while I made my way into the backseat. "The roads were practically empty, and Gardiner and DS Finchley were unpacking the Tender when I drove into the Yard. It helped that they knew me. Cut down on the explanations."

"I imagine it did." I didn't think Tom had any particularly fond feelings for Crispin—not like he did for Christopher—but he knows him well enough to trust that if Crispin told him there was a dead body, Tom could take him at his word.

I made myself comfortable and turned to watch as Christopher exited the building with a nod to the constable, and then came towards us. "I don't suppose anything interesting was said?"

"Everything I say is interesting," Crispin informed me as he made himself comfortable behind the wheel, "but if you mean did Gardiner say anything interesting, then no. They stopped unloading the Tender, Finchley went home, and Gardiner snagged a constable and followed me here. I don't know what they talked about, but nobody spoke to me, because we were in separate motorcars."

Of course. "How much did you tell him?"

"The basic information," Crispin said, as Christopher opened the other side of the motorcar. "Florence Schlomsky has been missing for a few days, and two days ago her parents got a ransom note in the mail. Tonight they dropped off the ransom. We followed the kidnapper and found the body. End of story."

He turned the motor on. The noise was loud in the quiet street.

"Succinctly put," I told him.

He smirked. "Thank you, Darling. Ready, Kit?"

Christopher nodded. "Let's go, and stand not on the order of our going, or however the saying goes."

I had my mouth open to quote the saying, but that was just as the H6 took off down the narrow street with a roar. Instead, I let the burst of air that hit my face blow the words away and rejoiced in getting away from the dank and depressing place where Florence had breathed her last.

WHEN THE KNOCK on the door came the next morning, I went to open it with visions of His Grace, the Duke of Sutherland, dancing in my head. When I pulled the door open and it only revealed Detective Sergeant Tom Gardiner, I considered myself lucky and invited him in.

"Christopher and Crispin are still asleep. If you'll give me a moment, I'll go knock them up."

I scooped up the pillow and blanket from the Chesterfield and bade Tom sit. "I'll only be a moment. Help yourself to anything you can find in the kitchen."

I headed for the hallway to the bedrooms even as I was speaking, and pushed open the door to my own bedroom, which Crispin was occupying, with no concern for the sleeping lord. "Rise and shine, St George. We have company."

He sat up straight in bed, looking confused and dazed and with his hair sticking out in every direction. I looked away as the blanket fell, leaving him bare to the waist. "It isn't..." His voice was froggy, and he had to clear his throat and try again, "it isn't my father, is it?"

I shook my head as I turned towards the wardrobe. "It's Tom. Just give me a moment to find a frock and some unmentionables, and I'll go change in Christopher's room. The lav is all yours."

"Thank you, Darling." I heard the rustle as he threw off the bedclothes, and kept my eyes averted as he stalked through the room and out the door in what was surely nothing much at all. Once the lavatory door was safely latched behind him, I scurried down the hallway with my summer frock and shoes, and entered Christopher's room with a brief knock. "Tom's here. St George is in the lav."

"Tom?" Christopher sat as upright as Crispin had at the news, but with rather more anticipation and less dread. His hair was sticking out every which way, too, and he was rubbing his eyes with his fists the way he had done when he was small. "Already?"

"It's seven-thirty. Practically time for elevenses." I pulled the pyjama top over my head and reached for my camisole. "I suppose he wants an early start, with a new crime scene to investigate and a fresh murder to solve."

"No doubt," Christopher nodded. "Better hurry up with that. Crispin will be here the moment he's done in the washroom, just to see if he can catch you without your clothes on."

"He wouldn't be so gauche," I said, even as I hurried to pull the frock over my head and smooth it down. "There. All safe."

And none too soon, either, since the door opened just a few moments later, and Crispin stuck his head in. "Morning, Kit. Darling."

He looked me over, but since I had managed to get the frock on just in time, there was nothing for him to see. He didn't look disappointed, but I smirked anyway. "What do you need, St George?"

"I came to raid Kit's closet," Crispin said, and pushed the door open. "Don't want to spend the day in black tie if I don't have to. You don't mind, do you, Kit?"

He walked in, wearing nothing but his trousers. I looked away, to where Christopher shook his head. "Knock yourself out. Just bring back whatever you borrow. You still have my flannel bags and pullover from the last time you rifled through my closet."

"You'll have to come down to Sutherland Hall and pick them up yourself," Crispin said, as he pulled open the doors to the wardrobe. "Let's see..."

"Excuse me," I told them both, "I'm going to go splash water on my face and brush my teeth. I'll see you both—and Tom—in the sitting room in a few minutes."

It was the reminder Christopher needed—that Tom was waiting—to get him out of bed and moving. As I walked out of the room, he had gone to join Crispin in front of the wardrobe, both of them peering in at the clothes as if they expected some sort of outfit to jump out at them.

By the time I made it out of the bathroom and then my bedroom, after taking a couple of minutes to paint my lashes and lips, everyone was gathered in the sitting room. Tom was sitting in the chair with Christopher perched on the arm, while Crispin was leaning back on the Chesterfield, one leg elegantly crossed over the other. Everyone was smoking.

"Refreshments?" I inquired when I walked in. "Breakfast? It's a bit early for alcohol, I suppose, but I could make a pot of tea or coffee?"

"Later," Tom said, with an air of authority. "Sit."

He nodded to the sofa next to Crispin, and I arched my brows and sat down.

"You too, Kit."

Christopher also arched his brows, but he slid off the arm of Tom's chair and took a languid seat next to me.

"So," Tom said.

There was silence. We sat there, side by side, and waited. It felt a bit like being called to the headmistress's office—or on the carpet before Uncle Herbert—but I honestly wasn't certain what crime I had committed, and I don't think the other two were, either.

"Why didn't you tell me about Miss Schlomsky?"

The question was directed at all of us, but I assumed—and so did he—that it was meant for Christopher. "That she had been kidnapped, do you mean? We tried. But by the time the ransom note came, and we realized that something was wrong, we couldn't find you."

"You must have known that she was missing before then?"

"We knew we couldn't find her," I said. "We knew that she hadn't shown up at the Savoy to see her parents, and that she wasn't in the flat. But it wasn't until the ransom note was delivered that we realized that she wasn't staying away of her own free will."

Tom nodded. "Tell me everything."

CHAPTER NINETEEN

WE TOLD HIM EVERYTHING, starting with the telegram
and Flossie's reaction to it, and ending with the discovery of the
body and Crispin going off to fetch the police. Along the way,
Tom asked questions about anything that wasn't clear, and by
the time we got to the end of the recitation, he nodded. "Excel-
lent, thank you."

"Our turn," I said. "Did the Schlomskys say anything last
night?"

Tom's lips twitched. "They said quite a few things."

I huffed. "You know what I mean. Anything interesting?"

"They suspect you of being involved," Tom said. "Or Mr.
Hiram Schlomsky does. Mrs. Sarah Schlomsky seemed to
believe your story about following the kidnappers to the house
in Southwark."

"Why wouldn't Hiram believe us? It was the truth!"

"You have to admit it looked suspicious, Pippa," the voice of
reason—aka Christopher—said. "If he saw us—or saw you two,
rather—on the church tower when he dropped off the ransom,
it's no wonder he thought you were involved."

"Not to mention that when he walked into the shack in Southwark," Crispin added, "and saw his daughter's body, I was holding a tire iron and Kit an oversized torch."

Ugh. Yes, when he put it like that, I suppose we did look somewhat suspicious.

"I had to promise him to test the tire iron for evidence," Tom told us. "I'm going to have to take it with me, St George."

Crispin waved a hand. "By all means. There's nothing on it but my fingerprints and a bit of dirt and grease."

Tom nodded. "I'm not concerned. While a tire iron is likely pretty close to the murder weapon, I don't think either of you was wielding it."

Good to know.

"Although while we're on the subject," Tom added, "I should also let you know that I stopped by Sutherland House this morning and spoke to Rogers. He assured me that there had been no young ladies in the house in the past week."

He glanced at Crispin. The latter smirked. "No, I've been a good boy lately. Although what my usual habits have to do with any of this..."

"He's talking about Flossie," I said, "you prat. And where she was kept during the time she was gone."

Tom nodded. "We also rang up Sutherland Hall, and Tidwell said the same thing. I hope he won't feel the need to tell your father about the inquiry, St George, but I thought I ought to let you know, in case His Grace brings it up."

"Much obliged," Crispin told him, but didn't sound like he was grateful. It's hard to, when you're speaking through gritted teeth. "Was that really necessary?"

"I'm afraid it was. Mr. Hiram Schlomsky was adamant that you be investigated thoroughly. Not only because you were holding a tire iron and standing over his daughter's dead body when he first saw you, but because you were also the last person to see her alive."

I watched the pretty pink color drain out of Crispin's cheeks, and he swallowed. "Surely not the last. The body was still warm when we found it. She couldn't have been dead more than an hour. I last saw her on Wednesday."

"She was alive somewhere between then and last night," I agreed. "And St George was with me on top of the church tower from about ten o'clock on. He couldn't have killed her."

"I'm afraid Mr. Hiram Schlomsky wouldn't take your word for it, Philippa," Tom said, "nor would I, to be honest. I know you'd lie for him if you felt it necessary."

I shook my head. "That's ridiculous, Tom. We were together. Hiram Schlomsky saw us himself."

"He saw you," Tom corrected, "and a young man with fair hair in evening kit. I have only your word for it that it was Lord St George."

"Mine and Christopher's. And Crispin's himself. Besides, who else do you suppose was with me? The *Graf* von Natterdorff?"

Crispin huffed. Christopher grinned.

"I'm familiar with Lord St George's feelings about his motorcar," Tom said, with a glance at Crispin, "so I can't help but be surprised that he allowed anyone else to drive it."

"It was between staying in the motorcar by himself, or going in the tower with Pippa," Christopher said, "and I'm sure I don't have to explain why—"

"Kit." The warning was clear in Crispin's voice.

"Never mind that," I said irritably. "Nobody cares, St George. It was Crispin and myself in the church tower, Tom. Christopher was in the Hispano-Suiza. He was as shocked as you are that Crispin was willing to let him take the motorcar, and he wasn't about to let the opportunity pass him by."

Crispin rolled his eyes, and it was Christopher's turn to smirk. I continued, "We stood on the tower and watched the kidnappers drive by, and then watched Hiram drive by, and then watched Hiram come back, and then watched the kidnappers come back, and finally we watched the kidnappers leave, with the ransom and with Christopher in hot pursuit. It took a half hour or so before he came back. For all that time, Crispin was with me at St Olave's. He was in no position to kill anyone. Except me, at any rate, and as you can see, I'm alive and well."

"And if you try to insinuate that Kit bludgeoned that unfortunate girl to death—" Crispin began, and Tom shook his head.

"Of course not. Kit wouldn't."

"But I would, is that it?"

"No," Tom said. "I don't think you would, either. But Hiram Schlomsky suspects you, and told me as much, and for everyone's sake, I have to investigate thoroughly, because that is my job."

"Well, he has an alibi," I said. "Unless I'm suspect, too, and you don't trust my word?"

"Of course you're suspect, Darling," Crispin said irritably. "Didn't you hear the man? You'd lie for me. Which simply isn't true, by the way, Gardiner. Philippa wouldn't spit on me if I were on fire."

"Of course I would," I shot back, equally irritably, because really, why say something so stupid? "I'll spit on you right now if you'd like. You wouldn't even have to be on fire—"

"Enough!" Tom's voice cut through the squabbling like a knife through butter, and we both—all three, since Christopher was sniggering—shut up. "I'll be taking the tire iron, St George. And the torch."

"Just as long as you don't take the whole motorcar," Crispin said. "I need a way to get home. And I would like them back when you determine that there's no evidence on them."

Tom nodded. "In exchange, I would like official, signed statements from all three of you as to what happened last night. You can come by the Yard later today and do it. But before you do that, let's go back to last evening. You saw Mr. Hiram Schlomsky deliver the ransom?"

"We saw him go into the church with a valise," I nodded. "And come back out without it."

"And it was the same valise you'd seen in the hotel room?"

Christopher and I exchanged a look. "I assume so," I said.

Christopher nodded. "No reason to think it wasn't. Why wouldn't it be?"

"Did you look inside it?"

We all shook our heads—when would we have had the opportunity?—and Tom continued. "Did you get the impression that he hadn't been able to come up with the money? It's a large sum, and not a lot of time to get it together."

"He intimated that he hadn't," I said. "Remember, Christopher? When we were in their hotel room, and we asked about it, he said, 'or as much as I could.'"

Tom arched his brows. "Kit?"

Christopher nodded. "He did say that."

"Do you think the kidnappers opened the valise and found it short," I asked, "and that's why they killed Florence?"

Tom opened his mouth, but before he could say anything—"It makes sense," Crispin said wretchedly. "Nobody does what was done to her without a whole lot of anger. Being stiffed the ransom might do it."

Tom nodded. "When I have a chance, I'll track down the bank and the money transfer and check the amount for myself. In the meantime, we'll count it as a likely motive."

He pushed to his feet. "And now I'd better get back to Southwark. With no electricity in the house, there wasn't much we could do last night. Now we'll start processing the crime scene and the body, and see what we can find."

"How will you identify her?" I wanted to know, and winced when I heard the words that came out of my mouth. Nonetheless, I carried on. "With her face... like it is?"

Tom arched his brows. "Is there any reason to think she isn't who we think she is?"

Of course there wasn't. Not really. But... "We didn't get a good look in the dark last night. I mostly saw the pink dress and assumed it was Flossie, since we expected it to be Flossie. And her mother hasn't seen her in almost a year, and didn't get a good look, either. I just thought..."

Tom sighed. "Do you just want an excuse to see the crime scene again? Or do you truly think there's something else going on?"

"It's not likely that something else is going on," I admitted. "The theory about the ransom being less than the demand makes sense. I just thought it was..." I swallowed, "interesting that someone would take the trouble to obliterate her face like that."

"And I won't say that you're wrong," Tom agreed. "It's just as well to make certain, I suppose." He glanced at the clock ticking away on the mantel. "The body should be in the city morgue in three hours. Go there and look at it. I won't have you interfering with my crime scene any more than you already have done."

I nodded. "Thank you, Tom."

"Don't thank me yet." His voice was grim. "I didn't get a good look either, in the dark last night, but what I saw wasn't pretty."

No, it hadn't been. And there was no part of me that wanted to see it again. But at the same time, the whole thing was niggling at me, and if going to view the body one more time would dispel that feeling of something being wrong—something other than the obvious—I was willing to put myself through it.

"I'll see you out," Christopher said and got to his feet. Tom nodded and did the same.

"Don't forget to come by Scotland Yard and sign your statements."

He nodded to the both of us before following Christopher towards the door.

"Am I free to go home after that, Gardiner?" Crispin called after him, and Tom turned to look at him, brows raised. "Before my father has an apoplexy and comes looking for me?"

"As long as you make yourself available for the inquest, should you be needed."

Crispin nodded. "Of course. Anything for Scotland Yard."

Tom huffed a breath and continued into the foyer. I shook my head at Crispin. "Are you simply constitutionally incapable of not being a prat, St George?"

He grinned. "I must be. Although I'll accompany you to the morgue before I go. Wouldn't want you to have to go through that without my bolstering presence."

I scoffed, and he added, more seriously, "In some ways, I've been closer to Flossie than you have. It won't hurt me to take another look, either."

It probably would, actually, him having been closer to Flossie than me. It wouldn't be pleasant for him to see her like that. But if he was willing, I wasn't going to turn down the support, nor the extra set of eyes.

"I would appreciate it," I said.

"Anything for you," Crispin answered.

• • •

AND SO IT was that three hours later, we presented ourselves at the city morgue in Golden Lane. By then, we had taken the time to put ourselves together properly, as well as have a hearty breakfast, which we needed after our late night, but which I regretted as soon as I walked into the mortuary. The sickly sweet smell of death and decomposition mingled with the vinegary burnt-match scent of formaldehyde, and my stomach did a quick flip-flop and threatened to turn itself inside out.

"Steady on," Christopher said, looking worried. I must have turned the color of old porridge, I suppose. Or a day old corpse, which seemed more appropriate for the occasion.

Crispin, meanwhile, put a steadying hand on my back. "There, there, old bean. Stiff upper lip."

"That's easy for you to say—" I began, and then I remembered who I was talking to. This couldn't be easy for him, either. "Sorry, St George."

"Never mind, Darling." But he didn't drop his hand from my lower back. "Let's just get it over with, shall we?"

We got it over with, and I have to say that it was one of the more unpleasant experiences of my life. One look at the corpse's head, and it was obvious that nobody would be able to identify her that way. It looked as if all the bones in her face had been broken, and there was nothing whatsoever there that anyone could recognize. Even her hair—that of it which wasn't sodden with blood—looked limper and more drained of color than usual. Florence had always had shiny, bouncy curls, and it was sad to see them lay limp and dirty.

The coroner's assistant, the one who had drawn the short straw and had to work on Sunday, mercifully covered the head as soon as we'd had a chance to look at it and shake our heads. But then there was the rest of the body to identify, of course. There was a strip of linen covering Florence's breasts, much as a brassiere would, and another strip covering her hips, but other than that, she was naked.

The violence had been almost entirely confined to her head. There were bruises around her wrists, where she had either been bound or someone had grabbed her, and also a few scratches on her legs and upper arms, but nothing apart from that.

I did my best, but it was almost impossible to reconcile the Flossie I had known, upright and vivacious, with the dead and mutilated husk of a woman on the table before me. I shook my head. "It looks like Flossie, but at the same time it doesn't."

Christopher nodded.

"I've never seen her nude," Crispin said, gaze distant as he looked at the body. "Her face, yes. I could have identified that..."

"Yes, me too. But you never got her out of her clothes?"

The assistant looked a bit shocked as his eyes flicked from Crispin to me and back, probably taken aback at my modern attitudes.

"No," Crispin said. "A snuggle or two in the lift, and in the front seat of my motorcar when I dropped her off places, but that was all. I've seen her all of four times, I think. Maybe five."

"I've seen her a lot more than that," Christopher said, "but never without her clothes."

He glanced at me. "I agree with Pippa. It looks like Flossie, but then again, it doesn't."

I nodded. Crispin tilted his head and opened his mouth, but before he could say anything, the bell outside in reception rang. The mortuary assistant looked at the door, and at us, and at the body, and back at the door.

"Go ahead," I told him graciously. "We won't touch anything."

Indeed, there was no part of me that wanted to touch any part of Flossie at all.

His eyes did the circuit again, from me to Crispin to Christopher to Flossie, and then back to the door as the bell rang again. After another moment's thought, he seemed to reach a conclusion and told us he'd be right back. He left the door open when he left, and that was how I heard the Schlomskys arrive.

Hiram's voice was a lot subdued from his usual American boisterousness when he informed the assistant that he was here to see Miss Florence Schlomsky. There was a pause, during which I assumed the morgue assistant debated as to whether he should ask them to wait, and then ask us to leave, or whether it would be a good idea or not to put all five of us in the same room with Florence's dead body at the same time.

Sarah must have read it as indecision, because she said, "Listen, my good man. That's my daughter you've got back there, and I want to see her."

She sounded strident, but she also sounded stuffy-nosed, as if she had been crying all night. And that was probably what did it. The next second, there were multiple footsteps coming down the hallway towards us.

"Damnation!" Crispin's eyes flicked over the room from side to side, searching for a way out that wasn't the door into the hallway. Barring that, I'm sure he would have been happy to spot a hiding place. When he saw neither, he squared his shoulders and faced the doorway like a little soldier.

Christopher and I exchanged a glance, and stepped towards him: one on each side, slightly in front.

Sarah Schlomsky came through the door first, and rocked back on her heels when she saw us.

Or perhaps when she saw the body. Or a combination of both.

At any rate, Hiram came through the door next, and ran into her. The morgue assistant had the sense to stay outside in the hallway instead of getting involved.

"You!" Hiram snarled. He was staring at Crispin, but then his eyes flicked to Christopher and back, as if he wasn't entirely certain which of them he was upset with.

"We'll go," I said, sidling towards the door on a trajectory that ought to take us past them without actually requiring anyone on either side to step out of their way. Behind me, Christopher nudged Crispin into motion as he brought up the rear.

"Not so fast," Hiram said, lowering his brows. "What are you doing here?"

He hadn't moved out of the doorway yet, and perforce, we had to stop.

"Attempting to identify the body," I told him, which might have been a bit cold-blooded on my part, but it had the benefit of being the truth. "Detective Sergeant Gardiner asked us to stop by."

Hiram looked from me to his daughter's body and back. And flushed. "This is outrageous."

The morgue assistant looked guilty, but didn't move to cover Flossie's body any more than it already was.

"There isn't enough left of her face to identify," I explained, even as I fought back a shudder. "We have to look at the rest."

"And do either of you know what my daughter's body looks like?" Sarah pinned both Christopher and Crispin with a fulminating stare. They both shook their heads, Christopher looking very chastised indeed, and a bit nauseated, while Crispin's face bore a preternatural solemnity that indicated that he, at least, had seen plenty of women's bodies in his life, but wasn't about to admit it right now.

"We've seen her bare arms and legs before," I pointed out. "Although I will say I never noticed the scar."

"Scar?"

I pointed. It was on Flossie's lower arm, at least three inches long, and it was recent enough that both the injury itself, and the stitches that had held it together afterwards, were clearly visible, like a white millipede traveling up Flossie's arm from her wrist to her elbow.

Sarah pulled the tip of a finger down it, tears gathering in her eyes. "She got this in the kidnapping attempt at Vassar a year and a half ago. This is my daughter."

She turned to the morgue assistant and repeated it. "This is my daughter."

He nodded. "Thank you, madam. And may I express my condolences on behalf of the City of London. We are sorry for your loss."

Sarah inclined her head. "Thank you."

There didn't seem to be much we could say after that, and we were intruding on a private moment anyway—the farewell between Florence and her parents—so I tugged on Christopher's sleeve and nodded to the door. He snagged Crispin and then all three of us sidled sideways. The mortuary assistant saw us go, and gave us a brief nod in acknowledgement, but neither of the Schlomskys reacted.

It wasn't until we were practically out of sight, that Sarah Schlomsky's voice reached us. "Miss Darling?"

I stuck my head back into the room. "Yes, Mrs. Schlomsky?"

"We're only here in England for a few more days. We could postpone our departure, but..." She swallowed, "London is no longer a place we want to linger."

No, that was perfectly understandable.

"We'll stay until we can make arrangements to take our

daughter home with us—" She glanced at the morgue assistant, who nodded, "but I could use some help packing up Florence's belongings. Since you were friends..."

She trailed off suggestively.

"Of course," I said, since it was the right thing to do, and furthermore, it was the only thing I could do. It wasn't as if I could refuse. "I would be happy to help."

"Thank you." At least she sounded grateful. "I'll call on you sometime this afternoon, if that suits."

"Please do," I said politely.

So that was that. Sarah turned back to her daughter's body, and we turned into the corridor and out of the mortuary into Golden Lane.

We walked in silence for the first minute or two, just enjoying the summer heat and sunshine after the cloying coldness of the morgue. And when we reached the Hispano-Suiza, parked in the lot beside the mortuary, we stopped for a cigarette and to enjoy the sunshine a bit longer before getting in.

"Was it me," Crispin asked, offering his cigarette case around, "or did something about that not feel right?"

I plucked a fag out of it and nodded. "The fact that Flossie is dead, and we can't even look at her face and recognize it? Yes, St George, I would say that something about that felt very much not right."

He rolled his eyes and turned to Christopher, who took a cigarette with a nod of thanks. "That's not what I meant, Darling, and you know it." Crispin dropped the case back into his pocket and pulled out a lighter.

"What did you mean, then?" I leaned forward so he could light up for me.

"Well..." He hesitated, with the flame two inches from my nose. "The scar, for one thing."

"The one on her arm?" I pointed to the cigarette.

He finally did as he was supposed to with the lighter, and nodded. "I didn't recognize it. And I swear I must have seen Flossie's arm before."

"She does wear opera gloves most of the time," I said, thinking back, "with her evening frocks. Although not always, and not with everything. And I'll admit I never noticed it either."

I blew out a cloud of smoke, and felt my nerves settle.

Christopher shook his head in agreement. "Thanks, Crispin. No, it's not the sort of thing you overlook."

No, it wasn't. Any more than you could overlook the Mensur scar on Wolfgang's face.

Crispin dropped the lighter back into his pocket, and we stood in silence a moment and let the nicotine do its job.

"Perhaps she tried to cover it," I suggested. "With sleeves and gloves if she could, and with makeup if she couldn't. Maybe that's why we never noticed."

Christopher nodded and Crispin shrugged, even as they both looked dissatisfied.

"I know it has been a few days since I saw her," Crispin said after another moment, "and she has perhaps not been fed a lot in the interim, and the opium may have taken a toll, even in just a few days of smoking it..."

I nodded for him to go on.

"—but did she seem a bit... diminished to you?"

"Smaller, do you mean?"

"Ye-e-e-es," Crispin said, dragging it out doubtfully. "Just... less, do you know?"

"Less alive, certainly." I took a drag of my cigarette and blew it out before I continued. "And you're right: they probably didn't feed her a lot, just kept her supplied with enough opium that she wouldn't care. So I wouldn't be surprised if she'd reduced a bit."

Crispin nodded. "And her hair... did it seem a bit— well, dull?"

"I didn't get the impression that they gave her a bath before they gave her back," I said dryly. "Five days of opium smoke probably didn't help, either. She was dirty. So was her hair. It's possible that that's why it looked limp and duller than usual."

Although I had noticed the same thing, so I couldn't say that he was wrong.

"What are you suggesting?" Christopher wanted to know, looking from one to the other of us. "That it wasn't Flossie?"

"Of course it was Flossie," I said. "Her mother identified her."

"From a scar neither of us have seen before."

There was a beat. Then—

"Why would her mother lie?" And if the dead girl wasn't Flossie, who was she?

"Insurance reasons?" Crispin suggested. "Perhaps there's some sort of payout on the ransom?"

"Perhaps. So how would that work? Hiram comes to London and kidnaps his own daughter?" Having gotten the idea from the attempted kidnapping a year and a half ago in New York, perhaps?

"Perhaps," Crispin agreed. "Then he sends a ransom demand to himself. He puts the money in the valise and drops off the valise, but he also gets the driver to pick up the valise again, and then he puts in a claim with his insurance company."

"But he's already a millionaire," Christopher pointed out. "Is he really going to break the law and put his own daughter in danger for a measly fifty thousand dollars?"

"In this scenario, his daughter wasn't in danger. She was in on it."

"And the dead girl is...?"

"Some random waif they picked up off the street?" Crispin suggested. "Someone with a surface resemblance to Florence who would be happy to spend a few days in a Southwark flop with as much free dope as she could smoke or sniff or otherwise use?"

"Or perhaps it's Ruth," I said. "The missing maid. She has to be somewhere, after all, and if Flossie's in on it, maybe they decided to murder the maid. Maybe the whole thing was a setup from the start."

There was a pause.

"Or maybe we're all mental," Christopher said, "and it's Flossie who is dead, and her mother knows her better than we do, and we simply never noticed the scar, because she took pains that we wouldn't."

Well, yes. That was possible, too.

Crispin tossed what was left of his cigarette to the ground and put his shoe on it. "If the excitement is over, I think I'd better head back to Wiltshire before my father sends out a search party. Or worse, drives up to Town himself."

"Has he done anything to replace Wilkins?" Without a chauffeur, I didn't think we had to worry, since His Grace wasn't about to motor his own car to London.

Crispin grimaced. "One of the grooms obliges when Father wants to go somewhere."

"I'll take a lift home," I said, "after we stop by Scotland Yard and sign our statements. I want to be there when Mrs. Schlomsky arrives."

Crispin nodded. "I know you'd never pass up an opportunity to sneak and pry, Darling."

"Naturally not. As if you wouldn't do the same, St George. I haven't forgotten the secret passage, you know." And all the secrets he had learned, eavesdropping on his grandfather's conversations with everyone else back in April.

"But of course." Crispin opened the car door. "In you go, Darling."

I went, and a moment later, so did all of us, in the direction of Whitehall and Scotland Yard.

CHAPTER TWENTY

SARAH SCHLOMSKY TURNED up in time for tea, but declined the offer of any. "No, thank you, Miss Darling," she told me as she stepped out of the lift on the second floor, flat key in hand. "That's not a custom we hold to in Toledo."

"What do you eat in the middle of the afternoon in Toledo?"

"We don't," Sarah said. "I don't hold with eating between meals. It'll ruin your dinner."

"Tea *is* a meal," I said, but I'm not sure that she heard me. Or perhaps she did, but simply chose to ignore me.

"In America, this is happy hour. People—" She said it as if they were a lesser life form, "—drink."

Drink? "I thought America was in the midst of prohibition." At least that's what Flossie had told me. How much she enjoyed being somewhere where she could go out and get a cocktail, when at home, she would have to sneak around.

Or perhaps I had chalked that up to being a facet of prohibition, when in fact, it was her parents she was hiding her drinking from.

"People still drink," Sarah said as she lead the way down the hall towards Flossie's door. "At home, at parties, at speakeasies. There's no way to legislate morality, more's the pity."

She inserted the key in the door and twisted it, and pushed the door open.

"Here we are." She stopped in the foyer and looked around. I did the same. Everything looked the same as it had done the last time I'd been here, as well as the last time she had been here. They were not the same time, of course, but she didn't need to know that.

"If you could start in here." She indicated Flossie's closet, aka the back bedroom. "None of this is anything I would want to bring home with me. Fold and stack everything, if you please, and we'll find a charity for it. Or perhaps some of the nice young ladies at the embassy would like something pretty to wear..."

Something seemed to strike her, and she turned to look at me, a quick up and down of my figure. "Anything you see that you like, Miss Darling, please feel free to keep for yourself."

"I'm afraid they're not really my colors," I said apologetically. "I'm not so fond of pink. And Flossie was a bit more... um... well-rounded than I am."

Sarah arched her brows. "Surely not? My daughter wasn't hefty."

"Oh, of course not." I would never say such a thing even if it were true, and in this case it wasn't. Flossie had definitely had a more womanly figure than I do, though. I tend towards the boyish, which is perfect for the current tubular fashions. Flossie had been more buxom, more of the Edwardian or even Victorian type. Her dresses would look like sacks on me, and as far as Christopher goes—whose color is definitely pink—they would be indecently short. And while Christopher might not mind that—he has good legs—mid-thigh is just a step too far, even for 1926. With the way hemlines are creeping upwards, we may get there eventually, but not for a while yet.

"If you can find a suitcase or trunk in this mess—" Sarah gave the room and all the lovely, expensive clothes a disparaging look, "tuck it away in there. Otherwise, just stack it on the bed, and we'll dig up a box later."

I nodded. "There's a trunk room in the cellar. I could go see if Flossie stored any of her luggage there?"

"If you don't mind," Sarah said, looking relieved, "that would be helpful. I'll start in the back, meanwhile."

"Of course." I headed down in the lift and informed Evans that I needed access to the trunk room. "There's something of Flossie's there, I assume?"

"Miss Schlomsky had a trunk when she arrived," Evans nodded, "and a valise. No furniture. That all arrived later, brand new."

Of course. Flossie wouldn't have crossed the Atlantic with furniture in tow.

Although from what her mother had told me, Flossie had bought her entire wardrobe new too, it seemed.

I took the key, and then the lift down to the cellars. They're dark and gloomy—the boiler is down there, along with the innards for the lift mechanism and the electrical board for the building and other things of that nature. The trunk room is directly opposite the lift, and I inserted the key in the lock and pulled the door open, only to find myself facing a wall of luggage.

I had never been inside before. When Christopher and I moved in, it had been with a trunk each of clothes from home. A lorry had followed with spare furnishings, and that lorry had taken the trunks back to Wiltshire once they were empty, and had stored them in the big box room at Sutherland Hall until we needed them again. Which we didn't expect we would. We had taken short weekend trips so far, to Wiltshire and Dorset and other places, but a weekender bag had always sufficed for that. A trunk is really only something you need for long voyages or big moves.

A lot of residents of the Essex House Mansions seemed to own trunks, and the trunk room was not organized in a manner that made sense to me. It took me several long minutes to walk around the room peering at each trunk in turn before I found Flossie's, marked with her last name and the number of her flat. I dragged it out behind me, locked the door, and then took the key back to Evans, before I took the lift—and trunk—up to the second floor and dragged it down the hallway and into Flossie's flat.

Mrs. Schlomsky heard me come through the door—or heard the trunk scrape across the floor—and she came into the foyer to greet me. "You found it. Good."

And then she got a look at the trunk, and her brows drew together. "That isn't Florence's trunk."

"It has her name on it," I wheezed. I straightened my back and tick-tocked my hips to work out the kinks before I added, "And her flat number. Look."

Sarah looked at it, but shook her head. "I can see that, Miss Darling. But I'm telling you, this isn't Florence's trunk. Not the one she left Toledo with."

I eyed it doubtfully. "Perhaps she bought herself new luggage once she arrived?"

"Why would she do that? Surely the time to buy new luggage is before you leave on a trip?"

It was a rhetorical question, clearly, because she went on without waiting for my answer. It was just as well, since of course I would have had to agree with her. No one buys luggage when they come home from traveling. Even if something's wrong with said luggage, the trunk goes in storage not to be considered again until the next time it is needed, and *then* a new trunk is acquired.

"Besides," Sarah said, still eyeing it critically, "this trunk is hardly new, is it? It has stickers and scrapes and scratches."

"Perhaps Florence bought it used?"

She gave me a look, as she should, really, since the suggestion made no sense. If Flossie wanted to replace her existing trunk, of course she would buy a brand new one.

"Could she be holding it for someone else? Ruth, perhaps?"

"If that's the case," Sarah said, hands on her hips and eyes still on the trunk, "where is Florence's trunk? Did you look to see whether there was another one with her name on it?"

I hadn't, although I had already searched more than half the luggage room when I'd come across this trunk. And surely they would have been stored together? "I can go back," I offered.

Sarah shook her head. "If it was there, you would have seen it. And no, to answer your other question, it isn't Ruth's trunk. Hers was black."

While this was brown. "What about Flossie's? What did that look like?"

"It was green," Sarah said. "Dark green, and bigger than this. A proper steamer trunk."

So this—clearly used, clearly brown—trunk didn't belong to either of the women who supposedly lived in this mansion flat.

"You are..." I cleared my throat. "You're absolutely certain that the women we saw today was your daughter, aren't you?"

"Of course," Sarah said, eyes flashing. "I'd hardly mistake my own daughter, would I? She lived with me for more than twenty years. Besides, there was the scar. I told you."

I nodded. "I'd never noticed the scar before. None of us had."

"Well, she'd had it for at least a year and a half," Sarah said. "She got it during that botched kidnapping attempt at Vassar year before last. Eight stitches. I know my daughter, Miss Darling!"

"Of course you do," I soothed. "I'm just trying to figure out why her clothes are different, and why her trunk is different, and why I've never seen her scar before, or her maid, for that matter..."

And when I put it like that, the explanation was obvious, wasn't it? If Sarah wasn't lying, and the body in the morgue truly was Florence Schlomsky, then the woman I had known for six months, the woman who had kissed Crispin in the lift and called Uncle Harold 'Your Highness'... was someone else.

"Just out of curiosity," I said, "can you describe Ruth to me?"

"The maid?"

Of course the maid. "You said she came to London with Flossie, correct?"

"She came over two weeks before Florence," Sarah corrected. "Someone had to be here to get things set up. We sent Ruth."

"And she was the one who contracted for the flat and arranged the furnishings?"

Sarah nodded. "Here and at the cottage in Thornton Heath."

"The...?"

"Cottage in Thornton Heath," Sarah repeated. "A country cottage. A chance to get out of the city to somewhere more pleasant." She smiled. "Ivy Cottage in Thornton Heath. It sounds rustic and peaceful, doesn't it?"

First of all, the Flossie I had known—not Flossie at all, as I now suspected—would have had no desire to get out of the city to the country. And secondly, no matter how rustic and peaceful it may have sounded—

"Thornton Heath is less than eight miles from Charing Cross," I said. And it was closer than that to Tooley Street and to the shack in Southwark. Someone could probably get from Southwark to Thornton Heath in twenty minutes after midnight on a Saturday.

If Flossie's parents had been paying for a cottage in Thornton Heath, it wasn't so Flossie—or the person pretending to be Flossie—could have a place in which to weekend. Nobody weekends in Thornton Heath. Sarah was probably imagining Dartmoor and *Wuthering Heights* or somewhere else equally picturesque, while in actuality, we were talking about a small town just south of London proper.

I hadn't seen any indication of rent for a cottage in Thornton Heath the other day, when Christopher and I had gone through the flat and all of Flossie's belongings with a fine toothed comb. No mentions of it, nor any paperwork related to it. That seemed a bit suspicious, if Sarah and Hiram had been paying for the place.

"Did you go visit the cottage this week?" I asked. "To check if Flossie was there, maybe?"

Sarah shook her head. "I had no idea it was so close to London. Florence and Ruth called it a country cottage in their letters. I assumed that it was... well, in the country."

Of course. "Flossie—the woman I thought was Flossie— never mentioned a cottage." I thought for a moment. Flossie— my Flossie, whoever she really was—had lived here, at the Essex House Mansions. I hadn't seen her every day, but I had seen her enough that I knew that she rarely spent time anywhere else. And this was clearly an occupied flat we were standing in, not a place someone spent a minority of their time. "You're certain the letters were from your daughter?"

"I know my daughter's hand," Sarah said, and she was undoubtedly right. Besides, if the girl in the morgue had been the real Florence, she had been alive until sometime last night. She would have been able to write letters to her mother.

Whether she had been in charge of what went into them, was a totally different story.

"Ruth also wrote to you?"

She nodded. "To keep us updated on things that were going on with Florence, you know. And the household expenses and such."

Ruth was in on the deception, then. Not that this whole thing could have been effected without her, really, but she would have had to have been, if the Schlomskys had heard from her throughout the past year.

"You never described Ruth," I said.

"Ruth?" She sounded confused.

"The maid. What does she look like? Or did, the last time you saw her?" If Flossie—the real Flossie—was the body in the morgue, she had spent her time in England somewhere other than here. But someone else had been spending her time here, pretending to be Flossie Schlomsky. That someone might have been Ruth.

"Short," Sarah said promptly, "and skinny, with a plain face and dishwater blond hair. It was long last time I saw her—I don't hold with bobbed hair on the servants; I much prefer a neat bun—but I suppose she might have changed that by now."

Something buzzed quickly into my head, but buzzed equally quickly out the other side. I decided not to try to chase it down. We were in the middle of an important conversation. "But she's definitely not a brunette?"

Sarah shook her head. "Definitely not. Dirty blond."

Not the woman I had known as Flossie, then. She had been

neither short nor skinny, and she definitely hadn't been a blonde, even a dirty one.

"Someone should go to Thornton Heath," I said.

Sarah looked at me.

"It's only a half hour away. And I should send a message to Tom. He's probably back at Scotland Yard by now."

They must be finished with the crime scene in Southwark, surely. It had been hours and hours since they began work on it. A couple of hours since we left the morgue and headed home, too. Enough of them for Crispin to have made it to Wiltshire, or at least somewhere close.

"And then we'll fetch Hiram and go to Thornton Heath," Sarah said.

I nodded, still distracted with my thoughts. We'd send a message to Tom, fetch Hiram, and go to Thornton Heath. And then we'd see what was what.

TEN MINUTES LATER, we were in a Hackney on our way to the Savoy. Our shared flat had been empty when I went to fetch my handbag, so Christopher must still be with Tom, wherever that was. We'd get to Whitehall eventually, and it wouldn't be too long, but the Strand was on the way, and so we stopped there first. Sarah asked the driver to wait, and I stayed with the cab while I waited for her to fetch Hiram and come back.

And so it was that I was leaning against a Hackney on Savoy Court when I heard my name spoken in a German accent. "*Freulein* Darling."

"*Graf* Wolfgang." I put on my best smile as I turned towards him, all the while wishing that I had put on a slightly nicer frock this morning. At that time we had been headed to the mortuary, though, to identify a dead body, and so I hadn't wanted to put on anything I really liked, since there was a chance that I might have to throw it away afterwards. I already had a hard time with the evening frock I had been wearing last night. I had loved it when I bought it, but after what had happened, I was ambivalent about wearing it again. It would always now remind me of Flossie, and of a woman with her face beaten to unrecognizability by a blunt instrument.

At any rate, there was Wolfgang, *Graf* von Natterdorff, in a stylish blue summer jacket, with a yellow patterned necktie and yellow pocket square. The combination played up both the blue of his eyes and the gold of his hair. He was carrying a walking stick, as well, a bit less ornate than the one Hiram Schlomsky habitually held—no buffalo head on this one, just a simple silver grip at the top—and he looked very handsome indeed, as evidenced by the many eyes that lingered upon him.

His lingered upon me. "Are you looking for me?"

There was just a hint of self-satisfaction in the question, as if it wasn't really a question at all.

"I'm afraid not," I said apologetically, "although I'm always happy to see you."

I simpered. He simpered back, and I added, "I'm waiting for Mr. and Mrs. Hiram Schlomsky to come back downstairs. We're on the trail of a criminal."

The smirk dropped off his face. "A criminal?"

"Their daughter was killed last night. We're going to her country cottage to see if we can find a clue to her killers' whereabouts."

Wolfgang blinked. "Alone?"

"There will be the three of us. And we'll stop by Scotland Yard on the way, to leave a message for Detective Sergeant Gardiner. It's his case." And if he was there, we'd take him with us. Naturally.

"And how will he feel about you chasing down clues on your own?" Wolfgang wanted to know, severely.

I imagined I would be hearing about it later, if Tom wasn't accessible and the Schlomskys and I ended up going to Thornton Heath by ourselves. But Tom wasn't in charge of me —I was a grown woman in control of my own destiny, not to mention my own safety—and it wasn't as if I wouldn't have tried to let him know.

"I'll go with you," Wolfgang said, just as the Schlomskys passed through the revolving doors and came into view. He didn't wait for me to agree, just turned to them with that formal little bow. "Madam. *Mein Herr*. May I introduce myself? I am *Graf* Wolfgang Ulrich Albrecht *von und zu* Natterdorff, and I am this lady's protector."

Oh, was he really? As if I didn't already have more than I wanted of those.

Hiram eyed him shrewdly for a second before— "Hiram Schlomsky. My wife Sarah."

Wolfgang clicked his heels. "A pleasure."

"Likewise," Hiram said, although with the way he looked at Wolfgang, bright-eyed and with his head tilted to the side, I thought he seemed more fascinated by Wolfgang's essential foreignness than he was strictly pleased at making the acquaintance.

"I shall accompany you on your quest," Wolfgang informed him.

It was presented as a fact, not a request at all, and Hiram's eyebrows arched at the high-handedness. He didn't quibble, however, just grunted, "Suit yourself," before handing his wife into the motorcar.

"Come along, Miss Darling," Sarah said, and her tone also brooked no interference. I slid into the backseat after Hiram. Wolfgang climbed in beside the chauffeur, and off we went.

Scotland Yard was next, ten minutes or so later, and as expected, Tom and Christopher were not sitting around waiting for me. Nor were Detective Sergeant Ian Finchley or Chief Inspector Pendennis. They were all off in a group somewhere, investigating, I assumed. I asked the constable on duty to pass along a message to Tom should he appear, and then we headed south.

The mews house in Southwark was also empty, except for a uniformed bobby standing guard outside the door. He informed us that the on-site investigation had concluded, but the crime scene had not been released, and so it would be guarded twenty-four hours a day, seven days a week, until Chief Inspector Pendennis decided that he was done and could let it go. The Schlomskys both looked gratified about this, and I guess that made sense, seeing as it was the place where their daughter had died.

I told this constable, too, to pass on a message to Tom should he return, and then I got back into the Hackney again for the journey to Thornton Heath.

IT ISN'T A LONG DRIVE, and a shorter one when you're in South London to begin with. It was less than forty-five minutes before we were rolling slowly through the hamlet of Thornton Heath, keeping our eyes peeled for the cottage the Schlomskys had been paying for since Flossie stepped off the boat in Southampton ten months ago.

"There." It was Sarah who spotted it first, perhaps because she was the most motivated to find it. "The small brick house over there. Is that it?"

"That must be it," I agreed, while the Hackney driver turned the Austin towards the curb outside.

The house was smallish and in no way ostentatious, situated on the edge of town with no close neighbors. It was also about as far from a picturesque country cottage as one could get. A detached two stories of red brick, square and blocky, with no more than two rooms up and two down, at a guess. There wasn't a flower in sight, but plenty of weeds.

Whoever had chosen this house, and had chosen to live here, didn't seem like it could be the same person who had chosen, and chosen to live in, the Essex House Mansion flat.

"The windows are dirty," Sarah said with a grimace.

I nodded. "If this is Ruth's house, she's been falling down on the job."

"I always suspected she was lazy," Sarah said. Her eyes burned as she looked at the house. "Do you think this is where they kept my daughter?"

"They didn't keep her in the house in Southwark. Not long-term." Not enough furniture, no running water.

No, the mews in Southwark seemed more like somewhere where they had gone to dump the body. They must have taken Flossie from here and driven her there on the day of the murder —yesterday—and then killed her and left her for us to find.

"There's a garage in the back," Hiram pointed out.

So there was. Small and dilapidated, with a few roofing tiles missing, but a garage, built with the same red bricks as the house. And with enough room to store an Austin Heavy Twelve-Four, should someone want to.

"I'll go peek inside," I said.

Sarah squinted at me. "Are you sure that's wise?"

"I sincerely doubt they're here," I said. "After last night, surely they're halfway to Calais by now."

That's what I would have done. Picked up the money, packed up anything important—not necessarily in that order—

and made tracks. Not only did they have kidnapping on their record now, but they had murder, as well. Whether that had been a facet of the plan from the beginning or not, it was done now, and the best they could do for themselves was get as far away from here as they could, as quickly as possible.

"We'll both go," Wolfgang said. He got out of the Hackney first, and then held the door for me.

"They're more likely to see us if there are two of us," I pointed out.

He gave me a look, and it was obvious that he wasn't going to relent, so I gave up on trying to talk him out of it and headed down the narrow drive that ran along the side of the small house to the smaller garage.

As it turned out, there were no windows on this side of the house, so there was no danger that we'd be seen by anyone inside. And the nearest neighbor was far enough away, and well enough hidden by overgrown hedges and untrimmed bushes, that discovery was unlikely from that angle, as well. I walked down the drive as unconcernedly as I would along Essex Street on a sunny afternoon, with Wolfgang right behind.

"Careful," he muttered when we reached the small garage. "Let me."

The small building had a pair of dilapidated doors in dire need of paint, inset with a row of windows at the top. I wasn't quite tall enough to look through them, and while Christopher would have lifted me—and Crispin likely would have too, all the while grumbling about having to get on his knees in front of me—Wolfgang stepped up on his own tiptoes and peered through the dirty glass on my behalf.

"A motorcar," he said after a moment's perusal.

"Like a Hackney?"

"Hmm." Wolfgang glanced over his shoulder at it. "Perhaps."

"Try the handle."

I took a step closer as he grasped it and turned. The door into the garage opened, and I got a glimpse of one headlamp and the front grille of a black Austin before I nudged Wolfgang out of the way.

He attempted to get in front of me, but I slipped around him. "We must make certain there's no one inside."

I stepped into the darkness of the musty garage, and felt a shiver of revulsion slither down my spine. This felt too much like last night for comfort.

The garage was empty, however. Or not empty: there was the motorcar, and scraps of wood, and other tools, and old oil cans, and spare tires... but no one was in the car, dead or alive. Whoever the killer was—and my money was on the chap in the cap who had driven the car yesterday—he hadn't seen fit to murder anyone else in the past few hours.

Or at least, if he had, he hadn't left them in the garage.

There was no valise in the motorcar. I did make certain of that. There was no bloody tire iron, either. Or a bloody wrench or anything else that could have served as the murder weapon.

By the time I came back out in the drive after peering through all the windows of the Austin, Hiram and Sarah had emerged from the Hackney, too, and had joined us.

"Anything?" Sarah wanted to know.

I shook my head. "The motorcar looks like the one from last night. But there's nobody in it. And no money."

"Money?" Wolfgang repeated.

"Fifty thousand dollars in ransom."

His eyes widened, but I waved the explanation off before he could ask. "The bloke who picked it up must have taken it inside the house. Or more likely taken it with him when he left. They must have had another motorcar waiting, I suppose. This one was used to transport poor Flossie, so they left it behind."

A shadow passed across Sarah's face at the reminder, and I wished I'd kept myself from rambling my thoughts out loud. To distract from having stuffed my foot in my mouth, I opened it again. "I wonder whether they left any clues inside."

We all turned to look at the back door of the cottage.

CHAPTER TWENTY-ONE

I'LL BE HONEST, I fully expected the Thornton Heath cottage to be empty. There was no reason to think it wouldn't be. These people had kidnapped a woman, had kept her locked up for ten months (or at least I thought they had), had turned her into an opium addict to keep her contained and quiet, and had extorted the best part of fifty thousand dollars from her father before murdering her in cold blood. (Extremely cold.) There was no logical reason why they would still be here, especially considering that it was the Schlomskys who had footed the bill for the cottage, and they could reasonably be expected to think of its existence at some point.

As a result, I had no qualms whatsoever about walking over to the back door and wrapping my hand around the knob and twisting. And when the door didn't budge, I also had no qualms about trying to come up with another way to break in. Perhaps there was an open window somewhere, that we—or that one of us; me, for preference—could climb through to get inside.

I stepped back and peered at the back of the house. If I had to slither in through a window, it would be safer to do it back here. There were no neighbors in sight—really, whoever had picked the cottage had done an outstanding job of finding an isolated, private place—and while the street out front seemed pretty quiet on a Sunday afternoon, it was still a street, and someone might come along it. Not to mention that the Hackney driver was still sitting out there, waiting for us to finish our business at the cottage.

No, if I was going to break and enter, it was much safer to do it back here.

"Boards on the window up there," Hiram muttered, gesturing to one of the first floor windows.

I followed the direction of his finger to the upper story, and nodded. Yes, indeed. Someone had nailed a lot of boards across the window from one edge of the frame to the other, probably sometime in the last year. Approximately ten months ago, I'd say.

"That must be where…"

I stopped without finishing the sentence. There was no need, after all. Hiram and Sarah could figure it out for themselves as easily as I could. If this was where Flossie—the real Flossie—had been kept prisoner since she arrived on English soil, that must be the room she had been kept in.

Sarah's eyes burned as she looked at the boards, jaw tight, while Hiram's hand clenched around his cane until his knuckles were white. I didn't envy the kidnappers whenever he came face to face with them.

"There's an open cellar window," Wolfgang pointed, and we all turned our attention to it.

Well, that solved the problem of who was going to go inside the house first, anyway. Not that anyone had discussed it so far, but I fully expected Wolfgang to put up a fight if I suggested that I go. Christopher would have fought, and so would Crispin have.

In this case there was no need. The window was small, and sunk below ground, into a narrow well lined with the same brick as the house itself. Hiram and Sarah were both too rotund to fit, and there was no way Wolfgang's shoulders would make it through. It would have to be me.

"Lower me down," I said, heading towards it.

"Absolutely not," Wolfgang answered.

I looked at him over my shoulder. "None of the rest of you will fit. It'll have to be me."

He shook his head. "I'm sorry, *Freulein* Darling, but I will not send you into the house by yourself. What if someone is there?"

"No one will be there. They would have to be stupid to still be here." I stopped in front of the window well, expectantly.

Wolfgang shook his head. "No."

"Fine." I crouched down on the edge. "I'll do it myself."

"I'll open the back door," Wolfgang said.

I peered at him, my heart sinking. Had I misunderstood something, and he wasn't one of the heroes? The man in the cap last night... could it have been Wolfgang? Had he made our acquaintance that day at the Savoy because he knew Christopher and I lived down the hall from Flossie—the fake Flossie—and he wanted to find out what we knew?

"What do you..." I began, and changed it in favor of, "do you have a key?"

"Of course not," Wolfgang said, with the suggestion of an eye roll. "If you would be so kind as to lend me two of your hairpins, I will endeavor to use them to pick the lock."

"Oh." My hand flew to my hair. "Of course."

That was much better. We could all go inside together. And of course he was one of the heroes. How could he not be, with such a dashing scar?

I pulled the Kerbigrips out of my bob and handed them

over, before tucking my loose hair behind my ear. "I've never seen anyone pick a lock before."

"It's a useful skill," Wolfgang said modestly as he wandered towards the back door with me right on his heels.

I imagined so. Not that I had ever imagined, up until a few months ago, at any rate, that I would ever have need for such a skill. But I watched avidly as he straightened one Kirbigrip into a stick and inserted it into the lock, and then inserted the other and began wiggling them both.

The Schlomskys, too, gathered around to watch. Hiram looked fascinated, just the same as I imagined I did, although Sarah seemed less impressed. She didn't comment on the many (illegal) uses of such a skill, but I'm certain she thought about them.

It was quick, anyway. Less than a minute, and Wolfgang slid the back door open, soundlessly. "I'll go first."

"By all means," I told him, and followed him into the house's kitchen.

And that was when I had to give up on the comforting notion that we were alone. There was scrambling from above our heads, the sound of rapid footsteps and shrill female voices, along with the lower (but no less startled) tones of a man.

MY FIRST INSTINCT was to back out of the kitchen and run. If we were right, and this was the correct cottage, and we hadn't made some sort of terrible mistake, the people upstairs were kidnappers and murderers. They had nothing to lose, and I didn't think we wanted to involve ourselves with them.

That was the worst case scenario. The best case scenario was that we had made a mistake and the people upstairs were innocent strangers, and all we had done was break into their house unprovoked. That possibility was better than coming face to face with murderers, but it was hardly a desirable thing to have done, even so.

So yes, I wanted to flee. Unfortunately, Hiram and Sarah had entered the kitchen now too, and between them behind me and Wolfgang in front, there was nowhere I could go. Especially when Hiram fastened his eyes on the ceiling, from behind which all the noise was emanating, and his face darkened to an angry brick red. His mustache bristled.

"Hiram!" Sarah said in warning.

He flicked her a look. "They killed our daughter, Sadie."

"We don't know that," Sarah said, although there wasn't much conviction in her voice. We all believed the same thing, and that was that we had caught the kidnappers in *flagrante*.

She had a point, however. We couldn't attack them without being certain. If Hiram went on the warpath and started swinging his cane, and he hurt somebody, and then that somebody turned out to be innocent of any crimes, we would be the ones in the wrong. Not only had we broken into someone's home, but we had attacked them.

I turned to Sarah and lowered my voice. "Are you certain this is the house?"

"It's the right address," Sarah said. "And it said Ivy Cottage on the gate."

"And you're certain you've paid for it?"

She nodded. "Positive. Ruth contracted for an apartment in London and a cottage in the country. I didn't realize the country—" She grimaced, "was quite so close to the city, but this is it. Ivy Cottage in Thornton Heath."

Well, then we weren't breaking and entering, at least. Not if the Schlomskys were the rightful renters of Ivy Cottage, and the ones who had been paying for it.

"Enough of this," Hiram said and pushed past me. He

raised his voice in a bellow. "Show yourselves, you yellow-bellied side-winders! Stand and fight!"

His voice echoed through the small house, and the scramble upstairs intensified. The voices rose in a sharp crescendo, and then steps entered the staircase and came clattering down. Hiram took a tighter grip on his cane and faced the doorway. Wolfgang took a step forward, next to him, so the two of them could stand side by side, protectively before Sarah and myself.

In the front of the house, someone took the last two steps of the staircase in a jump and then bounded through the receiving room into the dining room, where he became visible through the kitchen door. Meanwhile, lighter steps also descended the staircase above our heads, but at a more decorous pace.

The young man was clad in a tweed suit, but was hatless, and the light from the window shone on a head of heavily brilliantined black hair. His eyes were also black, or appeared so: wide and startled, the pupils enormous and surrounded by a thin ring of what might have been brown or hazel. He had a narrow face with a narrow jaw, and he was pale, but looked like he might have naturally olive skin, and the result was an unfortunate resemblance to porridge. He had a cricket bat clutched in one hand, knuckles white, and now he raised it threateningly.

"What are you doing here? This is my house!"

"That's him," I said. There hadn't been much light last night, and I had only seen him from the top of the St Olave's church tower, but the tweed suit was the same, and the general outline was the same, and so was his bearing and the way he moved. "That's the man who picked up the ransom."

His eyes flicked to me, and they hardened from anxious and startled to angry. But before he could respond, assuming he had wanted to, Hiram flung himself forward with a roar, cane swinging. It was all the young man could do to get his cricket bat up in time to save himself from having his skull split open.

As he stumbled back with a wordless bellow, the sound was echoed by a scream from the front of the house. "Sid! No!"

The call distracted Hiram for just long enough that the cane failed to make contact with Sid's head. Hiram stumbled forward, his equilibrium upset by the change, and then it was Sid's turn to swing the bat. It connected with Hiram's calf, and the latter stumbled back, swearing. Sid jumped back up to his feet, and then the screamer burst through the door from the front hall and staircase into the receiving room, and we got our first look at her.

And—

"Ruth!" Sarah said, and her voice was somewhere between shocked, appalled, and disappointed.

Ruth paid her no mind whatsoever, just flung herself at Hiram, claws out. And I do mean it literally: her fingers were curved like talons, and she was raking her nails down his cheek.

Even as I flung myself forward to keep her from sinking her claws into Hiram's face, I recognized her. Although the last— and first—time I'd seen her, she had looked quite different, in an expensive ensemble of royal blue chiffon with polka dots, standing in the lobby of the Essex House Mansions, waiting for Flossie for an evening at the theatre.

Now, a scowl contorted her plain face into something distinctly harpy-like. She was hatless, so I could see the dish-water blond hair Sarah had described—cut into a simple Dutch Boy that had nothing at all in common with Lady Laetitia Marsden's ditto. Laetitia, much as it pains me to admit it, has a lovely head of sleek, jet black, shiny hair that's regularly trimmed (probably with the help of a ruler) and which frames her face in a way that manages to simultaneously bring out her high cheekbones, the sleek line of her jaw, and eyes the blue of cornflowers. I may dislike her, but she's an exceptionally pretty woman.

Ruth wasn't pretty, nor was her hair particularly attractive. It was neither as sleek nor as shiny as Lady Laetitia's, and it hung limp around her plain, rather doughy face.

All of this ran through my head as I grappled with her, trying to catch her wrists to keep her nails from Hiram's face, at the same time as I did my best to haul her away from him. Hiram, meanwhile, swung about him with the cane, not caring who he hit, so I had to dodge that, as well, and now yet another individual joined the fray.

I heard a shriek, and the clacking of heels across the floor, a staccato, rapid rhythm, and the next moment, a hand had landed in my hair and fisted a handful of it. A second later I was yanked backwards, away from Ruth and Hiram. I squawked, outraged, but kept my grip on Ruth and pulled her back with me.

I heard a scraping sound, like metal on wood, and something from Wolfgang in German, but I was too busy to pay attention to it. I was already preoccupied with not losing my grip on Ruth while at the same time trying to dislodge whoever —not-Flossie?—was behind me. As a result, I was hanging onto Ruth with one hand, while I jabbed the other elbow backwards into the body of the woman behind me. She was soft, quite not-Flossie like in body shape, and as a result, what I was doing seemed not to have much of an effect. I wasn't able to hit her where it hurt.

Sarah had flung herself into the fray now, as well, but she also concentrated on Ruth, perhaps because Ruth had attacked Hiram, or perhaps simply because Ruth was someone she knew. Ruth must have betrayed Flossie, the real Flossie, and betrayed the Schlomskys, or we wouldn't be here.

This all sounds rather calm and collected, I expect. It

wasn't. It was an absolute, full on brawl, complete with screams and thuds, swearing from the men and shrieking from the women, furniture breaking and people rolling on the ground pounding on one another. I may make it sound orderly and chronological, but it was anything but. It also took place over a much shorter period than it takes to write or read—or for that matter experience. I can't imagine that it was much more than a minute or two from beginning to end.

The end came when something heavy hit the front door of the house, and then hit it again. In the back of my—admittedly rattled—mind, I suppose I probably assumed it to be the Hackney driver. We had left him outside on the road and requested him to wait for us—the last thing we wanted, was to be stuck in the wilderness of Thornton Heath with no way back to London. If he had heard the sounds of the brawl, it might make sense that he would come to our rescue.

That was if I had been able to string those kinds of thoughts together into a sentence, which of course I wasn't. By then, Sarah Schlomsky had taken Ruth out of my hands, quite literally, and had knocked her to the ground and was beating on her with her handbag. Sarah, I mean. She was quite a bit heavier than Ruth, and was sitting on top of her, giving Ruth no opportunity to buck her off. Ruth was squealing and trying to cover her face from Sarah's patent leather bag, but that was all she could do.

I, meanwhile, had my hands full with fake Flossie. And there the situation was quite different. I've always been a couple of inches taller, but she has always had me beat by a stone or two. As soon as I let go of Ruth in favor of throwing off the imposter, the fake Flossie had turned her attention to trying to throttle me. There was hair pulling and kicking and screaming and rolling, and hands wrapped around my throat, trying to squeeze the breath out of me. Black spots flickered in front of my eyes, and in the middle of it, as I said, the front door burst open and several sets of footsteps pounded into the front hall, and from there into the receiving room, and dining room, and kitchen.

"Police!" a voice bellowed. "Don't move!"

The light caught on something metallic that whistled through the air in my direction. Fake Flossie squealed as if she'd been stabbed—I found out later that she actually had been—and collapsed on top of me. I made a sound that was half scream, half moan, and tried to scramble out from under the limp body that was pinning me down, but I couldn't shift the—forgive the expression—dead weight.

Until someone wrenched her off me, and I was lifted to my feet.

"Philippa!" Wolfgang's voice said, and pulled me close to his chest.

I sagged in his hold for a moment—long enough to get a whiff of cigarette smoke and laundry soap and starch—before another pair of hands grabbed me and yanked me backwards. And then I found myself wrapped in Christopher's arms while he berated Wolfgang over my head.

"Good God, Natterdorff, have you no sense? Who brings a sword to a fist fight?"

Sword?

I tried to turn around so I could look for the sword, but Christopher was holding me too tightly. His frame was trembling, and so was his voice, and while I suspect that Wolfgang probably heard it as anger, I knew better: it was a reaction to fear. He had come into the house and seen me and been afraid of what had happened to me.

"You could have chopped Pippa's head off!" Christopher continued. "You came within a few inches of killing my cousin!"

"I was—" Wolfgang protested, but Christopher was beyond listening to reason.

"If anything had happened to her, we would have killed you, you realize that, don't you? Crispin or Francis or I, or my father... one of us would have murdered you in cold blood if you had hurt her!"

"Christopher," I muttered against his shoulder, at the same time as Tom's voice uttered a warning, "Kit."

I could clearly feel Christopher's reluctance, but he shut his mouth. And opened it again, to talk to me this time. "Are you all right, Pippa? He didn't get you, did he?"

I shook my head. "I have no idea what you're talking about. But no, nothing hurts."

That wasn't strictly true. I could feel the ache of blossoming bruises pretty much everywhere, and my scalp still tingled from having handfuls of my hair pulled viciously.

"There's blood on your face," Christopher said worriedly, peering at me.

I tilted my head back to peer back up at him. "I don't think it's mine."

He shook his head, but his eyes were still worried.

"Someone brought a sword to a fist fight?"

"Natterdorff," Christopher said, at the same time as Wolfgang cleared his throat.

"My apologies, Philippa. I didn't think I was close enough to harm you. It was not my intention to put you in danger."

Of course not. "I'm sure I wasn't in any danger," I said. And changed it to, "Or not from you. She was the one who tried to strangle me."

I straightened and took a step back so I could survey the damage we had done to the dining room and the aftermath of the brawl.

Christopher let go reluctantly, but he allowed me to step away, even as his eyes stayed on me.

Wolfgang was standing a few feet away, still clutching... yes, that was a sword in his hand. The handle was the same as that of the cane, so the blade must have been hidden inside it. A sword stick. How quaint and last century.

It must have been effective, though, because I was alive and well, while fake Flossie was sitting with her back against the wall clutching her upper arm, where blood had soaked through the pink sleeve of her frock. Her eyes were teary—I'm sure it must hurt—but they were also hot and angry. She sat quietly, however, with her mouth compressed into a thin line.

Next to her sat Ruth, with her blond hair in disarray and bruises coming up on her face and arms. Unlike the fake Florence, Ruth was crying softly: eyes red and tears running down her cheeks. Her skin was blotchy and her mouth slack, and she had her cuffed wrists resting in her lap.

Her boyfriend sat next to her on the floor, and that was where Tom and Ian Finchley, Tom's fellow detective sergeant, kept most of their attention.

Sid had also been cuffed, but behind his back. I suppose Tom and Finch thought there would be less of a chance that he'd try anything that way. And like fake Flossie, he looked angry, eyes burning and narrow jaw clenched. If looks could kill, we'd all be dead as doornails, including Ruth and fake Flossie.

Sarah and Hiram were huddled on the other side of the room. Sarah looked none the worse for wear, except for the fact that her hat had been ripped from her head and her hair was in disarray, but Sid must have gotten in a few shots on Hiram, who had bruises coming up on his face, and whose lip was split and swollen, and whose left sleeve had almost been separated from the shoulder of his jacket. Sarah was dabbing at the blood on his lip with a handkerchief and speaking to him softly.

Wolfgang, of course, looked like every woman's dream. The exertion had left him with a fine flush and slightly disarranged clothing and hair, and it was all to the good. He looked heroic, with his shoulders straight and his feet planted and the sword in his hand.

I turned back to Christopher. "Where did you come from?"

He pursed his lips. "Scotland Yard, where did you think? We drove in perhaps ten minutes after you'd been there, and got your message. And followed on as quickly as we could."

And had gotten here in record time and burst in immediately, since they hadn't had to wait to reconnoiter the garage and pick the lock on the back door before throwing themselves into the fray.

"Thank you for coming to the rescue," I said humbly.

Christopher snorted. "You seemed like you had it well in hand, actually, the four of you."

Perhaps. Then again, until Wolfgang started swinging about himself with the sword, we had seemed fairly evenly matched to me. Sid had youth and agility on his side, not to mention the motivation to avoid being arrested for kidnapping and murder, but Hiram had his cane and a lot of righteous anger. Sarah and her fake daughter were fairly evenly matched in height and weight, although fake Flossie was at least thirty years younger, and I could have taken Ruth had fake Flossie not gotten in my way. At least I thought I could have. She was small and slippery, and I'm not heavy, but I thought I was probably just a bit heavier than her.

But then Wolfgang had brought the sword stick out, and Christopher and the others had burst in, and here we were.

"St George will be sad he missed it," I said.

Christopher nodded. "I'm sure he would have enjoyed the chance to play hero."

"Well, then," Tom said, straightening after making sure that fake Flossie wasn't about to bleed to death. "Here we are. Would anyone like to tell me what's going on?"

He looked at Hiram and Sarah, and at the three captives, and at Wolfgang, and then at Wolfgang's sword. "I haven't seen one of those in a while."

Wolfgang flushed. It left the Mensur scar on his cheek quite visible, since it didn't flush with the rest of his face. "My apologies. I was afraid for *Freulein* Schatz's safety."

He looked about him for the wooden shaft of the cane.

"*Freulein...?*" Tom repeated, as Wolfgang spotted what he was looking for, hidden among the debris under what had been the dining table, and went to fetch it.

"Schatz," I said. "My father's name."

"No wonder His Lordship calls you Darling," Ian Finchley muttered, and Christopher told him, "That isn't why, Finch, as you very well know."

"Of course it's why, Christopher," I said. "Don't be ridiculous."

The look he gave me suggested that he thought I was the ridiculous one, and I rolled my eyes. And then Tom waved it all aside and said again, and not as a question this time, "Would someone please tell me what's going on."

CHAPTER TWENTY-TWO

WHEN NO ONE else spoke up—Sarah being busy with Hiram and Hiram being busy being attended to, and Wolfgang perhaps uncertain about the legality of his use of a sword cane —I took it upon myself to respond.

"You received the message we left, so you know what we're doing here."

Tom nodded. "Mrs. Schlomsky told you that Florence had a country cottage, and you decided to visit it."

"She was never gone from the Essex House Mansions for any length of time," I explained, "so I knew she didn't spend any time in it. Besides, nobody who wanted a country cottage to get away from London would take one here."

Tom nodded. "And of course, now we know that the woman you knew wasn't Florence Schlomsky at all."

Yes, we did. My eyes fastened on the brunette clutching her arm on the floor, and so did everyone else's.

"Name?" Tom wanted to know. And added, "Actually, let me give you mine first, so there's no question about what's going on here. I'm Detective Sergeant Thomas Gardiner with Scotland Yard, and this is Detective Sergeant Ian Finchley."

There was a pause when nobody said anything but when I could clearly hear confidence levels dropping all over the room. They'd been caught, fair and square, and by the authorities, and the game was over. There was no talking their way out of this.

"You are...?" Tom prompted.

"The blonde's name is Ruth," I said, when no answer was immediately forthcoming from anyone. "She was the Schlomsky's maid, whom they sent to England ahead of Florence to get everything ready for Flossie's arrival. And I heard her call the... um... the gentleman over there Sid."

Tom looked at him. And waited.

"Sidney Hodge," Sid said eventually, reluctantly.

"Thank you, Mr. Hodge. And when did you make this lady's acquaintance?"

Sid shot Ruth a look. If she had hoped that he would do something gentlemanly, something to protect her, she must have been disappointed, because he was quick to answer and made no attempt to soften the blow. "September of last year."

"Where?"

"My mother's auntie runs a lodging house in Putney," Sid said.

"And Miss Ruth stayed there?"

Sid flicked another glance at her. "She took the train up from Southampton to Waterloo station. Aunt Liz told me to go fetch her off the train. She was trying to make a good impression on the American millionaire, I suppose."

This time, the glance was at Hiram.

"You disapprove of Americans?" Tom asked gently, since Sid's voice, and the look he had leveled on Hiram, had certainly indicated something of that nature. "Or perhaps you disapprove of millionaires?"

"Well, it isn't fair," Sid said, "is it? That he should have so much, and so many of us have so little?"

There was nothing that could be said to that, since he was right. Or at least he was right as far as people like Crispin and Uncle Harold were concerned. People with inherited wealth, enough of it that nothing will ever be an issue for them, while so many people go without.

Although at least Hiram had worked for his money, as far as I understood it.

The millionaire didn't say anything in his defense, however, and Tom turned back to Sid. "So you fetched Miss Ruth at Waterloo. And took her back to your aunt's boarding house?"

Sid nodded. "Her and her friend."

"Her friend." All of our attention switched to the brunette next to Ruth on the floor.

"Myrtle Cavanaugh," she said, in Flossie's strident American accent. And unlike Ruth's tears and Sid's anger, there was defiance on her face, and no regret whatsoever. Not even regret over having been caught, although I suppose that must have been there, deep down.

"Miss Cavanaugh." Tom eyed her. "You met Miss Ruth on the boat? Or did you already know each other before that?"

"We met on ship," Flossie—Myrtle; and it was going to take me a moment to get used to that—said. "We were cabin-mates."

She leveled an unimpressed look at Hiram and Sarah. "All that money, and they couldn't even be bothered to pay for a private room for their servant to travel all the way to England. Had to throw her in with a stranger to save a few dollars instead."

Nobody said anything for a moment. Then Tom cleared his throat.

"So you met on the boat. And when you arrived in England, you took lodgings at the same boarding house?"

"By then, we had already fixed on a plan," Myrtle said.

"A plan for what?"

Ruth whimpered, and Myrtle glanced at her, but pushed ahead with what she was going to say even in the face of Ruth's distress. "A plan for getting the heiress out of the way once she got to London, and for having me take her place."

She smirked suddenly, in the direction of Hiram and Sarah. "I look a bit like her, don't I? Ruth said that I do."

The comment, not to mention the smile, was frankly shocking, a bit like a punch to the stomach, and it was no wonder that Hiram and Sarah both looked as if they had been slapped across the face.

"Evil," Christopher murmured beside me, and I nodded. Definitely evil.

Tom cleared his throat. "So you made a plan for what to do when Miss Schlomsky arrived in England. What did the plan entail?"

Myrtle flicked a glance at Ruth, or perhaps at Sid, or at both of them. "We made arrangements for the apartment in London and the cottage." She looked around at the dining room, indicating the space she was sitting in. "Sid nailed up the boards over the window on the second floor. When the heiress arrived in Southampton, Sid and Ruth drove all the way there to fetch her."

She snorted. "No train trip to London for the heiress. She was to be fetched directly off the ship."

Well, of course she was. It was understandable that Sarah and Hiram wanted Florence taken care of in every way they could, in a foreign country and among people who might not wish her well.

But at the same time, yes, I could see Myrtle's point.

"So Mr. Hodge and Ruth picked Miss Schlomsky up in Southampton," Tom prodded, and Myrtle nodded.

"They brought her here and we locked her in the room upstairs. Sid made sure she had enough opium and other dope to keep her quiet and happy. I moved into the apartment in Town, and we started to use the money. Every month or so, we made her write her parents a letter so they wouldn't suspect anything was wrong."

Tom glanced at Hiram and Sarah, a question in his eyes.

Sarah shook her head. "No. We didn't suspect anything. It was my daughter's handwriting, and there was no reason to believe she wasn't telling the truth about what she was doing. We believed she and Ruth lived together in an apartment in London, and that they had a little cottage they went to on the weekends sometimes. If I had had any idea..."

She trailed off, mouth flattening. Myrtle, damn her, tittered.

"And this went on for eight months," Tom asked, "with no problems?"

Myrtle shook her head. "Sid and Ruth kept the heiress contained. Sid got his motorcar and enough money that he didn't have to work for a living. Ruth got to play house with Sid. I got the apartment in London and whatever else I wanted—"

"And all you had to do was keep one girl imprisoned," I muttered.

She heard me, and gave me a glare and a toss of her head. "It's not like you've got any room to talk, Miss High and Mighty. You're living off your cousin's money, with your eye on the rest of the fortune, aren't you?"

Oh, was I?

"That's ridiculous—" I began, but then Christopher growled, and a second later, so did Wolfgang.

The latter took a step forward, and Myrtle rolled her eyes. "Oh, please. I have no idea who you think you are, but—"

"I," Wolfgang said coldly, "am *Graf* Wolfgang Ulrich Albrecht *von und zu* Natterdorff—"

"Sure you are," Myrtle said.

"He really is," Christopher told her, "and as for Pippa living off our money, of course she is. She's family!"

"But I have no designs on the title or fortune."

Nobody said anything, and I added, "Tell her, Christopher. Tell her that I have no designs on St George or his money."

Christopher rolled his eyes. "Of course you don't, Pippa."

Myrtle rolled her eyes, too. "Could have fooled me."

I narrowed my eyes. "I only took him away from you because it's inappropriate for an unmarried young lady to be snogging an unmarried gentleman in the lift."

Sarah made a distraught little moan, and Myrtle snorted. "Considering that particular gentleman's reputation, kissing a woman in an elevator is hardly the worst thing he's been accused of."

"Fine," I said. "I took him away from you because none of us wanted him involved with you. Even when we thought you were American heiress Florence Schlomsky, you weren't good enough for him. You were cheap and common and ill-mannered then, too, even when we thought you had money."

"But you believed me!" Myrtle said triumphantly. "You believed I was an American heiress."

I could hardly deny that, much as I would like to.

"Only because you were American," I told her bitterly. "Everyone knows that Americans are—" I hesitated, "different."

"But I fooled you." She sat back with a smirk. "I fooled all of you."

"Until this weekend," Tom said. "What happened?"

Myrtle scowled. "The telegram arrived. Miss High and

Mighty Darling over there delivered it. You always have to stick your nose into other people's business, don't you?"

"I was doing Evans a favor," I protested, "bringing it upstairs so he didn't have to."

She snorted. "So you weren't interested in what was in it?"

Of course I had been. Although there was no part of me that wanted to admit that.

"So the telegram arrived," Tom prompted when I didn't say anything, "from Miss Schlomsky's parents, informing you that they had arrived in England and would be in London in a day's time."

Myrtle nodded, and shot them a resentful glance. "No warning, nothing. No 'dear daughter, we are thinking of coming to visit.' One day, they were just there. On English soil, a few hours away, and threatening to destroy everything we'd worked for for almost a year."

Everything they had worked for? It didn't seem to me that there had been much honest work involved, but what did I know? I arched my brows at Christopher, who arched his right back. Ruth sniffled.

"What did you do?" Tom wanted to know.

"Rang up Sid," Myrtle said, with a glance at him, "and had him fetch me, and then we spent the rest of the night figuring out what to do about it."

"And the plan you came up with involved a false kidnapping, a ransom, and murder?"

"Well, we couldn't let them show up and see me pretending to be Flossie, could we?" Myrtle asked. "And we couldn't show them the real Flossie, either. So we had to come up with a reason why their daughter couldn't be there to meet them."

And they had settled on kidnapping. Which made a horrible sort of sense in the scheme of it.

It also explained a few things that had bothered me.

"So on Wednesday night, when Crispin dropped you off on the Strand…"

Myrtle smirked. "I walked across the street to Charing Cross and boarded a train for Thornton Heath."

Of course she had done. Nobody had dragged her forcibly off the street and into a motorcar. She had simply walked away on her own two feet.

"And last night?" Tom asked.

Myrtle eyed him. "We loaded up the heiress and took her to the house in Southwark—"

"How did you know about that?"

"Sid grew up around there," Myrtle said, with a flicker of a glance at him. Sid looked sour, but he didn't protest, or comment in any other way.

Tom nodded. "And then?"

"Sid went to pick up the money. And we came back here."

The way in which she phrased it was quite solid. That was what happened, nothing more and nothing less. But of course there was something fairly fundamental missing from the recitation, and of course we all realized it.

"And the murder?" Tom asked gently. "Who committed that?"

There was a moment of silence, one in which Myrtle flicked another glance at Sid and at Ruth. And then—

"Don't you dare, you bloody cow!" Sid growled. Ruth let out a sob, but after a moment, when she didn't say anything else, he continued, "I'm copping to the kidnapping and the thing with the money—"

The thing with the money? The ransom? Or the embezzling, basically, of the Schlomskys' wealth over most of the previous year?

"—but I'll be damned if I let you accuse me of a murder I didn't commit!"

"You didn't know there would be a murder?" Tom inquired. "Wasn't it part of the plan you concocted?"

Sid swung his head towards him and opened his mouth. And seemed to think better of it, because nothing came out.

"Of course it was part of the plan," Myrtle said. She gave her head a toss. "We couldn't leave her alive. We all knew that. There's no point in pretending we didn't agree to it now."

Sid opened his mouth, and then closed it again. And opened it again. "At least I didn't kill her!"

Ruth sniffed wetly.

"No," Myrtle agreed. "You didn't."

She sneered at him, actually sneered, as if being unable to commit coldblooded murder was something to be ashamed of, and Sid flushed angrily.

"So the murder of Miss Florence Schlomsky was always part of the plan," Tom said, yanking the conversation back on track, and everyone's attention turned back to him. Christopher squeezed my hand, and I squeezed back. "Is that correct?"

"Not always," Sid said. "At first, it was just about getting some of our own. Keep the heiress busy, spend the money."

"Keep her imprisoned while you slowly drain her father's coffers." Tom's tone was pleasant, but his face was not. His jaw was tight and his usually warm hazel eyes were hard as pebbles.

Sid squirmed a little. "I don't know why you'd want to put it like that..."

"That's the way it was," Tom reminded him. "But you had no plans to kill her."

"*I* didn't." Sid slanted a look at Myrtle. "Not then. *She* might have had other plans."

"As long as nobody knew anything, there was no need to kill her," Myrtle said, brows lowered. "We could just keep her, and keep the money coming. But when the parents showed up, it changed everything."

She slanted them a resentful stare, as if it were their fault that her plan of embezzlement had failed eventually.

"You didn't consider letting Miss Schlomsky go and cutting your losses?"

Sid shifted uncomfortably, and Ruth sniffed again.

"We talked about it," Myrtle admitted, almost reluctantly. "About killing the girl and getting rid of the body. About having Flossie Schlomsky disappear, never to be found again. Even about just leaving, and leaving her alive."

Sarah gave a little sob, and Myrtle flicked a glance at her before she continued, "But we had nothing to show for the past year. For everything we'd done. All the risks we'd taken. We'd lived well, sure, but we'd have to stop once the gravy train ended. I couldn't stay in the flat anymore, and Ruth and Sid couldn't keep the cottage. We'd have to go somewhere else and start over, and there was no money. So we figured we would get one more big score before we were done."

"The ransom."

Myrtle nodded. "It was only fair. If we'd known things weren't going to last longer, we would have saved more, but since we didn't..." She shrugged.

There was silence. I couldn't think of anything to say, frankly, and I think we must all be in the same boat. The sense of entitlement was staggering. The lack of remorse was disturbing. The acts of evil had been appalling, to say the least. Flossie's parents were huddled against the wall, pale and shocked. It looked as if all the fight had gone out of Hiram Schlomsky during the recounting of the plot to drain his fortune, or as much of it as they could get their hands on before they were caught. I would have expected him to curse and bellow and throw about him with his cane, but he just stood silently, clutching the cane in one hand and his wife's hand in the other. She was equally pale and speechless, her eyes dark with pain and her cheeks wet.

"You're awful people," I said to the group of prisoners on the floor. "I can't believe you did that. You deserve everything that's coming to you, and more."

Ruth avoided my eyes, and Sid just gave me a stony stare. Myrtle, however, smirked. "I fooled you, though. Didn't I?"

"Only because it never would have occurred to me that someone could do something so evil. You should be ashamed of yourself."

"Pish," Myrtle said. "Nature favors the strong. Survival of the fittest."

"Not anymore," Tom informed her. "You're all under arrest for kidnapping, for extortion, for murder..."

Christopher tugged on my hand. "Let's go. Tom can handle this."

I nodded, and let him pull me towards the kitchen door and the outside.

WE WERE STILL STANDING in the street outside three minutes later, when Tom and Ian Finchley came out herding the prisoners. Tom and Finch must have requested his help with the arrestees, because when they came out of the house, Wolfgang had a hand on the back of Ruth's neck and was pushing her along in front of him. Finch came first with a tight grip on Sid's arm, and Tom brought up the rear with Myrtle.

All three of them were stuffed into the back of the Tender, and handcuffs were fastened to hooks in the floor on both women's parts, and then Tom turned to us. "The parents went upstairs for a moment. You'll get them back to London when they come out?"

Christopher and I both nodded. The Hackney we had taken from the Savoy to Thornton Heath earlier was still here, and would suffice to get us all back to Town, even if we'd also have Christopher with us now.

"Come and see me at the Yard in the morning for statements. I'll be busy with this lot until then."

We promised that we would, and then Finch got behind the wheel of the Tender, and Tom climbed into the passenger seat, and the motor turned over, and...

"Give my love to Lord St George," Myrtle said cheekily from the backseat, and for a moment it was as if I was looking at Flossie again, the Flossie I'd thought I knew before all this happened: the American manhunter with the teeth, the boy-crazy heiress looking to trade her fortune for a British title... and then it all crashed down when Sarah Schlomsky's voice rose in a howl of grief from the upper floor of the cottage, and Christopher's hand squeezed mine, and the Tender pulled away down the street.

"Ready to go back to Town?" the Hackney driver asked, calmly as you please, as if he had missed everything that had gone on inside the house while he'd been sitting here, and as if Scotland Yard hadn't just driven away with three prisoners.

"Just as soon as the others come back out," Christopher told him, and the driver nodded. The three of us stood in silence and waited for Sarah Schlomsky's lament for her daughter to die away and for life to resume.

LETTER from the Right Honorable Viscount St George, Sutherland Hall, Little Sutherland, Wiltshire, to Miss Philippa Darling, Essex House Mansions, London:

Monday, August 16th

Darling,

Kit informed me that you asked Wolfie to come along on the hunt for Flossie's kidnappers instead of me. And not only that, but you allowed him to save your life? How could you be so careless? Now we're in his debt, and when he asks for your hand in marriage, we won't be able to say no.

StG

LETTER FROM MISS PHILIPPA DARLING, Essex House Mansions, London, to the Right Honorable Viscount St George, Sutherland Hall, Little Sutherland, Wiltshire:

Tuesday, August 17th

St George,
Pardon me very much for needing to have my life saved. At least I solved a kidnapping and a murder while I was at it. Where were you?

Oh, that's right. You were motoring through Wiltshire, probably snogging waitresses, as you usually do.

And 'Wolfie'? Really, St George? Is that a trace of jealousy I detect?

I'm sorry you missed the opportunity to play the hero, but that's what you get when you worry too much about what your father will say, you know. You should have stayed in London if you wanted to be part of the excitement.

For your information, if Wolfgang asks for my hand in marriage, and I decide I don't want to marry him, I shan't say yes. Saving my life doesn't mean he can command it. This is 1926, not the Regency. But I'll eventually want to marry somebody, and I don't see why I shouldn't consider him. He is handsome, wealthy, titled, and—as it turns out—brave. And the children would be beautiful. As far as I can tell, I could do worse.

Pippa

LETTER from the Right Honorable Viscount St George, Sutherland Hall, Little Sutherland, Wiltshire, to Miss Philippa Darling, Essex House Mansions, London:

Wednesday, August 18th

Hardly, Darling. He's German.

StG

LETTER FROM MISS PHILIPPA DARLING, Essex House Mansions, London, to the Right Honorable Viscount St George, Sutherland Hall, Little Sutherland, Wiltshire:

Thursday, August 19th

St George,

So am I, in case that fact has slipped your mind. Thanks ever so for the reminder, including the reminder of all the reasons why I have always despised you. I don't know why I ever thought you might have changed.

Don't bother responding to this letter. Go find Lady Laetitia and cry on her shoulder instead. In fact, just propose while you're at it, and spare the girl you claim to love the bother of having to turn you down. You and Laetitia deserve one another.

Philippa Marie Darling Schatz

THE LONDON TIMES,
MONDAY, AUGUST 23RD, 1926

Maurice, Earl of Marsden, and his wife, Countess Euphemia,

are pleased to announce the engagement of their daughter, Laetitia Grace, to Crispin Henry Jonathan Astley, Viscount St George. The groom-to-be is the only son of Harold, Duke of Sutherland, and his late wife, Charlotte. The couple will make their home at Sutherland House in Mayfair following their marriage at St George's, Hanover Square. Friends are welcome to attend the ceremony, which will take place at 11 o'clock on December 18th of this year.

Dear Reader,

First, the usual warning about the language: I'm not British. I'm also not American, but I've lived in the US for a good many years. While I learned British English first, the edges wore off during the 30+ years I lived across the pond. This book, like the others in the series, is a mish-mash of British and American English. There are lifts and flats and pavements instead of elevators, apartments, and sidewalks, but there are also odors instead of odours, and colors instead of colours, and because it takes place in 1926, there are motorcars and public call boxes from which one can ring people up, and attitudes and mores we're not used to these days. Pippa drinks cocktails and smokes cigarettes, because that was what independent young ladies did in 1926. It doesn't mean that I approve of drinking or smoking, or drink or smoke myself. It also doesn't mean that I want to take away anyone else's right to do so (as long as they keep their cigarette smoke out of my face, anyway).

The details of Herr Hitler's early exploits are unfortunately accurate. He planned a failed coup in November 1923, called the Beer Hall *Putsch* because it was planned in the Bürgerbräu Keller in Munich. Hitler wrote *Mein Kampf* while he was incarcerated in the aftermath of the *putsch*. Part I of *Mein Kampf* was published in 1925 and part II in 1926 by Eher Verlag. The first English-language editions didn't come out until 1933. We'll have to assume that Pippa either got her hands on a German copy of the book, or read the excerpts in a German language newspaper. Perhaps she was trying to brush up on her (other) native language.

German *Kurrentschrift* is a form of cursive that was used in Germany up until WWII, when the Nazi party banned it for being too 'chaotic.' It's based on medieval cursive, and looks a bit different from the standard British or American cursive we saw growing up. It is definitely harder to read, especially when you're not used to it.

A *Schmisse*, as mentioned in the story, is the kind of scar you end up with courtesy of a student duel. You mostly see them on the left side of the face because most people are right-handed. Mensur dueling was a popular pastime for upper-class students in Germany and Austria in the 1800s and early 1900s. The scars, alternatively called Mensur scars or *Renommierschmiss*, were a badge of honor, and the fighters went after them for bragging rights. There were cases of young men paying doctors to slice their cheeks open if they couldn't get the scars any other way, and there were also efforts made to make them heal badly so they'd be more visible. It was said that a man with Mensur scars would make a good husband, because he had proven himself to be brave.

St Olave's Church on Tooley Street in Southwark was a real place, which existed in various iterations from around 1018 until 1926, when it was torn down to make way for St Olaf House, a rather nice art deco style building which is part of London Bridge Hospital. The history that Christopher tells Pippa about it, is all true as far as we know.

Grosvenor Square has had an American presence since John Adams settled there in 1785. In 1926, it was the site of the American Embassy. Grosvenor Square is mentioned in many of Oscar Wilde's works, including *The Importance of Being Earnest* and *Dorian Gray*. As for the Bentley Boys, they were racecar drivers Woolf Bernato, Tim Birkin, Glen Kidston and Bernard Rubin, who bought adjacent flats and made the fashionable south-east corner of Grosvenor Square their home in the 1920s. The London cab drivers called it Bentley Corner for years afterwards.

The first Lyons teashop opened in Piccadilly in 1894, and after 1909, developed into a national chain. In the earlier years, the Lyons waitresses were nicknamed Gladys, but in 1924 the Lyons company decided to institute an update, and held a staff competition to choose the new name. Nippy beat out a long list of other suggestions, among them Sybil-at-your-service, Miss Nimble, Busy Bertha, Speedwell and Dexterous Dora. Presumably, the new nickname was meant to indicate how speedily the waitresses nipped around the teashop.

Before the Bobby Pin was invented in San Francisco, there was the Brit equivalent, the Kirbigrip or Kirby Grip. While the Bobby Pin got its name from the hairstyles of the 1920s, the Kirbigrip was made by the Kirby, Beard & Ltd. Company of Birmingham and took its name from them.

The business magnate's son who was kidnapped a couple of years before Pippa was born, was 15-year-old Edward Aloysius Cudahy Jr., who was snatched walking down the street in his hometown of Omaha, Nebraska, a week before Christmas, 1900. His father, Edward Cudahy Sr., was the owner of Cudahy Packing Company, and a very wealthy man. When a ransom note arrived asking $25,000 for Eddie's safe return,

Edward Sr. coughed up the money with no problem, and got his son back in one piece six hours later. The *Omaha Bee* said about it that Edward Sr. spoke very nonchalantly about the whole thing, as if he "had just dropped a nickel down a cellar grating."

$25,000 in 1900 comes to about $934,000 in 2024, so just under a million dollars in ransom. By 1926, though, you had to ask for $50,000 to get the equivalent of our $886,000. Still, it's a small price to pay for one's only son or daughter, isn't it?

ABOUT THE AUTHOR

New York Times and *USA Today* bestselling author Jenna Bennett (Jennie Bentley) has written more than fifty books, most of them in the genres of mystery and suspense.

For more information, please visit her website, www.jennaben-nett.com

If you would like to purchase one or more of Jenna's books, check your favorite storefront or visit Jenna's store, www.jennabennett.myshopify.com

Follow on Social Media:

www.ingramcontent.com/pod-product-compliance
Lightning Source LLC
Chambersburg PA
CBHW031320210726

48287CB00005B/1626